JUL 2007

S0-ADI-786

21 PROMS

Also Available

MISTLETOE: FOUR HOLIDAY STORIES

By Hailey Abbott, Melissa de la Cruz,
Aimee Friedman, Nina Malkin

FIREWORKS: FOUR SUMMER STORIES

By Niki Burnham, Erin Haft,
Sarah Mlynowski, Lauren Myracle

SUMMER BOYS
NEXT SUMMER: A SUMMER BOYS NOVEL
AFTER SUMMER: A SUMMER BOYS NOVEL
LAST SUMMER: A SUMMER BOYS NOVEL

By Hailey Abbott

SOUTH BEACH
FRENCH KISS
HOLLYWOOD HILLS

By Aimee Friedman

POOL BOYS

By Erin Haft

6X: THE UNCENSORED CONFESSIONS
6X: LOUD, FAST AND OUT OF CONTROL

By Nina Malkin

21 PROMS

Edited by David Levithan and Daniel Ehrenhaft

ELLENVILLE PUBLIC LIBRARY
40 CENTER STREET
ELLENVILLE, NY 12428

SCHOLASTIC INC.

New York Toronto London Auckland Sydney
Mexico City New Delhi Hong Kong Buenos Aires

If you purchased this book without a cover, you should be aware that this book is stolen property. It was reported as "unsold and destroyed" to the publisher, and neither the author nor the publisher has received any payment for this "stripped book."

No part of this publication may be reproduced, stored in a retrieval system, or transmitted in any form or by any means, electronic, mechanical, photocopying, recording, or otherwise, without written permission of the publisher. For information regarding permission, write to Permissions Department, Scholastic Inc., 557 Broadway, New York, NY 10012.

ISBN-13 978-0-439-89029-8
ISBN-10 0-439-89029-2

"You Are a Prom Queen, Dance Dance Dance" Copyright © 2007 by
    Elizabeth Craft
"All She Wants" Copyright © 2007 by Cecily von Ziegesar
"In Vodka Veritas" Copyright © 2007 by Holly Black
"Your Big Night" Copyright © 2007 by Sarah Mlynowski
"Off Like a Prom Dress" Copyright © 2007 by Billy Merrell
"Mom called, she says you have to go to prom" Copyright © 2007 by
    Adrienne Maria Vrettos
"Better Be Good to Me" Copyright © 2007 by Daniel Ehrenhaft
"Three Fates" Copyright © 2007 by Aimee Friedman
"The Question: A Play in One Act" Copyright © 2007 by Brent Hartinger
"Shutter" Copyright © 2007 by Will Leitch
"Geechee Girls Dancin', 1955" Copyright © 2007 by Jacqueline Woodson
"How I Wrote to Toby" Copyright © 2007 by E. Lockhart
"A Six-pack of Bud, a Fifth of Whiskey, and Me" Copyright © 2007 by
    Melissa de la Cruz
"Primate the Prom" Copyright © 2007 by Libba Bray
"Apology #1" Copyright © 2007 by Ned Vizzini
"See Me" Copyright © 2007 by Lisa Ann Sandell
"Prom for Fat Girls" Copyright © 2007 by Rachel Cohn
"Chicken" Copyright © 2007 by Jodi Lynn Anderson
"The Backup Date" Copyright © 2007 by Leslie Margolis
"Lost Sometimes" Copyright © 2007 by David Levithan
"The Great American Morp" Copyright © 2007 by John Green

All rights reserved. Published by POINT, an imprint of Scholastic Inc., 557 Broadway, New York, NY 10012. SCHOLASTIC and associated logos are trademarks and/or registered trademarks of Scholastic Inc.

12 11 10 9 8 7 6 5 4 3 2   7 8 9 10 11 12/0

Printed in the U.S.A.   40
First printing, March 2007

Table of Contents

You Are a Prom Queen, Dance Dance Dance
by Elizabeth Craft   1

All She Wants
by Cecily von Ziegesar   15

In Vodka Veritas
by Holly Black   26

Your Big Night
by Sarah Mlynowski   42

Off Like a Prom Dress
by Billy Merrell   68

"Mom called, she says you have to go to prom"
by Adrienne Maria Vrettos   71

Better Be Good to Me
by Daniel Ehrenhaft   84

Three Fates
by Aimee Friedman   107

The Question: A Play in One Act
by Brent Hartinger   136

Shutter
by Will Leitch   150

Geechee Girls Dancin', 1955
by Jacqueline Woodson   161

How I Wrote to Toby
by E. Lockhart   166

A Six-pack of Bud, a Fifth of Whiskey, and Me
by Melissa de la Cruz   183

Primate the Prom
by Libba Bray   192

Apology #1
by Ned Vizzini   206

See Me
by Lisa Ann Sandell   213

Prom for Fat Girls
by Rachel Cohn   225

Chicken
by Jodi Lynn Anderson   232

The Backup Date
by Leslie Margolis   243

Lost Sometimes
by David Levithan   262

The Great American Morp
by John Green   271

You Are a Prom Queen, Dance Dance Dance
by Elizabeth Craft

I hate my dress (pale blue). I hate my heels (silver). I hate my size 32D underwire Chantelle bra (nude) that my mom and the saleslady at Neiman Marcus made me buy to go with the aforementioned hated dress and hated heels. Yet here I am, wearing all three, standing near the snack table at P.S. 182's Mardi Gras–themed Junior–Senior Prom.

And all the while, my best friend, Emilie Lang, who's nearly six feet tall and strong from four years of playing volleyball, is squeezing my forearm so hard I can feel a bruise forming. But that's okay. The pain distracts me from the hate.

"He's dancing with Madison Trimabali," Emilie moans.

"He is?"

Emilie's been obsessed with this "he" since the middle of sophomore year when she was positive they shared a moment while filing into the auditorium for an assembly on the dangers of drunk driving. I glance in the general direction of writhing black tuxedos and pastel sateen gowns, trying to locate Madison's garish orange strapless number.

1

"If Trevor doesn't ask me to dance, I'm going to kill myself. I swear to God." Emilie jabs her finger in the air to emphasize how serious she is about the threat of suicide.

"I still have half a bottle of codeine from when I got my wisdom teeth out," I offer. "That and a bottle of Jack Daniels from your dad's liquor cabinet will at least put you in a coma."

Emilie gives me a look. I note that the bright blue streak in her blond hair contrasts in a not good way with her aquamarine lace bodice. "Why do I like you?" she asks.

There's no judgment in the question. She's genuinely baffled.

"I have TiVo in my bedroom," I remind her. "And I get to drive my dad's car on the weekend."

"Right." She nods, our friendship falling back into place. A person less obsessed with TiVo than I am might be offended, but Emilie and I understand each other.

At least, we did. Before the prom season started in earnest, and Emilie decided that since it's our senior year, we had to go. Apparently, eschewing traditional stuff like prom and basketball games is okay only to a point. Now that we're approaching graduation, Emilie feels we need to embrace "the high school experience." She says she wants memories. I tried pointing out that a last-ditch attempt to manufacture those memories by participating in activities totally foreign to us might defeat the purpose. But she's remained firm in her stance, and as a best friend, I feel compelled to support her.

"My breath stinks," Emilie says, her voice rising a couple octaves above normal. "It does, doesn't it?" She leans in and huffs at my face.

"You're fine," I tell her. "Crest fresh." Which is a lie. Her breath *does* stink, but being honest about it might breed hysteria.

"I'm gonna find Gavin," Emilie announces, referring to her date. "I'll get him to dance, then I'll maneuver him close to Trevor."

I consider pointing out that scheming to dance *next to* one's crush might fall into the pathetic category, but similar to the breath situation, I decide against it. "Maneuver next to Trevor. Check."

My own date, Adam Edwardson, is nowhere to be seen. Fifteen minutes ago, I sent him to the vending machines next to the guys' locker room in search of a Fresca. I tried to drink a cup of the punch the prom committee provided, but in addition to being spiked with several kinds of competing hard liquor, I hate punch. Fresca, on the other hand, is very refreshing. I wonder if Adam decided he'd had enough and snuck out of the prom. Maybe I'll get an apologetic message from him on my cell phone in the morning.

"Wish me luck." Emilie gives my arm one more squeeze, then race-walks toward the crowd to locate Gavin, who's most likely too drunk off spiked punch to realize that he's merely a pawn in my best friend's Machiavellian pursuit of true love.

I drift closer to the snack table and shove a fistful of broken Lay's potato chips into my mouth. They're in a bowl next to a mangled King Cake, an apparent Mardi

Gras staple. Too late, I remember I hate Lay's potato chips. Aside from the grease factor, tiny crumbs stick between my teeth, where they'll probably stay until I floss two or three weeks from now. Fastidious, I am not.

I am, however, the kind of person who slows down to look at horrible car accidents. It's that instinct that compels me to turn my attention back to the dance floor. I see Emilie and Gavin, grinding to the Norah Jones cover the band is playing. As promised, Emilie seems to be subtly but determinedly guiding Gavin toward Trevor and Madison. I wonder if, in her zeal, Emilie has stopped to notice that Trevor and Madison are now making out.

My wondering is interrupted when I feel a presence behind me. I fantasize that the presence is a prom-hopping serial killer who has approached to put me out of my misery. Alas, I turn to find Adam Edwardson, slightly sweaty and holding a can of Fresca.

"Sorry it took so long," he says, half-panting. "The vending machines only had Pepsi so I ran to the 7-Eleven down the street." His expression borders on triumphant as he hands me the Fresca.

"Thanks." I'm sort of caught off guard by the lengths Adam went to in order to acquire my soda. Sprinting to a convenience store in one's tux qualifies as above and beyond. I hate it when people go above and beyond. It makes me self-conscious and a bit nauseated.

Then again, Adam is an above-and-beyond type. He's one of those science-loving guys just close enough to being labeled a geek or a dork that he overcompensates by being so genuinely nice to everyone that they have no choice but to like him. I took his niceness into account when I asked him to prom.

4

"Ayla?" he asks. It's weird to hear him say my name for some reason. Maybe because I'm still rattled by the heroic dash to 7-Eleven.

"Yeah?" I take a sip of the Fresca, its grapefruity goodness sliding down my throat in a way that makes me glad to be alive.

"Doyouwannadance?" The words are softly spoken and run together, but I manage to capture the sentiment behind them. Years of watching TV with the volume on low while doing homework has trained me for moments like this.

"That's okay," I tell him. Out of the corner of my eye, I can see Emilie and Gavin. They're now a mere one couple away from the still-grinding Trevor and Madison, and Emilie is waving her arms wildly as she bops her butt in Trevor's direction.

I turn my attention to a GO RAIDERS banner that's strung permanently across the gym. The fact that it's sagging under the weight of brightly colored streamers depresses me. I hate streamers.

Adam looks around the gym, too, clearly hoping his gaze will land on something worthy of conversation. I know I should make an effort, maybe ask about his Fresca-buying adventure. But there's a lump of resistance in my throat. I feel any attempt at a good time will validate Emilie's stance that the prom is an experience worth having. To atone for what an awful person I'm being, I hold out the can of Fresca, offering him a sip.

He takes the can and gulps. There's a weird intimacy to it. Someone watching might think we're a couple. I hate couples. As far as I can tell, they're always smug on the outside and miserable on the inside.

"Let's get our picture taken," Adam suggests, handing the can back. His fingernails are extremely clean. I imagine his pre-prom fingernail-cleaning ritual. "It'll be fun."

At the far corner of the gym, there's a line of couples waiting to be photographed in front of fake Bourbon Street. In case the Mardi Gras theme isn't clear, Ms. Gleason, who teaches European history, is standing at the front of the line, passing out plastic strands of beads to everyone before they pose.

"I'd rather not get in on the whole Mardi Gras deal," I inform Adam.

"Why?" He looks confused. The expression on his face reminds me of Emilie's, earlier, when she couldn't remember why she liked me.

"Hurricane Katrina?" I remind him. "Considering New Orleans is currently a wasteland of grounded shrimp boats, wrecked houses, and abandoned cars, I don't exactly feel comfortable whooping it up."

Adam shrugs, his shoulders straining the material of his rented tux. "I don't know. I thought it was a nice idea."

"Oh." Somehow, he's managed to make me feel small. I hate feeling small. "Anyway, it means Fat Tuesday. This is Saturday."

"Good point." He smiles, and I feel better. I hate that his smile makes me feel better, because that implies I'm weak, that I need the approval of others to feel okay about myself.

"Thanks again for the Fresca," I say for no apparent reason. "It was very refreshing."

He nods. For a couple of moments, neither of us says anything. I study the couples milling around the gym and on the dance floor, all adorned in their plastic beads, not a care in the world. I think, not for the first time, that humans need to be subdivided into a number of different species. There would be one species for pedophiles, another for homecoming queens and football captains, a third for geniuses who cure cancer or spend their life getting to the bottom of pi. I don't know what my species would be, except that it's not represented anywhere in this gym.

"Are you sure you don't want to dance?" Adam asks finally.

"Positive," I assure him. "I'm good just hanging out here."

I don't add that I hate to dance. I hate it more than my dress or my heels or my size 32D underwire Chantelle bra. I hate it more than the prom.

"Do you mind if I ask someone else?" he asks. "I mean, since you don't want to?"

The question floors me. The last thing I expected when I asked Adam Edwardson to the prom was that he would leave my side in the pursuit of a dance partner. During one of our physics experiments last semester, I clearly heard him state that he does not get his groove on whatsoever. Given that Adam has overly long legs and an obvious aversion to drawing attention, the news didn't surprise me.

"You *want* to go out there?" I'm looking at him closely for signs that the old Adam Edwardson has been replaced by an identical alien replica.

"It's the *prom*," he responds. "That's what we're supposed to do. Dance." He smiles again. "Didn't you get the manual?"

"But you said you *don't dance*," I remind him. "You said you have no rhythm and that given a choice between medical interrogation and doing the Electric Slide, you would choose the medical interrogation."

He gives me a look. "Do you remember everything everyone says, or is it just me?"

"Everyone." And it's true. Conversations get stuck in my head for years. My dad says it's a gift, but he's wrong. It's actually quite annoying.

"Anyway, I wasn't suggesting we do the Electric Slide. We could just get out there and sort of move back and forth." He sways a little to show me what he means.

"Huh." I'm forming my next thought when I see Emilie making a beeline for Adam and me.

"She looks happy," Adam says, noticing Emilie, too.

He's right. Even from here, I can see that her cheeks are glowing from more than the blush she had me apply five hours ago. "Yeah."

"Is that bad?" he asks.

"Why would it be bad?"

"You tell me."

Adam is probing. I hate probing. Luckily, Emilie reaches us before he can delve further into my thoughts on the topic of happiness.

"Gavin threw up," she announces. "Nobody even noticed."

"Ah, memories." I'm being sarcastic, but she doesn't pick up on it. Probably because Gavin wasn't the only one hitting the punch.

8

"Trevor and I had major eye contact," Emilie tells us, beaming. "Something is definitely in the air."

"Emilie's in love with Trevor," I explain to Adam. It doesn't seem fair to leave him out of the loop.

"He's a good guy," Adam says, giving Emilie a little pat on the back. "You'd make a cute couple."

Once again, I'm astounded by Adam's general niceness. He's got to know that Trevor doesn't know Emilie's alive, yet he doesn't hesitate to join in her enthusiasm. Suddenly, I get an idea.

"Since Gavin's out of commission, you two should dance," I suggest to them. "I'll watch."

Emilie's head bobs up and down, but Adam shakes his. "Maybe you should see how he's doing," he tells Emilie. "What with the puking and all."

She sighs. "I guess I'd be a pretty shitty date if I didn't, huh?"

Adam shrugs, not wanting to *say* it, but clearly thinking that's the case. I feel stymied. I hate feeling stymied. Nonetheless, I can hardly force the two of them to twirl off into the Mardi Gras night.

Emilie grins. "Next time you see me, I'll be in Trevor's arms. Guaranteed." She takes off, jigging a little to the Maroon 5 song the band is playing as she goes. I marvel at her ability to live in perpetual denial. She will *never* be in Trevor's arms. I know that as sure as I know that I will never wear these heels again.

"Don't say you didn't have your chance," I say to Adam in the awkward silence that Emilie leaves in her wake. "I tried."

"Can I ask you something?" His intonation goes up at the end of the sentence, like he wants my permission, but my gut feeling is that he's going to ask regardless of my response.

"Sure." I wonder what's coming. It could be anything from my bra size to my opinion on how to solve world hunger.

"Why did you ask me to the prom?" Adam is looking straight at me, his brown eyes curious, one eyebrow slightly raised.

"Because you're nice and smart and I knew you didn't have a date," I reply. There are other reasons, but Adam doesn't need to be privy to them.

"Bullshit."

"Excuse me?"

"Nice and smart?" he repeats. "You're more complicated than that."

"I didn't even want to come to the prom," I admit. "But Emilie had her heart set on it. . . . I didn't want to let her down." The information is veering toward personal, and I feel uncomfortable. Under most circumstances, I hate feeling uncomfortable. But with Adam, it's sort of interesting, like a science experiment.

"Still doesn't explain why you asked *me*," he says. "Maybe at some point you'll reveal that particular secret." He's staring at me like he *knows* something. Like he's read my nonexistent diary or taken a spin in my mind.

"I doubt it." I tug at the bodice of my hated spaghetti-strap dress to turn his attention toward my 32D cups and away from this little conversational interlude.

"I know you a lot better than you think," he continues, undistracted by my somewhat hefty bosom. This comes out sounding like a challenge, whether he meant it to or not.

"You don't know me," I assure him. I keep myself shrouded, metaphorically speaking, from the world at large. It keeps life simpler.

"I know you're scared," Adam says. "I know you walk around wearing your protective shell, pretending you don't care what anyone thinks, because deep down you think they won't like what they see."

My heart starts beating fast. I go to take a sip of my Fresca and discover the can is empty. I look at my feet, and then back at Adam. I open my mouth to speak, but nothing comes out.

I've been seen.

Adam picks up on my verbal paralysis and takes his cue. "I also know that if you'd open up and let people know you, they'd be in for a treat," he continues. "Despite all your hard work to convince me and everyone else that you're an abyss of negativity, I'm not buying it."

"You're wrong," I respond finally. "About all of it."

Adam stares at me, into the abyss of negativity. He seems to be weighing something. "I'm going to leave now." His tone is pleasant, as if he's delivering a fair-weather report. "You ever wanna tell me the real reason you asked me to be your date, I'd really like to hear it."

I don't protest. I simply watch him walk away, relieved. For me, prom is almost over. All I have to do is find Emilie and tell her I'm leaving. I can still get home in time to watch *Saturday Night Live.*

Heading toward the dance floor, where I see Emilie's head moving above the other girls, I tell myself that I'm glad to be rid of Adam and his analytical dismantling of my personality. I want to be alone. I love being alone. At the edge of the dance floor, I position myself to get

Emilie's attention. I assume she revived Gavin, who's most likely resumed his intake of punch.

And then I see her. She's not dancing with Gavin. She's dancing with Trevor. And they're not just dancing, they're talking. He smiles, she laughs. It doesn't look like drunken, prom laughter. It looks like the real deal. Emilie guaranteed the next time I saw her she'd be in Trevor's arms, and she was right.

I think of all the times I told her to forget about Trevor. I think of how she'd just shake her head and say I didn't know what I was talking about.

She was right all along. I was wrong.

What if she'd listened? Where would she be now? But I know the answer. She'd be right next to me, holed up in my bedroom with a pizza and sixty hours of TiVo to watch. Emilie wouldn't be living. She'd be hiding.

Just like me.

My feet start to move. Even in the heels, I make good time as I head toward the gymnasium door, toward the huge painted sign that says THANK YOU FOR COMING TO MARDI GRAS. In my peripheral vision, I notice Principal Maughn standing by the exit, at the ready with more beads and a watchful eye for intoxicated students. I blow by him, pushing open the heavy door and bursting into the warm May night.

The parking lot is a sea of cars and rented limos. I know he won't be here, but I keep moving anyway. I have to. Even outside, I can hear the band.

"Ayla?" Adam's voice comes from behind an SUV with a GO RAIDERS bumper sticker. He steps out, and under the parking lot light his skin is pale, almost like he's an apparition.

12

"You were right," I admit. "About all of it." He grins. I think he's not surprised to see me, although I can't be sure. "I'm ready to tell you . . . the reason . . . about why I asked you."

I don't usually speak like this, with hesitation. But what I'm about to say is the truth, and it doesn't roll easily off my tongue. He nods, encouraging.

"It's because you said you don't dance," I explain. "I hate dancing." But that's a lie. I stop, force myself to rewind and tell the truth. "Actually, I'm scared of it. Terrified, in fact. The idea of everyone watching . . . thinking I look like an idiot. I couldn't bear the thought of prom if I had to get in front of that band and . . . *do something*. I thought you'd be safe. That you wouldn't want to dance."

He closes his eyes and inhales deeply, as if he's savoring the moment. "Finally."

"And it's not just that," I go on, the words rushing out now. "I'm scared of everything. Where to sit at lunch. What to say in class. People." I take a breath. "I hate being scared."

"Then stop." Adam walks out of the light and into the dark, closer to me. "I'll help you."

"You can't."

"I can."

I shake my head. It can't be that easy. Except he has such kind eyes that I want to believe him. I want to live. "How?"

"Take my hands," he says softly. "You are a prom queen. Dance, dance, dance."

I hold my breath. Every cell in my body is screaming to run. But his eyes, those kind eyes, hold me in place.

Inside, the band has transitioned into something that sounds like zydeco music. I picture Emilie, ecstatic, grinning at Trevor.

"There's no one to see us," Adam continues. "I'll even close my eyes."

I know that if I do not do this, I will regret it forever. I reach out, and Adam clasps my hands. His skin is smooth and dry and reassuring. I exhale. I can do this. We can do this.

Adam and I start to sway. I move my hips, and then my feet. I shut my eyes, and I think he shuts his. I listen to the band, and I imagine that we're on Bourbon Street in the middle of Mardi Gras. There are thousands of people, and some of them are looking at us. But, for once, I'm not scared.

As the song ends and another begins, I keep a tight hold on Adam's hands. I'm free, and I don't want it to end. This is my prom night. I love my dress. I love my shoes. I love my size 32D underwire Chantelle bra.

And someday, just maybe, I will love to dance, dance, dance.

All She Wants

by Cecily von Ziegesar

1. Winter break junior year Mum and Dad and Alex leave Brooke behind with chicken pox while they set off to Kauai for three weeks. Happy Holidays! Brooke becomes obsessed with Netflix and even more obsessed with Molly Ringwald because they look alike — except Brooke's eyes are blue and bigger, her hair is straight and blond, and she is probably shorter, although just as gawky as Molly. Maybe they don't look alike at all, but she is still obsessed and watches *Sixteen Candles*, *Pretty in Pink*, and *The Breakfast Club* in constant rotation. Just like Molly in those movies, Brooke's never had a real boyfriend. She doesn't go to a big suburban public high school with school buses and lockers and a cafeteria the way Molly does, though. She lives in Manhattan and has to wear a kilt to school. Her school lunchroom looks like a restaurant in an Austrian ski chalet, with padded wooden armchairs, cloth napkins, baguettes, and brie. In *Pretty in Pink*, Andie sits at a table with her friend Duckie in the gigantic, crowded school cafeteria, drinking diet soda out of a straw and moping about the prom. Brooke's school is called St. Agnes, named after the patron saint of young virgins, and doesn't have soda or a prom.

2. It's not like she doesn't have friends, but they are all away, snowboarding in Zermatt or flambéing themselves in St. Bart's. Her best friend, Katherine, is in Namibia of all places, looking at animals through binoculars and flirting with her safari guide, whom she has bragged all about in e-mails. Apparently he is "hung like a zebra," which leads Brooke to wonder how Katherine would know, since Katherine is even more of a virgin than she is. Plus, she looked it up in the *National Geographic Encyclopedia* in her dad's library and zebras' are actually pretty small, like Shetland ponies', so maybe being hung like one isn't really something to brag about. She wonders how old Molly Ringwald was when she lost her virginity for real. Like, was she still a virgin when she played Andie in *Pretty in Pink*? She seems bitchier in that than she does as Samantha in *Sixteen Candles*. When she's Claire in *The Breakfast Club* she just seems confused, which makes sense. First she was a virgin — *Sixteen Candles* — then she was thinking about maybe not being a virgin anymore — *The Breakfast Club* — and then she wasn't — *Pretty in Pink*. Or maybe she's just a really amazing actress, which actually goes without saying.

3. Brooke is so bored. She'll do anything to not be this bored. Her housekeeper, Ana, is living with her while the family is away, but Ana would rather watch reruns of *The Apprentice* and eat spray cheese on Triscuits all day than play Hearts with her. Besides, Brooke is sixteen, she can amuse herself. Of course, she's basically housebound, due to her illness, but her Central Park West apartment building is big enough — surely there must be someone to hang out with. Like maybe the boy in 1C? Mum is always complaining about the families in the ground-floor apartments, which apparently are rent-controlled. Probably his family doesn't have enough money to go snowboarding in Switzerland. Probably they have a Christmas tree with presents underneath it. But he probably doesn't have a prom, either — most schools in the city don't. Maybe he'll want to come to *her* prom.

4. She knocks on the door to 1C, which faces the building's laundry room. She didn't even know the building had a laundry room because her family's washer/dryer is in their apartment, off the kitchen. Not that she's ever used them. Ana does all the laundry. Twice a week it appears in her drawers, neatly folded and smelling clean.

Brrrring! The doorbell sounds exactly like the in-between-periods bell at her school. An excessively fat woman answers the door, draped in something that could be called a dress, but could also be some sort of bathrobe-like garment. A caftan? It is black, with shiny silver piping, and was not made by Carolina Herrera.

"You want my son?" the woman asks in a thick Slavic accent, her fleshy lips frowning beneath her mustache. "*Lazy*, so lazy! He listens to iPod all day."

Brooke doesn't know what to say to that since she's been watching *Pretty in Pink* all morning, trying to figure out if the hair dye she ordered from drugstore.com to match Molly-as-Andie's would come out looking right, or if it would turn her blondish-brown hair irreversibly magenta.

"I wondered if maybe he wanted to come upstairs?" she asks boldly. "I've been sick and I can't go out."

The woman disappears down a narrow corridor, leaving Brooke standing in the half-open doorway. The apartment smells like boiled lentils and Bounce. The boy comes down the corridor toward her. He's darker and shorter than she remembered him, but he has this amused-by-life look that she likes. She won't be shy with him.

"Hey," he says. "I'm Taylor." He laughs, like he knows his name is stupid; his parents just named him that to fit in with their environment.

She smiles. "Want to do something?"

5. They don't even talk in the elevator but she can't stop smiling. She doesn't even care that she has little scabs all over her face and hands. Actually, she has little scabs all over her body, but in her jeans and white J.Crew turtleneck sweater, he can't see them. He can see how much she looks like Molly Ringwald, and he knows the scabs will heal. They sit in the den, on the floor, with their backs against the sofa, eating Pringles, drinking ginger ale, and watching *The Breakfast Club*. He makes the biggest crunching sounds she's ever heard. When Molly kisses Judd Nelson and gives him her diamond earring, Brooke sort of lurches in Taylor's direction and they start kissing. Brooke takes her sweater off. This is further than she's ever gone with a boy because the only time she's ever really kissed any boy is at Camp Pokomoonshine in the Adirondacks, where she went for four years. Last summer she was a CIT. Kissing Taylor feels just like watching a great Molly Ringwald movie she hasn't seen before. He has chin stubble that makes him more manly than Gary from camp, and he doesn't put her hand on his crotch the way Adam, Gary's bunkmate, did. Taylor waits for her to put her hand there herself, which she doesn't, because she barely knows him and it's only like eleven A.M. and putting her hand there seems more like a nighttime activity. Brooke has the feeling Taylor's kissed a few girls in his lifetime, but none as Mollyish as she.

"Can you come over later?" She yawns, Molly-like, pretending not to be into him. "Like, tonight, at eight?"

6. She spends the entire afternoon in her parents' dressing room, trying on her mom's gowns and feeling very much like the doll Edith in her favorite children's book, *The Lonely Doll.* Thank goodness she doesn't live with anyone named Mr. Bear, who would spank her if he caught her wearing the $7,000 Carolina Herrera goddess gown Mum wore two years ago at the Costume Institute Gala at the Metropolitan Museum of Art. It is blue, but if she wanted to be specific about the color, she would probably call it Aegean Blue, because it looks like the sea in Greece when the sun is setting and the air smells like ripe olives. She can imagine Taylor touching the dress but she can't imagine him taking it off without ripping it, because it has about forty tiny hook-and-eye closures down the left side of the bodice. She will just have to take it off herself.

7. Taylor rings the bell at 7:54 — making it obvious that he's into her. Ana, the housekeeper, answers the door because Brooke is in her room mixing punch. She can hear him walking down the hall toward her room, his sneakers squeaking on the freshly waxed parquet floor. Her *Absolutely '80s* compilation CD is on constant replay. Right now it's playing Brian Ferry's "Slave to Love."

He knocks on the door. She dims the lights and then opens it. He doesn't have a corsage or anything. He hasn't even changed his clothes. She tries not to feel disappointed. He would have if he'd known, but how could he have known?

Brooke hitches up her gown, which is a size or two too big. "Don't say anything. I know it's kind of weird, but I'm pretending we're at the prom." Her neck, shoulders, and arms are bare but the scabs don't look bad with the light dimmed.

She closes the door behind him to keep her nosy housekeeper from spying on them. How nice her bed looks, so perfectly made with its pretty white seersucker-and-lace bedspread from Tocca Home. She sits down on it. On her bedside table, Maraschino cherries dance in the cut-glass Baccarat crystal punch bowl, which she has filled with ginger ale, Veuve Cliquot, Tanqueray gin, and apple juice. She ladles out a goblet of punch and drinks the entire thing. She'd thought when it got dark, things would feel different. She could pretend they'd known each other all their lives and this was the night. But Taylor just stands there in his dorky Levis and kind of ugly black button-down shirt and definitely ugly white leather basketball sneakers. He looks like Emilio Estevez. Ew!

"What grade are you in anyway?" she asks, licking her lips with a Molly-esque combination of standoffishness and allure.

"Tenth," he answers, folding his arms defensively across his chest.

He is so out of there. "My parents are coming home in a sec," Brooke lies with a shrug. "My brother got pneumonia so they're flying back early." How anyone could get pneumonia in Hawaii, she has no idea, but it sounds authentic.

8. The next day she visits the laundry room just because she likes the smell. At least it's somewhere to go besides the elevator or the lobby. Taylor is there, with another boy who looks a lot like him, only older and taller, folding their laundry.

"This is my brother, Michael." Taylor pats Michael's shoulder like he's proud of him for being so good-looking and tall. "He goes to Columbia."

Even Brooke is impressed, although she knows she shouldn't be. Her brother, Alex, applied early to Columbia and he's a total loser.

"Brooke has a really nice room," Taylor says like he wants his brother to know that he's been in her room.

Michael is folding a pair of black Calvin Klein boxer briefs in a very manly, matter-of-fact way. He grins and hauls a frayed white towel, with the word FLORIDA emblazoned on it in faded orange letters, out of the dryer. "Taylor is in love with you," he confides to Brooke with an amused twinkle in his nice brown eyes. "He took, like, four showers this morning, he was thinking about you so much."

Brooke blushes. She isn't exactly sure what Michael means about Taylor's showers, but she doesn't really want to know, either. It's not that she doesn't like Taylor; he just didn't sweep her off her feet the way he was supposed to on prom night. "I'm so bored," she tells the boys with listless insistence. "Want to come up and watch a movie with me or something?"

Michael folds another pair of black Calvin Klein boxer briefs. It's Christmas Eve and his Columbia friends have all gone home. He's probably bored, too. "Sure," he answers for himself and Taylor, who glares at him, like Michael always steals his girlfriends.

9. "I thought your family came home last night," Taylor says in the elevator.

"Well, they didn't." Brooke shrugs her shoulders, already annoyed with his forlorn white leather basketball shoes. Not that he's so bad. He isn't. He's nice. He's a good kisser. And he doesn't ask annoying questions or assume she's desperate because she goes to St. Agnes. According to her dickhead brother, Alex, who goes to St. Hugh's, all St. Agnes girls are smart, nerdy, and horny because they're all repressed virgins. Alex's friends actually knock on her door sometimes and say, "Do you want me to get you laid? Because Alex says you need it bad." Then they laugh, like they're just joking. But if they're joking, why do they even bring it up? Taylor isn't like that, but there's something so completely next-door-to-the-laundry-room about him. Like he only emerges to go to school or something. Michael's sexier — a much more obvious prom date — but even he's got a little too much laundry room in him.

10. Outside, it's snowing. Brooke leaves the boys in the den with the TV remote and heads into her parents' dressing room to change. At first, she'd planned

22

on wearing her mom's black Vera Wang with the little mink bow on the bodice. Now that it's snowing, she puts on the flowing white Oscar de la Renta gown with the mohair corset. It's a total snow queen outfit, like something Barbie would wear in one of those freaky animated all-singing, all-dancing Barbie movies Brooke used to watch over and over back in first grade. *Barbie the Snow Princess of Icetopia.* Or, *Brooke Fenton, Prom Queen!* All she's missing is a diamond tiara. She heads back into the den in bare feet because her mom's shoes are all size ten and she's only a size eight.

"Holy shit," Michael exclaims when he sees her. Weirdly enough, the boys are watching *The Breakfast Club.* Or maybe it's not weird. Taylor probably thinks he can kiss her again during the Judd–Molly kiss scene. Brooke pads over to the window to watch the snow fall. It's getting dark already. The bare limbs of the trees in Central Park are stark white.

The boys scoot apart and she sits down on the sofa between them, fanning the voluminous white skirts of her gown all around her until the sheer white silk touches their jeans. She can feel them trying not to look at her, as if waiting for her cue. To do what, though? She doesn't even know what she wants with them. It's just fun to wear a pouffy dress and flirt a little. It might be more fun to be in Namibia riding an elephant with a guy hung like a zebra, but that's not an option right now.

11. They watch the whole movie and then they watch *Top Gun* with Tom Cruise, one of Alex's favorites and Michael's, too, apparently. Brooke considers putting her hand on Michael's leg, just to see what happens,

23

but then he falls asleep just before Tom Cruise's best friend, Goose, dies. She stops the movie before it's even over. With its fighter planes and Goose-dying scene, *Top Gun* has never factored into her prom-night fantasies. She stands up to check out the snow again, ignoring Taylor completely. All of a sudden the soundtrack to *Sixteen Candles* comes on. Spandau Ballet.

> *Bah bup-bup baah bah*
> *You **know** this **much** is **true** . . . !*

She turns around.

It's gotten dark but the glow of the snow through the windows makes the room look almost candlelit. Taylor holds out his hand. "Dance?"

Brooke realizes how much he actually looks like Jake from *Sixteen Candles* — at least he will in a few years. And Sam never really knew Jake, Brooke realizes, it was just the idea of him that she liked. Brooke likes the idea of Taylor, too. "Oh, he's just this guy from my building," she can hear herself explaining over the phone when Katherine returns from Namibia. She walks over and puts her hands on Taylor's shoulders. He puts his hands on her waist and they rock from side to side. She smiles up at his nice dark eyelashes and thick eyebrows. If they were really in a Molly Ringwald movie, he'd say something like, "Merry Christmas, Brooke," and then kiss her.

She closes her eyes. And then he does — he says it.

"Merry Christmas, Brooke."

Now he's more than just an idea. She keeps her eyes closed, tilts her head back, and kisses him. It's exactly like the scene at the end of *Sixteen Candles* when Jake and

Sam sit on the dining room table with Sam's birthday cake between them, kissing. Except they're in the city and it's snowing and Michael is splayed out on the sofa, snoring softly. Maybe it's not like any movie. Maybe she and Molly and Taylor and Jake don't have anything in common. But who gives a shit? The prom is all about dancing and kissing a boy you've always secretly liked, and she's doing it, she's finally doing it.

In Vodka Veritas

by Holly Black

Wallingford Preparatory has two tracks. One is for kids who want to get into the good colleges that private boarding schools — even ones in New Jersey — are supposed to help you get into. The other track — the one not mentioned in the brochures — is for rich kids kicked out of public schools. It's probably been that way since before they let the girls in, back when this place was just the one building that's boarded up on the edge of the campus. Put on a jacket and tie every day and all sins are forgiven.

I've been at Wallingford five years — since I got expelled from the seventh grade for making a knife in metal shop. But I wasn't being psycho like the girls here think. If some asshole jock threatens to jump me after school because I made him look stupid in homeroom, I'm not going to just take the beating like a good little geek. My skinny ass wouldn't have exactly won in a fair fight, so I didn't play fair.

My mother says that I don't think about consequences until it's too late. That might be true.

But seriously, most of the reasons why Wallingford girls think I'm crazy are stupid rumors. Like it wasn't my fault that after the school trip to France, everybody said I brought back the head of some guy who got into a motorcycle accident on the Rue Racine. Come on, anybody who believes that is a moron! How would I have gotten a head through customs? They won't even let in some Anjou pears. And painting my fingernails black is a cosmetic choice, not a symbol of my eternal devotion to Satan. It's also one of the only things I can do to get around the dress code — makeup is allowed, and the handbook doesn't specify only on girls.

Yeah, so I guess you picked up on my lack of school pride. Want to know what Wallingford is really like? Every year, they send out a fund-raiser to restore Smythe Hall — that boarded-up eyesore I mentioned earlier — and every year the only thing that gets built is an addition on the dean's house. That's also why we have to have our prom in our own banquet room. Sure, it's better than a gymnasium, but the public school kids get to dance and eat rubbery chicken in the ballroom of a Marriott.

It's not like I don't do any extracurricular activities, though. I'm the founder and president of the Wallingford gaming club — the Pawns. Our shtick is to break into empty classrooms and project PlayStation games on the whiteboard or jerry-rig Doom 3 tournaments with our laptops. Sometimes we even go old-school and play paper-and-dice Dungeons and Dragons. It's my job to decide. That pretty much makes me Lord of the Losers. Which is great if you want a Phantom Blade with a Fiery Enchantment, but not so great if what you want is a date to the prom.

Luckily, my best friend, Danny Yu, VP and secretary of the Pawns, doesn't have a date, either. There are many reasons why I love Danny, but the biggest one is that he's the only person at Wallingford as crazy as me.

Like one time, when he was home sick, he saw some daytime talk show that had a bunch of KKK members on it and gave out their official website. So Danny flips open his laptop and sends them an e-mail: *I am very interested in starting my own chapter of the Klan. Can you tell me what thread-count sheets we should wear?* A half hour later, he sends another one from a different account: *Do you believe that white bread is racially superior to other breads?* They never e-mailed him back.

Come on, you can't blame that shit on DayQuil. That's plain genius.

So it's the week before prom and we've already been shot down a couple of times. We're in Latin class and we're supposed to be translating something about Dionysus. Danny's going over our seriously limited prom choices instead.

"I could ask Daria Wisniewski," he says. "She likes comics."

"She has that creepy doll with the goggles she takes everywhere. Odds are she'll put it in a matching prom dress and bring it along."

"It could be your date, then," Danny says. "Perfect."

"What about Abby Goldstein?" I list off the reasons this is a good idea on my fingers. "Hot. Redhead. Talked to me twice without actually needing to."

"Dude, she'd never go out with you. Not even if she had a nasty fetish and you were the only one discreet and desperate enough to take care of it."

"Very vivid — that fantasy of yours. Weird that it's about me, though."

"Boys," says Ms. Esposito. She's tiny, shorter than a sixth grader, but not someone you want to piss off. She drinks coffee all day long out of a thermos that has a French press built right into it. "How about you tell me what the Bacchanalia were?"

I stutter something, but Danny turns nonchalantly on his chair and smiles his most ass-kissing grin. "The festivals of Bacchus, called Dionysus by the Greeks. People got drunk and had big orgies."

Some of the class laughs, but not Ms. Esposito. "He was called Dionysus by the Romans and Bacchus by the Greeks, but otherwise essentially correct. Now, can anyone tell me what the maenads were?"

We can't.

"No? Well, if we're going to continue reading the story of Orpheus, it's important to know. It was said that the mysteries of Bacchus inspired women into an ecstatic frenzy that included intoxication, fornication, bloodletting, and even mutilation. They would tear those not engaged in celebrating Bacchus limb from limb."

The class is silent.

"Xavier, can you read the first paragraph in Latin?" Ms. Esposito asks. She looks satisfied, like she knows she can freak us more than we can freak her. As Xavier starts to read, Danny turns to me.

"Let's not go," he says.

I'm still thinking about wild women streaked with mud and dried, black gore. In my mind, it's kind of hot. "What?"

"Let's get into our rented tuxes, take pictures for our parents, pretend we're off to get our dates, score a bottle of booze, and do something dumb, something different."

His kiss-ass grin has not faded and I realize something about that smile. It's kind of smug. Charming but smug.

I'm torn. On one hand, it sounds like a pretty good plan. On the other hand, it's a plan I didn't come up with. "Let's break into Smythe Hall," I say. "Do some urban exploring right on campus."

"Genius." His grin widens into a smile and the naked, crazy girls fade from my mind.

The night before we're supposed to go, Danny calls me. "Um, dude. I feel like a dick, but I have a date. I'm going to the prom."

I'm in my dorm room, downloading episodes of *Veronica Mars* and googling the old school. I was going to tell him that there were photos on Weird NJ of the place. I was going to tell him that supposedly someone remembered having a prom there. I have maps and everything printing in color off my ink-jet.

My hamster, Snot, runs on his wheel and I hear only the *clack, clack, clack* of the metal because I'm not speaking. Snot's been hiding the choice bits of seed from his food bowl for the last half hour but now he's finally decided to kick his night into high gear. Lucky him.

"Who?" I ask.

"Daria," he says. "She asked me, man. And she has a friend who could go with you —"

I don't wait to hear who the spare friend Daria Wisniewski's willing to throw in to sweeten the pot. I don't ask if it's her stupid doll. I just hang up.

He calls back twice, but I just let the phone buzz. I look at the tuxedo hanging on the door of the closet. I look at the floorboards, at the one I pried up to hide the half bottle of Grey Goose liberated from my parents. Now it seems like a half bottle isn't nearly enough.

My roommate left for his dad's house this afternoon. He and his date are taking the SATs in the morning and then going straight to prom. I'm not sure if he thinks that's like foreplay or what. Anyway, I'm glad he's not here, because my eyes burn like I just got dumped.

I know I'm not supposed to cry over a guy standing me up. So I don't. But I have to practically break my knuckles against the brick wall outside my window to manage it.

By the time I get to the abandoned part of the school on prom night, I'm already drunk.

The good thing about living at a private school is that you know how to break into places. You learn how to break into other guys' rooms to take their hot cocoa mix and soup cups. You learn how to break into unused classrooms because that's the only place you can really set up a bunch of computers for a tournament. If you're like Danny and me, you learn how to grappling hook out of your dorm room and break into the cafeteria because sometimes what you really need is a sandwich.

So, basically, I take off the hinges. No problem if you're sober, but it takes a while for me and I have to set down my bottle. Then I almost knock it over. The glass makes a hollow sound and scrapes over the concrete. I snatch it up by the neck and stumble inside, leaving the door just leaning there, sagging from the knob.

Inside, the dust is so thick that the cuffs of my pants are already white with it. The walls are wainscoted in wood, and along the water-streaked boards, I see the outlines of where paintings once hung. I take another sip. The vodka no longer burns as it goes down. I feel like I'm drinking water.

I loosen my tie and a kind of giddiness comes over me. It's much cooler to be here than at the prom. I bet Danny forgot to get Daria a corsage and she's already resenting him. I bet they're taking stupid posed pictures in front of some kind of draped cloth and a vase full of red, red roses. I bet that the food is tasteless and the music is bad. I bet he's forgotten that we were going to wear tuxedos on our little breaking-and-entering expedition and had to rent whatever was left. I imagine him in light blue with a ruffled shirt. That makes me almost laugh out loud, but my smile turns sour when I realize that it would actually be *funny* and I see us both in them, exalting in our dorkitude.

Maybe I should have just sucked it up and taken the pity date. I wonder if Danny is pissed that I hung up on him, if he thinks that I'm afraid of girls. Suddenly, I'm morose. Being drunk by myself in an old building doesn't seem as edgy as it did moments before. It seems sad and a little pathetic.

Just then, I hear a sound down the hallway. I get up, clumsy with booze. My fingers and tongue are so numb that it's almost pleasurable to stumble. I know that it could be one of the rent-a-cops the school's probably crawling with or even one of the administrators, but my drunk brain can't help conjuring up a girl. In my fantasy, she just got dumped by her jock boyfriend, she's stunningly beautiful, and she goes back to the prom with me on her arm.

I walk in the direction of the sound and I see candles flickering. In the center of a large room, six robed figures funnel dark liquid into silver flasks. At their center is Ms. Esposito. I'm so surprised that it takes my brain long moments to catch up with what I'm seeing.

I stumble a little and they all look at me. The whole thing is so surreal that I start to laugh.

"*Ave*," one of them says. I walk a little closer and I see Xavier. He's second board in the chess club, which makes him a member of the Pawns.

I salute him with my almost-empty bottle of Grey Goose.

"*Potestatem obscuri lateris nescis*," he says. Some of them laugh nervously.

I frown, trying to figure out what he's saying. "Did you just tell me that I don't know the power of the dark side?" More laughter.

Xavier grins and turns to the others. "He's okay," he says. "He passed the test. Besides, I can vouch for him. He's down. And besides, *cornix cornici oculos non effodiet*."

A crow doesn't rip out the eyes of another crow. Nice.

Looking at their faces, I suddenly realize I know them. It's the Latin Club. Diego, Jenny, Ashley, Mike, and David. And their advisor, Ms. Esposito. Geeks, one and all. My people.

"What are you doing?" My words come out slurred.

"Bringing Bacchanalia to Wallingford," says Jenny. "And you're going to help us."

I picture Jenny streaked with mud and blood, rolling around in an orgiastic frenzy, but the image doesn't stick.

"*Quomodo dicitur Latine?*" says Ms. Esposito.

33

I know that one. She wants Jenny to only talk in Latin.

"*Paenitere*," Jenny tells her.

It's then that I notice Mike's gleaming dress shoes and the sequins at Ashley's throat under her robe. A crazy grin grows on my face as I realize they're wearing prom clothes. All this creepy shit aside, I finally get it. They're going to spike the punch. This is a prom prank of epic proportions.

Danny won't be part of it. He'll be slow-dancing like an idiot. He'll feel left out.

"*In vodka veritas*," I say and tilt back my bottle, pouring the last of it down my throat. I choke a little, but I swallow anyway. *In vodka is truth.*

Ms. Esposito doesn't smile, but she does hand me a vial of the whatever-it-is. I'm thinking Everclear. "*Nunc est bibendum*," she says. *Now it's time to drink.*

They snuff out their candles and strip off their robes near a closet. The gleaming wood and lack of dust point to them meeting here before, maybe lots of times.

"Wow," I say drunkenly to Xavier as we cross the quad. "This is pretty awesome. I had no idea Latin Club was so cool." And I hadn't. I'd always pictured the Pawns as the big geek rebels. I'm actually a little intimidated. I kind of want to join.

He grins. "*Quidquid latine dictum sit, altum videtur.*"

That one takes me a while, but I finally figure it out. *Everything's better when you say it in Latin.* I restrain myself from rolling my eyes.

As we're about to enter the banquet hall, Mike turns to me and says, "*Cave quid dicis quando et cui.*" Basically, be careful what I say.

My plan is to be careful where I stand. I'm sure I stink of vodka and I bet that my eyes are glassy. Any advisor gets a whiff of me and I'm going to get hauled out of here.

"Look," Xavier says, leaning close to me, and I'm startled to hear him speak English. "The rest of them probably don't care what happens to you, but I want to make sure you understand. That stuff in the vial is an antidote. Take a quick sip and you won't be affected."

"But . . . aren't we just spiking the punch?" I ask.

He laughs. "No way. Look around. People are drinking water and soda and energy drinks. No one drinks punch out of a central punch bowl anymore. That's out of some eighties movie."

I look around. The theme of the prom is Under the Sea. Blue, white, and gold streamers hang from the ceiling, and the tables are covered in sea-green chiffon cloth. Someone has spray painted real shells gold and scattered them on the tables, hot gluing them around napkin rings. Stenciled numbers mark the round tables. I think I see Danny across the room, sitting at one of them, next to Daria. He has his arm draped over her shoulders.

But Xavier's right. Servers are clearing plates of cake, but there's no table with a cake on it. No punch bowl beside it to spike. "Wait, so what are we doing exactly?"

"Dude, aren't you tired of the beautiful people lording over you?"

Of course I'm tired of it. I nod.

He tilts his head toward the stage and the DJ. The shimmering lights of the dance floor reflect in the lenses of his glasses, obscuring his eyes. "They think they're so

35

smart, but all they do is screw up, screw around, and screw off. Tonight, they'll see their own true natures. You'll love it. One steaming-hot plate of revenge coming right up."

Across the room, I see Ms. Esposito lift her hands. She starts chanting, and next to me, Xavier starts chanting, too, with a wink in my direction. They're speaking low and I can't make out the words over the music. I feel weird, violent, and too hot. I want to yell at Danny; I want to feel my knuckles bruise against his jaw.

Xavier smacks the side of my arm. I look at him and he's miming at me to drink something. I remember the vial in my pocket and take a sip. It tastes too sweet, like fortified wine. Immediately, I notice that I'm breathing like I'm already in a fight. I shake my head. Everything's fine. I'm fine.

I turn toward the dance floor. Couples are grinding against each other, hands roaming over satin. Boys start unlacing their ties and shrugging off jackets. That's funny, I think.

Across the room, Jenny and Mike are leaving. Ashley takes a picture of the headmaster as he leans down to kiss Ms. Perez, our newest and youngest English teacher. Surprisingly, neither of them seems to notice the camera.

Behind me, Xavier laughs. I start walking toward where I saw Danny and Daria last.

Couples are no longer dancing — they're kissing and groping. A few have moved to lying on the floor together. The captain of the football team knocks the shells and plates off the table and throws Missy Carthage on it. He climbs on top of her.

It's all happening so fast. Someone hits someone else. I don't see how it starts, but there is a sudden knot of fighting.

The music has stopped and only human sounds fill the silence. The camera flashes again.

"What's happening?" someone asks. There's a girl in a shimmering green dress with one sleeve and a heavy ruffle on the bottom. Her hair is spiked up and saturated with glitter and her eyes are heavily outlined in black kohl. Her skin looks blotchy around the neck like she's getting hives. She slouches against the doorway.

She doesn't even go to this school.

"You should leave," I say, but then a boy catches her hand and pulls her into a kiss. She groans.

I grab her hand and pull her back to me. The boy lets go and she slides into my arms. Her mouth comes against mine and we're kissing. I've only kissed three girls before and none of them kissed me like this, like they never wanted to stop, like they don't care about breathing. I pull back from her and she frowns, like she doesn't know where she is.

I shake my head, but that just makes me dizzy. The floor is carpeted in sequined gowns and black tuxedos. On top of them, bodies move together. I see the math teacher, Mr. Riggs, among them, writhing around with Jacob White and Nancy Chung. Amy Gershwin's purple bra is around her waist, like a belt, as she crawls toward them.

Across the room, three cheerleaders corner another cheerleader and swipe at her with their long, manicured nails. Scratches mark both her cheeks.

I stumble forward and see Danny. He's lying half

underneath a table, kissing Hannah Davis, who turns and kisses Daria Wisniewski. None of them is very dressed. Hannah is wearing Wonder Woman underpants.

There's a part of me that figures Danny deserves whatever happens to him at that point. I know it's an asshole thing to think, but isn't this what he hoped would happen at one of the prom afterparties anyway? Would he really have turned down a threesome with two girls? I mean, sure, everyone is going crazy, but aren't they just giving in to what they really desire? Isn't he?

And it's not like I could stop him.

Then I think of the vial in my pocket. There's still some liquid in it. But then, maybe he wouldn't want me to stop him.

"Danny," I say, still not sure. I want him to do something that will make him familiar again.

He turns toward me and his face is blank with desire.

I take out the vial, because I don't care what he wants or if he deserves it. I just want him to be Danny again.

"Drink some," I say, but he's kissing Daria and not paying any more attention. I get down on the floor. Someone is pulling off my jacket. I let it go.

Hannah Davis puts her lips to my neck and I reach over her to try and force Danny to drink, but everyone shifts and I'm afraid I'm going to spill the antidote.

So I take a swig and hold it in my cheek. I press my lips to his and when his mouth opens under mine, I spit it all out. Yes, okay, that's technically a kiss. Technically, I kissed Danny. But it worked.

"Dude," he says and stumbles to his feet. He looks like he just woke up out of a dream.

I have no idea what to say to him. "The Latin Club is totally evil," I blurt.

"The Latin Club?"

I can understand why he's confused.

"We have to stop them," I say, but they're not even here anymore. They've already succeeded, taken photographic evidence, and gone home.

Danny picks up a pair of pants. Three kids are doing body shots off the limp form of the assistant headmaster. I don't even know where they got the liquor, but I think I see blood near his neck.

"What can we do?" Danny asks. Daria pulls at his pant leg and he stumbles, wide-eyed. "This is nuts."

"I know where they keep their stuff," I say, and he follows me from the banquet hall and out into the night. We run across campus to Smythe Hall. A few kids are out on the lawn, dancing around naked to the delight of the underclassmen hanging out the windows of their dorm.

Inside the abandoned building, I feel my way through the dusty rooms to the closet. My empty bottle of vodka is still there, but it looks unfamiliar, as though it's a relic from a hundred years ago.

The closet contains a moth-eaten lion cub skin, which is both scary and gross, a bunch of goblets, and an almost-full bottle that smells and looks just like the antidote.

"I know what to do," I say, and I explain my kiss/spit technique.

Danny raises his eyebrows higher than eyebrows should go. "Your plan is that we kiss everyone."

"Basically, yes," I say.

"Teachers included?" he asks.

I realize I'm looking at his mouth when he talks. I remember the way his lips feel. I'm a moron, but I think I get it. I finally get it.

"Everyone," I say. "Teachers. The basketball team. The administration. Hot girls. *Ever-ry-one.*"

He laughs. "It's genius," he says, "but definitely evil genius."

"Is there any other kind?" I quip.

So we kiss our way through the entire junior class. I make sure to plant a good one on the headmaster. It's pretty awesome to spit in his mouth.

When we're done, we round up Daria and Hannah and go out to a diner. We eat in silence, but Danny and I keep grinning at each other and finally we just start laughing, which the girls so don't appreciate.

"Sorry I was kind of a dick," I tell him after Daria and Hannah go back to their dorm. "And sorry we had to suck face to save the school."

"You're not sorry," he says, and for a moment the words hang dangerously in the air, able to mean too many things. "You got to kiss Abby Goldstein," he finally finishes and we can both laugh.

"And you," I say, surprising myself. There I go, not thinking about consequences. I'm not even sure I know what I mean. No, I know what I mean.

"Yeah?" he asks.

I nod miserably. He knows what I mean, too.

"That's cool," Danny says. "'Cause I'm such a stud, huh?"

"You're such an asshole," I say, but I laugh.

*   *   *

40

The next Monday is bizarre. Classes with juniors are almost entirely quiet. Lots of kids aren't even there. The underclassmen are buzzing like crazy with rumors. It's the first time I've ever seen knots of seniors, sophomores, and freshmen all gossiping together. Drugs, they're saying. A cult. It's kind of hilarious, except that people got hurt. The assistant headmaster is still at the hospital, but his wife e-mailed his resignation.

I've got to admit it, I'm finding myself strangely full of Wallingford pride.

Of course, Mike and Xavier and all the rest of the Latin Club glare at me when we pass in the halls. I don't think they're all that mad, though. Whatever blackmail scheme they got going is probably kicking into high gear. I'm sure they'll all be buying new computers by the end of the week.

Still, I'm a little nervous as I roll into Latin.

Danny's already there and he grins as I sit down next to him. "Dude," he says, "want to go to Western Plaguelands tonight for a raid? I heard about a sunken temple in Caer Darrow with lots of purple drops."

"I'm on it like a bonnet," I say.

All things considered, he's a good best friend. Maybe better than me.

Ms. Esposito walks by my desk, holding her coffee. *"Antiquis temporibus, nati tibi similes in rupibus ventosissimis exponebantur ad nece,"* she says, which I think means that if we were back in the good old days, I'd be left out on a windswept crag to die.

She smiles.

I'm so registering for German next year.

41

Your Big Night
by Sarah Mlynowski

You were worried it wouldn't happen. Terrified. Smashing-a-headlight-while-taking-your-driver's-test terrified. Ever since Shane dumped you again, this time for The Model (some sophomore named Reese who supposedly had appeared in some random catalogues), you knew that you had HAD to get a date for prom.

But terror be gone! TheMan, the screen name belonging to Brent Booster, your blue-eyed and sexy yearbook editor (with whom you occasionally e-flirt while working on page layouts) has just written you the delicious words you've been waiting for:

TheMan: wanna go 2 prom together?
Or is asking you sexual harassment?

Yes, yes, yes! You don't write that, obviously, since you are trying to appear cool. You take a deep calming breath, lift your feet onto your desk in an attempt to stretch and therefore relax, and type:

Drew: Sure
TheMan: sure it's sexual harassment?

Drew: Sure I'll go to prom with you. ☺

But then you worry. Why does he call himself TheMan? You hope he is being ironic.

Your own screen name came from your ex. When Shane met you back when you were fourteen, he thought you looked like Drew Barrymore. Now everyone you know calls you Drew.

But more than Shane's screen name, you worry about Mandy, Brent's on-and-off-again girlfriend for the past year, who, though not on the yearbook staff, often hogs the yearbook couch, fridge, and Internet access. Should you ask about her? No, you decide. You should not.

Drew: What about Mandy?

You nervously pick at your split ends while waiting for a reply. You're pretty sure Mandy and Brent are finished. In fact, just today you witnessed her throw her bio textbook at his head after third period. You wish you had the guts to throw a textbook at your ex. But that would show him that you care. Which you don't. No way, no how. It's kaput. Finis.

TheMan: so over

So perfect! Two months before prom and you already have a date. And you need a date, if you want to make Shane jealous. Which, of course, you don't.

*　　*　　*

"Don't go with him," your best friend Jen warns you the next day in gym.

You, Jen, and your other best friend, Kyra — the three of you clad in hideously fluorescent orange gym clothes — are lying side by side (first Kyra, then you, then Jen) on identical blue and smelly foam mats. This month your phys ed teacher has become obsessed with Pilates and is making you all engage in a form of painful sit-ups called hundreds, where you lie on your back and pulsate a hundred times.

"Why" — you exhale as you pulse — "not?" You are trying harder than you normally would, in an attempt to get into shape for prom.

"Because he's going to get back together with Mandy and you're going to get screwed," Jen says matter-of-factly.

"He wouldn't have asked me if he was planning on getting back together with Mandy," you point out.

"It's a risky move." Kyra stops exercising and turns on her side to face you. "Why don't you want to come with us in the Winnebago?"

You roll your eyes. You are not going to prom in an RV. And you are not going to prom with girlfriends. Any other time, any other occasion, fine, but this is *prom*. You need a date. You can't have Shane thinking you can't get a date for prom. Seeing you on the arm of another guy will make Shane realize what he has lost. Which will make Shane fall in love with you all over again. Not that you'd take him back. No way. Not this time.

At least, not right away.

Fine. You admit it. You want him back. Maybe. And making him jealous is the way to his heart. It's worked before, and it'll work again.

"We saw you roll your eyes," Jen says, still hundreds-ing. Unlike you, she is superathletic (plays intramural soccer and Connecticut community baseball). She can even multitask easily, i.e., work out and talk at the same time.

"It's going to be fun," Kyra says, re-tying her long black hair into a ponytail. "Don't you want to spend the night with the people who are actually important to you and not some random guy?"

"Brent isn't random," you say. "We've been on year-book staff together for three years. Plus we e-flirt." The IMs and e-mails were always harmless, although you used to leave them open on your computer so Shane would see them. Making it look like another guy was interested in you always made him more attentive. Much more effective than all those times you'd call him (after not hanging out for a week) and bug him not to take you for granted.

"You e-flirt whenever he's fighting with his girl-friend," Jen reminds you. "Then they get back together, and good-bye, IM buddy."

"He's not getting back together with Mandy," you huff.

"I don't like Mandy," Kyra says. "She's so snobby."

"I don't like her either," Jen says. "She's so blond. I have to watch her every morning, bobbing up and down in her cheesecake convertible."

You shake a fistful of your blond hair at her. "Hel-lo?"

"You know what I mean. It's blinding. Like a spotlight glaring into your eyes."

Mandy lives two doors down from Jen and never offers her a lift to school. Luckily, Jen has you to pick her up.

"Don't you think he'd make a good prom date?" you ask, deliberately steering away from the topic of exes. "Picture him in a tux."

"You guys would look good in pictures," Kyra admits.

You lay your head back on the mat, close your eyes, and visualize these so-called pictures. Yes, you would look good together. Not as good as if you were going with Shane, but still good.

"I understand wanting to go with a boyfriend," Jen says, "but since none of us has one, it's stupid not to go together."

"Are you saying I'm stupid?" you snap.

She is obsessed with the Girls Only Winnebago. She read about it in a teen magazine and became convinced that all senior unattached females should do it. Instead of bringing dates, a bunch of girls have their pre-prom party in a chauffeured Winnebago, go solo to the prom, and then party all night in the RV.

You're not crazy. Are you? Most people want a date for prom, don't they? Your friends act like you're the first person in the history of the world to want to be paired up for the friggin' thing. Though if they knew the real reason you're so desperate to go, they might be more understanding. Of course, they might also have you institutionalized. Either that or chain you to a brick wall until the whole thing is over.

"I'm not saying you're stupid," Jen says. "I just don't understand why it's so important to have a date."

Shane always wants what he can't have, but no way are you going to remind them of that important little tidbit. *"I am not going to let you go through that again,"* Jen would say. *"How long do you think it would take before he breaks your heart another time?"*

"Let her do what she wants," Kyra cuts in. "It's her senior prom. She has to make a decision that she'll be happy with for the rest of her life."

Jen snorts. "You make it sound like a tattoo. It's just a dance."

Just a dance? Easy for Jen to say, considering she already went last year with her then-senior boyfriend. "I want the whole shebang," you announce. "A date. A corsage." Shane to realize his mistake.

"We're going to get ourselves corsages," Kyra says. "Come on, Drew, are you in?"

"No, I'm not in. I want to go in a limo."

"But the Winnebago has a king-size bed!" Kyra exclaims. "How cool is that?"

"What do you need a bed for if none of you even has a date?" you ask.

"Jumping," Kyra says. "And watching movies."

"More like napping," you mutter. "Because that's how bored I would be in the Winnebago."

You spot Brent and Mandy chatting by the water fountain.

Uh-oh.

Calm down. They're just talking. Nothing to be worried about. Nothing wrong with a little chit and chat.

*   *   *

47

When Brent tells you that he and his friends have rented a limo, you cheer.

And then you buy The Dress.

A gorgeous pale pink Nicole Miller dress that makes your mom tear up when you model it for her. She buys you a matching (on sale!) pink wrap because Connecticut nights can be cool in May, and one-inch silver heels that don't give you much height but will keep you comfy and able to dance all night. You are *so* not making the same mistake you made at your cousin's wedding last fall. You wore three-inch strappy heels that gave you blisters the size of your thumbs and forced you to hold on to table-tops for balance.

Tabletops — and Shane. He was there, holding your hand, showing off his dimples, telling you that you looked beautiful, making you feel beautiful. And special. Until the next week when Jen told you she saw him making out with The Model in the back row of a James Bond movie.

You're on your way home from school when you spot Brent in the passenger seat of Mandy's car.

I'm going to be sick, you think.

You IM him later that night.

> Drew: What's the story? Are U
> and Mandy back together?
> **TheMan: no . . .**

You do not like the look of those ellipses. This is not good. Not one bit. What should you do? You decide to pretend that all is normal and that this doesn't affect prom at all. He is not going to ditch you. They were just talking, right? *Right???*

You're on your way to Spanish when you spot a whirl of hair: blond (hers) and brown (his). It reminds you of your favorite chocolate-and-vanilla-swirl frozen yogurt. (Not that your prom diet allows for frozen yogurt.) It's them. And they're kissing. They're practically eating each other's mouths.

Also not good.

You try to catch him alone, but he is stapled to Mandy's mouth for the rest of the day.

"Told you," Jen says. "There's still room in the Winnebago."

"Please come, it will be awesome!" Kyra squeals. "We are going to have a huge slumber party afterward and watch movies all night!"

"I have a date," you scoff.

"Not for long," Jen taunts.

You are vigorously doing hundreds when you see the IM:

TheMan: hey Drew . . .

Damn ellipses. You breathe in, breathe out, then type:

Drew: Yup?
TheMan: Mandy and I are back together.

@&$%! You are far too well mannered to type what you're thinking. Instead you write:

49

Drew: Good for you guys.

Log off, your inner voice warns. Save the prom! Save the prom! Quickly log off before he can —

TheMan: the thing is . . .

No, no, no!

TheMan: she wants us to go to prom together. You understand, right? U can still come in our limo. It fits 12 people and we're only 8. Interested?

It is not fair that Mandy and Brent have gotten back together in time for prom while you and Shane have not. You log off before you tell him where to shove it.

"You were right," you tell Jen, while slamming shut your locker.

"No kidding. So you'll come with us in the Winnebago? It's not just me and Kyra anymore. Lisa Gilmore and Janna Finestein are in, too. We're aiming for five people, so with you —"

You can't take this today. "I'm not coming in the Winnebego. I'm going to Plan B."

"Which is —"

"Powell."

Powell has been your best male friend since fourth grade. In the third grade he used to pick his nose and try to wipe the boogers on your hair and you would kick him in the butt. That summer you called a truce. (Though

50

he still occasionally tries to gross you out and you still occasionally give his ass the boot.)

Jen shakes her head in clear dismay. "I cannot believe you'd rather go with him than with us."

"He's a good friend, just like you. Except he happens to be male." Sure, you would never go out with him before — but that was pre-prom. Now you can already picture it as clearly as if it were a romantic comedy playing on the movie screen in your head. Buddies forever, and then you decide to go to prom as friends. But what's this? You can't believe how cute he looks in his tux? He thinks you are a vision in pink? You're grooving to some pop song when suddenly the band begins to play "Your Body Is a Wonderland" and at first you're smiling but then a serious expression settles on your faces as your bodies come closer and then closer and you can barely get a pinky finger between your ligaments. . . .

But then, just as you are about to start hooking up on the dance floor, Shane cuts in and tells you that he has never stopped loving you. Who should you choose? How could you hurt Powell after so many years of friendship? Powell makes your decision for you when he kisses you on the cheek and says, "Go for it." And you all live happily ever after.

At lunch, you tug Powell toward an empty classroom by his too-long, torn-sleeved jersey. "Gotta talk to you."

He lets you guide him and then hops onto the teacher's desk. "What up?"

Your turn. But you're suddenly nervous. "So," you begin. "How are you?"

He waves his brown paper lunch bag at you. "Hungry."

Ask him! Just pop the question. What's the big deal? You've been friends for years. There is no reason for your palms and armpits to be suddenly sweaty. No reason, damn it! Unless you've been holding a love torch for him for years and you've only just realized it this very second?

Nah.

"So," you begin again. "What are your plans for the next few months?"

He raises an eyebrow. "Um, exams?"

"And after exams?"

"College?"

He is not making this easy. "And before college?"

He laughs. "Summer?"

Is he trying to kill you here? You're going to have to just blurt it out in one quick word: *"Andwhataboutprom?"*

"You mean who am I going with?"

"Yes, who are you going with?"

He opens his lunch bag, reaches inside, pulls out an unwrapped sandwich, and starts munching. "Not sure yet. You're going with Brent, right?"

"That didn't work out as planned."

"No?" he asks while chewing. "So who are you going with?"

Is he hinting? Is that hope you hear in his voice? "I was thinking that maybe it would be fun if *wewenttogether, whatdoyouthink?*" Your words come out faster and higher than you expected, like the way your voice sounds on an answering machine.

He stops chewing and cocks his head to the left. "You and me?"

"Yes."

"Oh."

"Oh" is not the answer you wanted. You were angling for more of a "*That's a great idea, Drew! Brilliant! What time should I pick you up?*"

"Wouldn't that be fun?" you squeak.

"Well . . ."

Pause. A pause so long you can feel your hair turning gray. "Well, what?"

He shrugs. "I kind of want to go with someone I like."

You don't know what to do with that statement. "Excuse me?"

He laughs. "That didn't come out right. But I was thinking of asking Becky Darien."

Becky Darien is known as Backseat Becky. A nickname she gave herself.

"Sleazeball," you say. "You don't like Backseat Becky."

He laughs again and slides off the desk. "I could."

You kick him in the ass. "You're that desperate for action on prom night?"

"Why are you always kicking me?"

"Because you deserve to be kicked."

"Is it so wrong to want to Get Some on prom night?"

"Yes! It is!"

"Is that any worse than just wanting a date on prom night? Why don't you just go in the Winnebago? Look," he continues, "maybe we can work something out. I want action and you want a date. If you're willing —"

You kick him again.

*　　*　　*

53

Prom is three weeks away. You, Jen, and Kyra are sitting on Kyra's tiled kitchen floor, eating your usual: tortilla chips dipped in Kyra's mom's homemade pizza sauce. Truth be told, you're more fake-eating than eating, since you want to lose five pounds before prom. If you lose five pounds, you know you will look your best. Your ultimate. (The pink dress, which you bought with a slimmer you in mind, is a smidgen too tight.) You want to look the way you looked when you and Shane first kissed back as freshmen. Five pounds less and tanned. Five pounds less, tanned, with whiter teeth. Yes, it is finally the time to try those Whitestrip thingies again. Only this time you'll have to avoid swallowing them.

"I just need to find another date," you say as you fake-nibble on a tortilla.

Kyra picks up a chunk of tomato with her chip. "I heard that Shane and Reese are going in Brent's limo."

You freeze at the sound of his name. Shane's name, that is, not Brent's. You assumed he would be taking Reese to prom, but hearing it somehow makes it official, which makes you want to throw up. It's not fair that your ex-boyfriend, the guy you were planning on going to prom with since you first started high school, is taking some random sophomore.

Jen flicks Kyra in the knee. "Why would you even bring him up?"

Jen and Kyra are the ones who had to deal with you every time you and Shane broke up. Who had to follow you to the bathroom when you started crying so hard in class that you couldn't breathe. This last breakup was the hardest — on them as well as you. They convinced your parents to let them take turns sleeping over because you

54

were too depressed to sleep. But they think you're over it now, and you are . . . sort of. You're over it because you know what it takes to get him back.

Last spring, you and Shane decided (actually *he* decided; you merely nodded your head) to date other people, and he spent the summer dating a lifeguard named Meredith. You hoped all would fall back into place when school started, but on the first day of class you spotted him with a cheerleader named Cecelia, and your hopes deflated faster than a punctured water wing. You didn't want to call him, but you caved. You knew you sounded pathetic, but you didn't care. You wanted him back. Not that it did any good. And then you started dating Ethan Shappell. He was sweet and made you laugh. You finally stopped wishing that every time the phone rang it would be Shane. Of course, as soon as you stopped caring, your cell rang and it *was* Shane. Shane who was bored with Cecelia. "I miss you," he said, and your mouth went dry, and your heart was in your throat, and Ethan who? And then you and Shane were back on, back together, back on track. Until The Model.

"Because," Kyra says, bringing you back to the here and now, "she should be glad that she's not going with Brent. Then they'd all be in the same limo."

If you're all in the same limo, then Shane will see what he's missing, up close. You can already smell his salty, buttery scent.

"I don't want to talk about Shane," you say. "I want to find a new date."

"But who?" Kyra asks as tomato sauce dribbles onto the tiles.

"But why?" Jen asks as she passes Kyra a napkin.

55

"I don't know," you say. "Help me brainstorm."

"What about Jeff Odom?" Kyra asks.

You shake your head. "He's going with Melissa Fields."

"Ethan Shappell," Kyra suggests. "He really liked you last year."

"Alesha Zelnick," you say.

"I got one!" Kyra exclaims. "Nick McNearly!"

Hmm. You reach for the last chip in the bag and take an extra-small nibble while contemplating the suggestion. Nick is a nice guy. He helped you with an assignment just last week. You lent him a pen. You always say hello and wave when you pass each other in the hall. He's also going to MIT next year, which will make Shane (who applied to all the Ivies but only got into his safety school) go ballistic.

"He's a possibility," you say.

Jen grabs the empty bag and tosses it into the garbage can. "I *cannot* believe you'd rather go to prom with Nick McNerdy than with us."

"You are so mean," Kyra says. "Don't call him that!"

"Gimme a break," Jen scoffs. "You know he's a nerd. It doesn't mean he's not a nice nerd. I'm sure he'll end up running Microsoft when he's older and being a kazillionaire, but he's still a nerd. And I know Drew agrees. We have math together and he picks his cuticles all through class and leaves the skin in a pile on his desk."

"That's not nerdy," Kyra points out. "That's disgusting."

You brush away their concerns with the back of your hand. Nick is tall, dark, supersmart, and semi-handsome in a Clark Kent kind of way. Maybe in a tux he'll turn into a superhero. A tux *and* a manicure.

You wait until the bell rings and then gently rest your hand on Nick's shoulder. You were planning to engage him in small talk, but you're too nervous and too afraid to look at the mound of cuticles piled on his desk, so you just blurt out, "Nick, do you want to be my date for prom?"

His pencil case falls from his ripped-up fingers and lands on his chair. "Me?" he yelps.

"Yes."

"You want to go to prom with me?"

"Uh, yes?"

"I would love to go with you —"

Hurrah!

"— but I can't." His face crumples. "Heidi asked me at lunch and I said I'd go with her."

Damn. "That's too bad. Well, have a good —"

"I wish you had asked me first. I would rather have gone with you. Will you be my date at the movies on Saturday instead?"

After asking him to the prom, you couldn't exactly say no, could you?

"Do you want to share a box of Junior Mints?" Nick asks as you reach the front of the concession line. He picks at his fingers while he waits for your answer.

"I think I'll have my own, thanks." You don't want his fingers anywhere near your food. And anyway, you always order popcorn. The smell reminds you of Shane.

"I can't believe you went out with Nick McNerdy," Jen says from across the cafeteria table.

"Actually, I had a lot of fun," you say. If he weren't

moving to Boston and if you weren't still in love with Shane, you would even consider going out with him again. "He's a really good —" The rest of the words in your sentence get caught in your throat like they're coated in the low-fat peanut butter you're fake-eating. When you first sat down, you saw that Shane and The Model were sitting only a few tables over, eating pizza. You could have dealt with that. But now his fingers — his surely greasy fingers — are running their way through Reese's light blond hair, and the very sight of it is making you sick. And then he gives her the look, his eyes crinkled with attraction and laughter. The look he used to give you.

"You have to ignore them," Kyra says softly.

You can't. You want to, but you can't. You lay your sandwich back down on its tinfoil wrapper, then roll the foil between your fingers, your gaze masochistically glued on the happy couple.

"What an asswipe," Jen spits. "Don't they realize that you're right here?" She pulls out her phone and sends someone a text.

"What are you doing?" Kyra asks.

"Texting Daniel Heller. And getting Drew a prom date. He's an ass, but he's hot."

Your heart leaps. "Who's Daniel Heller?"

"The pitcher on my baseball team. Do you remember him? Kyra called him Hot Heller last spring. He goes to Farmington High. You were with Shane then, so you didn't come out with us that often —"

Kyra whistles. "I remember. He was gorge."

"I think I do," you say. "He has reddish hair and looks

a bit like he could play the high school quarterback in a teen movie?"

"That's the one. You'd think red hair would be hideous, but he somehow makes it hot. *Red* hot, get it?"

"Why haven't you fixed him up with *me?*" Kyra whines.

"Because he's a total jerk. Calls all women hon. And is so anal you would not believe. Irons his baseball jersey. He doesn't deserve a date like Drew, but if she's so insistent on going to prom with a date, he'll do. At least he'll look good in pictures." She looks down at her phone. "He wants to know if you're the blond friend."

"That's me," you pipe up.

Jen keeps typing and then gives you a thumbs-up. "He's in. You, my dear, have a date."

You can't keep the smile off your face. You look over at Shane's table and the word *hah* is at the tip of your lips, but you swallow it down. Yum. Tastes good. And it's all you're allowed to eat for the next week, since your plan is back on and you really have to look your best.

It is one week until prom and you are sitting on your carpeted floor doing leg lifts as you talk to your perfect prom date via phone. Gorgeous, built, perfect Heller.

"The party should be cool," Heller says.

"Definitely." You can't wait to see the look on Shane's face when he sees you looking your hottest with Hot Heller. Hah!

You have lost five pounds. You have whitened your teeth. You have visited a tanning salon. You have found the perfect date. You have even convinced Brent that he owes it to you to squeeze you and Hot Heller into his and Shane's limo.

You and Heller will look so good together that Shane will die and want you back.

"You're going to pick me up in the limo, hon?" Heller asks.

He has taken to calling you hon. This would probably annoy you more if not for the fact that you're hoping Shane will overhear and interpret it as a sincere term of endearment.

"Actually," you say, "would it be possible if you came over here so my parents could take some pictures?"

He sighs. Loudly. "How am I supposed to get there?"

"Any chance your parents would let you borrow their car?"

"It's not the car that's the problem. I have a BMW X3. But I intend on getting wasted and don't plan on driving."

"Oh. Of course. Can your parents drive you here?"

"What am I, twelve? Why don't I just take a cab?"

You breathe a sigh of relief. "That would be great, thanks."

"No problem. Obviously, I expect to be reimbursed."

"Of course," you say quickly. You remind yourself that while he's sounding a bit jerky, he is doing you a favor by coming to prom. By being your hot date so Shane can fall in love with you again.

Hopefully.

"I have a sweet tuxedo tie I'm going to wear," he says. "What are you wearing?"

"A pale pink dress."

"Oh, I don't think so, hon."

"Sorry?"

"I hate pink."

You wrap the phone tighter around your wrist. "You hate pink?"

"I have red hair. Trust me, you should wear something black. Or white. White is cool."

"I didn't think of that." He's right. What are you going to do? You don't want to clash with your date. "I guess I can look for a new dress." The tag is still on the gown. You hope they have it in other colors.

"Good plan. It should be a cool night."

You hope not. Because the pink wrap was on sale and you can't exchange it.

Hot Heller rings your doorbell at 5:22, twenty-two minutes later than he was supposed to.

"Come in, come in," your dad says, ushering him in.

Wow. His nickname is not for nothing. "You look great," you say, which is clearly an understatement. He's gorgeous. Tall, broad shoulders, chiseled cheekbones, big smile. Perfect teeth. And his hair isn't red-red, it's more of a strawberry blond. A strawberry blond that would not have clashed with your pink dress. But no matter. Your black dress looks hot. Hot as in attractive. Although with its long sleeves, you might get a little warm, too, but it's all you could find at the last minute. It's a bit funeralesque, though in a sexy way. He is wearing a black tuxedo tie instead of a bow tie and he looks like he could be in an ad for groomsmen.

"Nice to meet you, Mr. . . . ." Heller looks at me and shrugs. "I don't know your last name."

Your father visibly balks.

"Let's just take some pictures," you say quickly, and usher Hot Heller to the porch.

"You're not going to wear those shoes, are you, hon?" he asks as he hands you an all-white corsage.

"Sorry?"

"Don't you want to be taller? Why are you wearing flats?"

You look down at your pretty silver shoes. They're not flats. They have a heel. Sort of. "They're comfortable."

"But you're way shorter than me. Whatever. It's your prom. If you don't care, I don't care."

But you do care. You want to look your best. You know that as soon as Shane sees how amazing you look, how skinny and tanned and manicured and smiley you are, how taken you are with another guy, he will want you back. Seeing Heller will make his face turn a nice shade of Hulk green. He will want to push his slutty sophomore Model aside and play with your hair and whisper in your ear that he is sorry and that he still loves you.

You excuse yourself and change into your black three-inchers. What were you thinking, picking *comfortable* shoes? This is not about comfort. You hold tightly to the banister so that you don't slip down the stairs.

"Better, hon," Hot Heller says.

You think you might dislike Hot Heller. But he is doing you a favor and you should appreciate it. "Thanks for coming with me," you tell him.

"I don't mind. Although I almost said no when Jen e-mailed me that her friend needed a date. I assumed she meant her other friend, the one I met last spring."

A large pit has lodged itself somewhere in your esophagus. "You mean Kyra?"

"The fat one with black hair."

You're now quite sure that you dislike him. In fact, you're pretty sure you detest him. You consider taking your high heel and punting it into his crotch. Instead you say, "Kyra *isn't* fat," and remind yourself that after tonight you will never have to talk to him again.

You and Heller stand there alone on the porch, not speaking. You have nothing to say to him. Nothing whatsoever. You look out the window and watch as the limo rolls down your street and parks in front of your house.

"The limo we had for our prom was much nicer," says Heller.

You're not sure *detest* is a strong enough word. *Hate? Loathe? Abhor?*

You calm yourself down, wave to your parents, suck in your stomach, open the limo door, dip your perfectly straightened hair inside, and say in your most demure voice, "Hello."

You sweep your eyes over the four already-seated couples to locate Shane and The Model, who are pressed up against each other in the backseat. Shane looks adorable in his tux, as you knew he would. He's opted for a black bow tie, which he is already tugging. The Model is wearing a short gold dress that shows off her long legs. In your opinion, it's not quite prom appropriate.

You scoot onto one of the side seats and Heller follows behind. Then once you're sure everyone has ogled his hotness, you smile extra brightly and say, "Hi, everyone, this is Daniel Heller. Heller, Peter and Lindsay,

Mike and Bonnie, Adam and Farrah, Shane and Reese."
When you reach the happy couple, you widen your eyes
as though you are pleased to see them. You grip your
leather seat as the limo pulls down the street.

Shane is studying Heller. Then he turns to you, and
you feel his eyes on you, slowly, carefully taking you in.
Eyes flickering with interest.

It's working!

You move your hand from your lap to Heller's knee,
Shane's eyes following it like a bouncing ball.

He shuffles a few inches away from The Model. "Hey,
Drew," he says. "You look really good."

"Thanks, Shane, that's really sweet of you," you say in
the most dismissive tone you can conjure up. Instead of
looking at him, you focus on your date and pick a thread
off the top of his jacket. "Heller, you look fantastic in
your tux."

"Thanks, hon."

Out of the corner of your eye, you watch Shane flush.
He moves a little farther away from Reese. He's now staring at Heller. "Hey, man, what school do you go to?"

"I was at Farmington."

Reese leans in. "Really? I have a ton of friends there.
Do you know —"

"What college are you going to?" Shane asks him,
interrupting.

Yes, yes!

"Yale," Heller says, his chest inflating. "You?"

Shane scowls. "Oh. Rutgers."

"Shane?" Reese says, nudging him. "Can you cut the
tag in the back of my dress? It's scratching me."

What, does she think he walks around with scissors?

Shane is too preoccupied with you and Heller to answer. "Shane? Hello?" she asks again, sounding annoyed.

Finally, you turn away from Heller's lapel and turn to Shane. He looks deep into your eyes. And you can't look away.

"You really do look amazing," he says.

"Thanks," you say, your voice lowering. Whispering.

It's the look. He's giving you the look.

Heller puts his arm around you, pulling you into him. Shane flinches.

Everything is unfolding just the way you planned. By the time you get to the prom, Shane will be begging you to get back together. You should be happy. Ecstatic. This is what you want.

Isn't it?

"Shane?" Reese repeats. "Can you pay attention to me, please?"

Shut up, you want to tell her. Not because she's interfering with your plan, but because she reminds you of you. The way your voice sounded when you'd call Shane, reminding him not to take you for granted. The way it sounded when you'd beg him to get back together with you.

It's getting hot in here. It's too soon for this kind of weather. Damn unreliable weather. It was supposed to be a cool evening. Damn long sleeves. And Heller's tuxedoed arm is starting to feel like a weight on your shoulder.

"Can I open a window?" you ask the group.

"What about my hair?" one of the other girls complains.

"I'll help you," Shane offers, reaching across your lap for the window.

Sure he will. Tonight. But where will he be tomorrow? Shane wants you now because he can't have you. And then it hits you. Maybe you wanted *him* because you never really had him.

"Just turn the air on, hon," Heller says.

Your arms are hot, your neck is hot, your face is hot. You're burning up. You play with the controls over your head, but it doesn't help. You can't cool down. You can't relax. Instead you're wondering, is Reese's name even Reese? Or is that just what Shane calls her? The way he named you Drew.

The air's not working. What kind of limo doesn't have air?

You are still turning the question over in your mind when you pull onto Mandy's street. And that's when you see it. It's huge. It's white. It's the Winnebago. And it is currently reversing out of Jen's driveway.

You bet your friends are having a blast. While you're just — hot. And uncomfortable.

Yes, you found a date. Yes, you're making the boyfriend who got bored with you want you back. But you're not sure you want him back anymore. The only thing you are sure of is that you never did like the name Drew. And you're not too crazy about "hon" either.

Before you can change your mind, you press the intercom button and tell the driver, "Can you pull over, please?"

"Mandy's house is farther down the block," one of the girls snaps.

You exhale slowly. Your stomach juts out just a bit, but you no longer care. All you care about is spending the night with people who matter. People who always

66

make you feel special. "I know. I'm sorry about this, but I'm going to have to bail."

Everyone stares at you like you're speaking a foreign language. Can't compute.

"But the prom hasn't even started," Heller whines.

"I know," you say. "Unfortunately, you're not the right date for me. But feel free to enjoy the limousine. Here's twenty bucks for the cab. And I'm sure the driver will drop you off at home if you ask nicely."

The limo pulls to a stop and you dash out the door. "Wait!" you scream, your arms flailing above your head, running toward the Winnebago, not caring about how crazy you look, not caring about the knives pinching and stabbing your poor feet.

Your friends' faces are pressed against the trailer windows watching you, their excited shrieks audible through the glass.

The Winnebago stops and the door swings open. And then you, the girl formerly known as Drew, climb aboard.

Off Like a Prom Dress
by Billy Merrell

It isn't that I want to look older, but that I don't want to feel so
    young.
Like all my life I've watched those movies, and every time

the girl becomes the princess in the end. Either she was all along
or the dress transforms her. She's ringed in wind and music

and the prince gallops up with a ceremony and a kiss
and her childhood ends with laughter and some otherworldly
    light.

Now that's an ending! And all I have is a prom and the promise
of the kiss after. Maybe a party at the last second. And then
    nothing.

So when my mom said I couldn't take Jonathan dress shopping,
that it simply wouldn't be right if it wasn't a surprise,

I told him to come along anyway, afraid if he didn't choose it too
he wouldn't choose me. And maybe he'd gallop off

and the music would end and I'd be left sitting there
with a souvenir cup or a candle with the date stamped on it.

Mom drove me to the mall and Jonathan trailed two cars behind.
Once we were there he stayed out of sight until the last second

when he'd wave a thumb to show if I looked "hot."
Satin and tulle, gray lace over burgundy blush — No.

Red amulet, white corset, and the billowing — No.
And of course everything I loved he loved and Mom hated.

My mom made my dress, she reminded me. How could I forget?
But that was a long time ago, in Idaho, and she can't sew,

so why bring it up now? And of course we argued,
and of course the fun trip turned into neither of us speaking.

Jonathan shrugged and waved goodbye. And Mom
pretended not to see him. *What do you want?* she asked
    finally.

This shouldn't be about him. Unless he plans to wear it.
I want a dress that will change as I dance, or that will change me.

But I couldn't say that. Not really. The sun was setting
as we walked to the car. We drove west with it my eyes.

I want a dress. And to be allowed to look as pretty as possible.
And that's it. It isn't about what the magazines say, or
    Jonathan.

Well, in that case, can you keep a secret? And I could.
She turned on the light in the attic and we climbed the stairs

and I started to hear that music. She found an old box
and handed it to me to carry down. Once in my room

we peeled back the old tissue and lifted the gown
like a sea-green sea, choppy and faint until it bloomed.

I stepped into it, let it up over my shoulders.
Looking then at the mirror I saw: moon over midtown,
the small lights of the buildings off the water.

I love it, I told her. Which was true. And its simple lines
and how I fit inside it perfectly. I began to dance
right there in the quiet as she put the tissue in the empty box.

I danced in place with my eyes closed and the sea settling,
thinking of Jonathan in a matching green tie, his eyes lit
by that odd light, and everything began to change.

"Mom called, she says you have to go to prom"

by Adrienne Maria Vrettos

It will be too hot to sleep in the attic room soon, and I'll move down to the screened-in porch that stretches along the whole left side of our house. If you look at our house from the bottom of our hill, it looks like either the porch is too heavy or the dirt is too soft. Either way, our house is sinking, porch-side first.

Philip and I set up on the porch in the summertime, on metal beds with pancake mattresses that smell like the summer camp Mom bought them from. We make them cozy with sheets and pillows from inside the house and use opened-up sleeping bags as blankets. The beds go on one end of the porch, with wooden crates for end tables, and ridiculous jangly lamps that Mom kept from when she was in college. On the other end is our Summer Living Room, with the overstuffed and flowery living room furniture we keep in the barn for winter, so we can wrap up in blankets and open the barn doors and sit on the couches and watch the snow come down.

For now, though, my room in the attic is made just cool enough by having all my windows open to a breeze that's woven with a late-spring chill. I'm happy. It's been a long time since me and my cat, Drox, have gotten to cuddle up together for a night of sci-fi and antihista-mines.

"You're not supposed to have him up here," Philip says when he opens my bedroom door and sees Drox attempting to burrow himself into the warm space between my neck and the pillow.

"I took an antihistamine," I say, not looking up from my book.

While Philip digests this, he presses his big toe against the end of the loose floorboard in the doorway, making the other side of the board rise a full two inches before he lets it drop back into place. "Mom says that doesn't matter," he finally says.

I shrug. "Mom's working overnights this week."

"I know that," Philip says, popping the floorboard up and down again. Then he yells, "Don't tell me things I know already!"

The reason my big brother yells things is because when he was born he didn't get enough oxygen to his brain. You could call him stupid, but that'd get you a punch in the mouth for being a liar. Call him slow and you won't get punched, but you will get spit on because even if it's sort of the truth, it's an asshole way to say it.

He's a normal pain in the butt like anyone else's older brother, he just can't do addition and sometimes you have to explain why a joke is funny. He can drive, and could live on his own if he wanted. And also he doesn't have a heart of gold or a way with animals. One day some girl is going to look into his river-water eyes and fall right in. And she's not going to care that he won't be the one to balance their checkbook.

We had to get Philip clinically diagnosed as slow

before the school would pay for him to have special tutoring, because they just wanted to put him in special ed and be done with it. Even though we as a family have nothing against kids that ride the short bus, Mom knew all Philip needed was a little extra help. The school disagreed, so we sued them and Philip got tested. Knowing that those white-coats were trying to see if he was stupid did a number on Philip's self-esteem, but at least it got him his tutors.

Even though we won, it took them a while to get Philip what he needed. That's because back then Mom was still a tax evader and it was a sore spot with the town. They thought if she didn't pay taxes, her kid shouldn't get pricey extra help, and plus they were all still cranky they lost the lawsuit about the NO TAXATION WITHOUT REPRESENTATION! signs in our front yard. So Mom agreed to pay taxes and back taxes and forward taxes and the school board sped up the paperwork and Philip got his tutors. Once we're both out of school, though, we all agree Mom can get back to evading taxes, since she seemed to like it so much.

"I know you know," I say. "I'm just telling you that's why it doesn't matter that the cat's up here."

"Oh," he says. "So this is what you're doing tonight?"

"Yep," I say, going back to my book.

"Well," he says.

Wait a minute. I cock my head to the side and look at him. "Philip, why'd you come up here?"

"Well." The floorboard is popped in and out of place a few more times. "Mom called, she says you have to go to prom."

"Nu-uh!" I shout, jumping off my bed and stomping

73

over to where Philip is now staring with intense interest at his toe. "She said if I went to graduation, I didn't have to go to prom! Philip!"

Philip looks at me. "I think that she might of changed her mind," he says quietly, trying not to smile.

"It's no fair!" I yell. Then I yawn.

We stand there in silence.

"Do you have a dress?" he finally asks, eyeing my kitty slippers.

"She really said I have to go?"

"Yes."

"Or what?"

"She didn't say."

We both think about this.

"What do you think I should do?" I ask.

"You could go in a suit," he says.

"No, I mean should I go to prom?"

"Do you want to go?"

I sigh at him.

He shrugs. "Don't go, then."

I nod and picture Mom coming home tomorrow morning and tickling my chin until I wake up and tell her about prom. It's not that she's deluded, or in denial, or that she doesn't know exactly what school's like for me, she's just . . . terminally hopeful. She thinks that your own joy can be separate from the people around you, that things like graduation and prom are happy memories to be, even if you have no one to share them with. She's big on me participating in my own adolescence, so at least I'll have something to reflect on in the future.

I sigh. "Do we have any suits?"

He shrugs. "The one from school court."

"I thought we burned that."

"Oh yeah," he says. "Maybe Mom has a dress."

"All she has are pantsuits and scrubs," I say, looking longingly to where my cat is now curled and purring around my book. "Could I just wear my nightgown? It's like a dress."

"Let's see what Mom has."

Mom has seven smart pantsuits and four sets of slightly mismatched scrubs. I decide not to wear either after we discover that I can actually fit my whole body inside a leg of her pants and disappear entirely by holding the waist up to my neck and ducking down. When I stand up straight again, Philip says, "It's like you're being born."

Mom does have one dress. It's her office party/school court dress. It's royal blue and has a giant belt, but at least it's silk. I hold it up in front of me in the mirror.

"Try it on," Philip says.

I go into the bathroom and put it on.

"It's a prom night miracle!" I yell to Philip from where I'm standing in front of the mirror.

Philip opens the bathroom door, looks at me, and laughs.

"Or not," I say, spinning so he can see how the dress expands to almost eat me alive.

"It's big," he says.

"Mom's big," I remind him.

"Don't tell me things I know already!" Philip yells. I yell it with him, to keep him company and let him know I know.

Like I said, Mom's a big lady, so even when I use the last hole on the belt, it hangs off me.

75

"I'll get the staple gun," Philip says, moving toward the door.

"Mom might get mad," I say. "But it was a good idea. I'll wear it like this." I stand with my arms akimbo, one hip thrust to the side.

"Sassy," Philip says.

"How long do I have to stay?"

"She said two hours. And say good-bye to the principal before you leave, because she's calling him Monday to make sure you were there."

I think of something and gasp. I gleefully yell, "Hey!" which gets Philip's attention. Then I yell, "I can't go to prom. I don't have a ticket."

Philip looks at me.

"She bought me a ticket, didn't she?"

He pulls a thick triangle of folded paper out of his pocket and hands it to me.

"God, she's such a stinker." I sigh. "Will you give me a ride?"

"You have to ride in the back."

"Why?"

"I melted your part of the front seat."

We say good-bye to Robert, who's drinking orange juice at the kitchen table, on our way out. He's the boarder who's lived with us for years. He has greasy glasses and a whole other family in Idaho that he doesn't see.

The passenger seat in my brother's truck is melted down to a lump. Strangely, or maybe not if you know my brother, everything else in the truck is perfectly fine.

I sit in the back, on top of a bale of hay he has tied down.

"It's prickly," I say.

We end up beside a parade of limos on the two-lane into town, winding our way toward school. Some of the back windows are down in the limos, and I can see glimpses of oiled knees and suspicious-looking soda cans being passed around. There's also lots of shrieking. They don't see me, since Philip's truck has a wicked lift on it, and all they'd see if they looked out the window are the hand-painted blue flames that burn their way down each side. As we get nearer to the turn onto Schoolhouse Road, the shrieks get louder and Philip slows down so he's the last one in the train pulling onto the narrow road leading to school.

We don't follow the limos up the driveway to the school. Instead, Philip pulls over by the sign reading PROM TONIGHT! I climb out of the back and lean into the cab. We both look through the windshield at the school. I'm already working on forgetting its angles. Philip, though . . .

"Ten o'clock, okay?" I say to him.

He nods, still staring at the school.

"Don't wait here, though," I say.

"Why?" he says, before yelling, "It's five hundred feet!" He points to the wooden marker Mom and I put into the ground to show him how close he could come to school.

"Because," I say, "they'll come ask you what you're doing here, and we don't have bail money right now."

"I'm not doing anything wrong."

"You know that doesn't matter."

"Did everybody laugh at me when it happened?" he asks.

"No," I say, even though a lot of people did. I mean, it's funny, right? The slow kid bringing a potato gun to school for science fair and getting expelled because it's technically a firearm.

"Yeah, they did," he says.

"Some of them did," I say. "But not all of them."

"Who didn't?" he asks, finally turning from the school to look at me.

"Your friends didn't," I tell him, and he nods.

"And you didn't?"

"Not once. What time are you picking me up?"

"Ten o'clock."

"Okay."

I walk up the driveway. At the entrance to the school, couples are lined up, waiting to go in and have their pictures taken and then have a big entrance into the gym. In line there's lots of squeals and hugs and comparisons of suits and dresses and passing of badly hidden flasks. Every time the door opens you can hear music from the gym, giving people a twenty-second window to show off their moves, then the doors close and they look stupid dancing to the crickets.

I get in line behind Drew Barker, who's a senior, and his too-much-younger girlfriend. She's holding on to the crook of his elbow and trying to make nice with the senior girls who hate her.

My appearance sparks mild interest.

Behind me are two people I don't know. She is in pink, and he has a bow tie to match.

It turns out Drew and his jailbait date are friends with the pink people. They've all started talking to each other, first sort of over my head, then around either side of me.

Now they've sort of surrounded me and are talking around me like I'm a campfire until it's jailbait 'n' date's turn to walk through the doors. The Pinks try to follow.

"I'm next," I say, stepping in front of them and nodding at the gym teacher, who is on door duty.

"Whatever," Mr. Pink says, trying to lead his date past me.

"I said, I'm next." I step in front of them again. He decides to take this as funny. He laughs. It's an ugly laugh.

"What does it matter?" Ms. Pink asks, her voice more grating than I'd imagined. "Why do you need to get inside, anyway?"

All I say is, "I'm next," as the gym teacher opens the door and I walk through.

Ms. Pink calls me a bitch. The door closes behind me before I can bark at her.

I know why the Pinks assumed I'd let them go first. It's because of embarrassment. They're embarrassed by me, and they assume I'm embarrassed of me, too. And if I'm embarrassed, then I won't ever want to make any sort of attention-grabbing scene, like telling the teacher when one of them takes my seat, or refusing to slink out of class because the teacher's run out of birthday cupcakes. No. I will stand there in front of the teacher's desk till she goes and gets me a HoHo out of the vending machine in the teachers' lounge.

They have the photography area set up in the front hall of the school. I wait till jailbait's done and then sit on the stool in front of the blue-sky-with-puffy-cloud backdrop.

The photographer looks at me for a second, then looks expectantly at the door.

"Just me," I say.

"And you want your picture taken."

"No," I say. "I thought this was the bathroom. Was I not supposed to pee on the stool?"

The photographer blinks at me. I really don't want to have another fight with him. I know he remembers me from school picture day earlier this year, when he tried to get away with taking just one picture of me before yelling, "Next!" He'd given everyone else at least three shots each. That day I had stayed seated on the stool while we yelled at each other, until the principal came over and made the photographer snap two more pictures after whispering something involving the word *litigious* in his ear.

Now the photographer is saying, "Okay, then." And looking through the viewfinder. His finger rests on the button, and I flash him a *live long and prosper* as the camera clicks.

"What did you just do?" he asks, but I'm already off the stool, standing in front of his little table with my hand out for him to print out the picture and give it to me. He prints it out and hands it to me.

"And a frame," I say. He gives me a frame.

Inside the gym the terrible dancing is already well under way. I strut my way toward the center of the dance floor.

On the way there, I see Norah. We were friends when we were little, then her mom opened her front door for a Bible-thumper that rang the bell, and Norah got all new church friends and stopped drinking soda. Then last year her mom left the church and now Norah and I talk in the halls and ride the bus home together. She says she and her mom miss their church friends some-times. I like Norah because when I think of her I think, *She's of the world, like me.* The other kids here, they think the world is full of people like them. But it's not. It's filled with people like Norah, and like me. I've seen them at emergency rooms and car impound lots, and peace marches and the DMV. I know that I'm not as alone as people here want me to think. I've got a whole world out there waiting for me, and they've just got each other.

Norah's dancing with the quiet kid from art class who's always making moony eyes at her. Norah's dress is a prom night miracle. I recognize it right off. It was her mom's, and Norah and I used to dress up in it when we were little kids. It fits her perfectly. Norah sees me as moony art boy is dipping her, and she jumps up to hug me.

"You're here!" she yells.

"Wow, Norah," I say. "You look really pretty."

She spins around and giggles, then fingers the silk of my dress.

"It's so soft!" she says, smiling at me. She glances at Mr. Moony and whispers, "He came over and talked to my mom and convinced her to let me go."

"That's great," I say to her, and then I say it to him, "That's great." He blushes.

"Want to stay and dance with us?" she asks.

"No. I'm going to go dance in the middle."

"Okay." I love Norah because she doesn't warn me not to go.

There is a knot of bodies in the middle of the floor. They have their arms slung around each other's shoulders because the DJ is playing "their song," the one that was always on the radio the summer they all went down to a beach house where they had fights and lost their virginities. I've heard the stories. They are all crying and vowing undying love for each other, even though I think it's a little early in the night for that. The song ends, and the hugs turn to screams when the DJ starts playing the next song, which is a sweet cut off a new album that's on permanent repeat on the stereo at my house.

There's scattered laughter as I walk across the floor. They think it's funny that I can walk to the rhythm. They'll think what's next is funny, too, I'm sure, because what they don't know is that I can *dance*.

I can shake it, drop it, and pop it. My Robot is unbeatable and I can Mashed Potato, too. I don't do the Worm because that's for amateurs. My mom and Philip and I and sometimes Robert dance all the time. My mom can flip all of us over her back when we swing dance, and I'm sure Philip could flip me but he's not allowed to because he lets go too soon or too late, and if I get a concussion they might jail him. All our living room furniture is on special sliding discs that we ordered from the TV, so we can spread out and have ourselves a dance-off. Mom usually wins these — because of her poundage she can make dance moves look like an army invading. She's the living room champion. But I can lay it out here, in front of these amateurs, and I do.

I dance the bejeezus out of the song, and the next one, and the next one after that. Some people laugh and try to dance with me, some against me, a few try to nudge me off the dance floor, but I dance on. I go to school here, like everyone else, and if Mom says I'm going to have a prom, well then, I'm having myself a prom. I'm drinking the free punch.

Philip's waiting for me in his truck at the bottom of the school driveway when I get there. We smile at each other through the windshield.

"Let's set up the summer porch tonight," he says as I walk by his window. "I already put out the beds."

I climb into the back of the truck. He's put a blanket on top of the bale of hay, which I appreciate. He takes the long way home, through the fields and over the ridge. The wind blows my hair, sending it shooting out in front of my face. Through the tangle I can see the blue-black sky, and the stars.

My brother likes to drive. I am going to leave this place one day.

Better Be Good to Me

by Daniel Ehrenhaft

Intro/Count-off

So there are some things you should know.

My name is Zack. I was once seventeen. Now I am balding and pudgy, but I'm okay with it. My wife is okay with it, too. Or so she says. She can say anything, though, because she's still beautiful. (Jerk.) To cut to the chase: We are the parents of a seventeen-year-old; let's call her "Harper" — screw it, that's her real name — who is about to go to her prom. With a boy named Randy. Yes, Randy. None of this may seem like a big deal, except that Harper's mother and I lost our virginity to each other the night of <u>our</u> prom. (Or the boarding school equivalent; more on that later.) By luck or fate, we ended up at the same college. Once there, we dated in earnest. Senior year, we conceived Harper. We married soon after. We were both twenty-one.

No, I don't have any regrets. No big ones, anyway. Personally, I get a kick out of being a decade younger than any other parent in Harper's class. All the dads are fatter and balder than I am, including Randy's — a boost for my self-esteem. But whenever my wife and I admit to new acquaintances that, sure, we can trace our roots as a couple back to the prom (or the boarding school equivalent), we inevitably get the: "Oh my God, it's so romantic you were high school sweethearts!" And we both chuckle to ourselves, because even though we were and are in love, the truth is a little stranger than that.

So now, Harper, I turn my attention to you. Your mother and I are thrilled you had no interest in attending boarding school. We love having you home. We also think that Randy is a nice kid: polite, quiet . . . he could lose the lip pierce, but whatever. The point is, consider this a cautionary tale. Just because Randy is your prom date, you don't have to sleep with him. (Besides, Randy's best friend may be more your type. Kidding. Jesus. Awful joke. Pretend I didn't say that. . . .) NO SEX AT ALL!!! NO DRINKING OR DRUGS!!! YOUR MOTHER AND I WANT YOU HOME AT 1 A.M. AT THE LATEST!!!

Oh, and one more thing. Seeing as this story takes place in May 1986, you may not get many of the references. For your convenience, I've included a glossary at the end.

I: Prisoner of Your Love

"Mom, does liking this song make me gay?"

My roommate stares at himself in our closet mirror as he asks me this question. He stares in the mirror a lot. But tonight he has an excuse: He has just donned a tuxedo, and he is adjusting a paisley bow tie. (A real one, not a clip-on like mine.) Seventeen, and he's an expert at tying bow ties. His other skills include skeet shooting while high, pilfering from his trust fund, and hitting on Miss Wyatt, our 19th-century comp lit teacher, who sometimes flirts back.

The song at issue is Tina Turner's "Better Be Good to Me."

It blares from his stereo, a kick-ass piece of equipment — a Bang and Olufsen. Unfortunately, the right speaker is positioned at the head of my bed, where I am sprawled in my boxers and T-shirt. These days, you can't turn on 105.9 FM ("Connecticut's Classic Rock, from AC/DC to ZZ Top!") without hearing some horrendous two-year-old Tina Turner track. I expect this sort of crap from MTV. MTV broadcasts a steady barrage of synthesized cheese, performed by androgynous clowns. The Thompson Twins? I can't identify the gender of a single member. Not that it matters, but still . . . how can any self-respecting classic rock DJ segue from Bad Company to semi-new Tina Turner and not feel shame? This is wrong.

"Yes, D," I finally mumble. "Liking this song makes you gay. Very, very gay."

He smirks, not taking his eyes off himself. "But Tina Turner is tight with The Who. Remember *Tommy*? She was The Acid Queen."

"Speaking of which, how are you feeling? Anything melting yet?"

"Nothing is melting. Not even that pimple on your nose."

"Blow me."

He winks at me in the mirror, his dilated pupils glittering like two black marbles. "I can't blow you, Mom. I already have a date."

I laugh and grumble. I wish something *would* melt the pimple on my nose.

Earlier this afternoon, my girlfriend, Marci Wolf, offered to lend me a stick of cover-up for tonight's "huge rite of passage." (Her actual words, I swear.) She smiled straight into my nose as she did so. I brusquely informed her that I do not wear cover-up. The Thompson Twins wear cover-up. Tina Turner wears cover-up. Not me.

II: Entangled in Your Web

My roommate's name is DePaul Adams. His family controls the entire U.S. shipping industry. (Or something.) In recent months, he has taken to psychedelics with the all-consuming zeal of a religious fanatic. He is Dorchester Prep's Timothy Leary, a self-appointed guru of chemical mind expansion. Give him an excuse; he'll drop a tab of acid. He drops it before lacrosse practice. He drops it for late-night cram sessions. He dropped it one Friday morning to "deal with Chapel," even though the drug's effects tend to last at least twelve hours, so by dinner he was still off in the land of looking-glass porters and marmalade skies. Tonight, he has dropped it in celebration of the Spring Ball, the aforementioned rite of passage and Dorchester's sad parody of a prom.

He's also my best friend.

When my Grandpa Joe died this past winter, DePaul sent a letter of condolence to my mom so breathtakingly elegiac that it made her cry. He was hallucinating when he wrote it. Oh, and he keeps two dwindling sheets of Daffy Duck Blotter in our mini fridge (still over a hundred tabs) — more than enough LSD to get us both expelled, and probably enough to land us each a stretch of ten-to-twenty in a federal penitentiary.

III: Hot Whispers in the Night

"You should get dressed, Mom," DePaul says. He tears himself from his reflection. "The chicks will be here soon."

"Turn this garbage off first," I groan from my bed.

"Never!" He cranks the volume and starts to jig around the room — his bow-tied, tuxedoed body a sudden squidlike cross between a Deadhead and the cast of *Beat Street,* arms flapping in waves, a blissful smile on his face.

I laugh again, but I am depressed. I am depressed because DePaul is happier than me, and he always will be, even without the LSD. I am depressed because he is going to Princeton in the fall, whereas I am going to NYU (I didn't get into Princeton), and because he never gets zits, and because I am stone-cold sober. Furthermore, DePaul owns his tuxedo. I rented mine. My parents are not billionaires. My family has not bequeathed me a trust fund. My bow tie is neither real nor paisley; it is fake and black, like a waiter's.

Mostly, I am depressed because DePaul wants me to have fun tonight, and I want to have fun, too. But I can't. I have a secret.

Not that I mention any of this. I've never mentioned it. I've never even *hinted* at it. I came close to whispering it to a certain someone once, late at night, off campus, when we were both drunk . . . but I stopped myself. Like I'm doing with DePaul right now.

Instead, I tumble out of bed and start climbing into my own tuxedo — while my best friend continues to jig, and Tina Turner's overplayed atrocity continues to blast from his thousand-dollar speakers.

IV: I'm Captured by Your Spell

Fifteen minutes later, there's a knock on our door.

"The chicks," DePaul whispers to his desk lamp. He and the lamp have been chatting for a while now. His eyes are all pupil; the irises have long since disappeared.

I scowl at him. My fake bow tie is asphyxiating. The cummerbund threatens to flatten my kidneys. Every item of clothing suffocates me in some way, down to the rented black shoes and socks. Yes, I've rented socks. The guy at the tuxedo place insisted on it, claiming my own socks were "too thick" and wouldn't match the rest of my "ensemble." (Too thick?) Dressing in one of these things is tantamount to extortion. It ran me $197.35 — $2.65 shy of my monthly allowance; $2.65 doesn't even cover my acne medication. It barely buys a sandwich. I vow never to wear a tux again.

DePaul tries to scowl back, but ends up giggling. I shuffle over to our door and open it. The chicks are indeed here, DePaul's girlfriend and mine. Side by side.

Rebecca Weiss and Marci Wolf.

Rebecca is a freshly showered vision, her long red curls still damp (she refuses to use a blow-dryer because of "the static"). She's applied a dash of eyeliner, but no lipstick. She's not even dressed formally. She's in *sandals* (I can see her red-painted toes) and a rumpled skirt and a loose-hanging Indian print blouse (I don't think she's wearing a bra, either) . . . and every article of clothing accentuates every curve of her flawless porcelain body, right up to her eyes . . . those wondrous, slinky, hazel eyes.

Conversely, Marci hides her eyes behind freakish chlorine-blue contacts. She's slathered on about an inch of makeup. Blond hair = blow-dried. Silver hoops dangle from her ears like a pair of hollowed-out air hockey pucks. Her strapless pink dress reminds me of the gruesome bridesmaids at my aunt Irma's wedding. (Irma was a newlywed at the age of fifty-three. She married an accountant named Melvin Lewis, who is kind, but resembles a four-hundred-pound pork roast.) Needless to say, Marci is not wearing sandals. She is wearing high heels. They are plain and black, like my tux.

Marci smiles straight at the zit on my nose and says, "Hey, handsome!"

V: Captured!
So, in case you haven't figured out my secret —

I am an asshole.

Plus, yes, I am in love with my best friend's girlfriend. Call it cliché, call it pitiful or whatever you want, but there's another problem on top of all that.

Rebecca and Marci are also roommates. And best friends. Like DePaul and me.

In other words, I am not only in love with my best friend's girlfriend, I am in love with my girlfriend's best friend. And she is the same person.

Evil, I know. Confusing, even. But to clarify, it's not just a crush. It's empathy. It's *feeling* (the feeling I could never have for Marci): for Rebecca's acerbic wit, for her redheaded bohemian beauty, for how she hates MTV but secretly enjoys it. For how she loves Van Halen circa 1978–1984 as much as I do, and thus believes Sammy Hagar should be shot. For how she laughs so hard that she loses herself. And for the braces she once wore, because now that they're gone she's hotter and knows it.

If only I loved Marci . . . if only I even *liked* Marci enough not to be bored with her and irritated by her (evil again, but true) . . . if *only*, everything would be perfect. DePaul and me, Marci and Rebecca: two pairs of roommates and best friends, hooked up with each other. There is no better boarding school scenario. After all, sex at Dorchester is tough to schedule. Sex generally occurs when one's roommate is out. So imagine, if your roommate could sneak out and trade places with your significant other's roommate . . . why, all four of you could be having sex every night of the week!

But sneaking out has never come up among us. For one thing, it's traditionally up to horny males to initiate such liaisons, and DePaul won't make a move. He seems as bored with Rebecca as I am with Marci. (How? HOW!!! Is he *that* blind?) And I am too much of a wimp to sneak out — even for sex. I am too much of a wimp to have sex, period. I am a virgin. I want the first time to be amazing, and I'm scared it won't be with Marci. Maybe that's weak, but I don't care. Finally, on a practical level, DePaul is often tripping too hard late at night to do anything else except chat with his desk lamp.

VI: Oh, Yes, I'm Touched by This Show of Emotion

"I said, hey, handsome," Marci repeats. "Hello? Zack? Anybody home?"

I force a smile. "Sorry. Hey, Marci. Thanks. You look beautiful."

Marci sighs and brushes past me into the room, her heels clattering. My eyes meet Rebecca's for a moment. She smiles back, but I detect displeasure. I can't blame her. I really wish I weren't such a jerk or a liar. Rebecca's best friend deserves someone better than me; she deserves someone better *to her*. Chalk it up to inertia. Or chalk it up to a simple probability: If I break up with

Marci, I will in all likelihood wind up on Rebecca's shit list — a place I refuse to be.

"Rebecca's in a pissy mood," Marci announces.

"Why's that?" DePaul asks.

"Because she found out yesterday that she didn't make it off the wait list at Stanford. She's pissed because now she's going to NYU. As if that's a bad college. You know where I'm going? Oberlin! Picture a bunch of drugged-out cellists in a godforsaken wasteland — no offense on the drugged-out part, D — but seriously . . ."

Marci's voice fades into nothingness. *Rebecca is going to NYU???*

Rebecca snickers and shakes her head. DePaul furrows his brow at her, as if genuinely concerned. (He's most likely puzzling over how she has morphed into a unicorn or a giant daffodil.) Part of me rejoices — the part reserved for unwholesome fantasies. Suddenly, I am ecstatic that I didn't get into Princeton.

"Zack, you got into NYU, too, right?" Rebecca asks me point-blank.

"Yeah. Actually, my parents already sent in the tuition deposit."

She wriggles her eyebrows. "Mine, too. Maybe we'll get mugged together. Or better yet, we can buy switch-blades for protection, and every once in a while we'll hijack a taxi to go visit DePaul in his ivory tower. Princeton is only two hours from the ghetto."

I burst out laughing.

Marci turns to me. "What's so funny?"

"Uh, I . . . um, nothing. Sorry. It was just what Rebecca said — about the ghetto, and about us going off together to the ivory tower. I mean, with the switch-blades. New York City is not that dangerous. . . ." I don't finish. I don't even know what the hell I'm talking about. Whatever it is, it can't be good. Silence falls over the room.

"So, D, how do I look?" Rebecca pipes up. She glares into the black holes that should be DePaul's eyes. "Zack just complimented *his* girlfriend."

DePaul studies her for a moment. "You're shimmering?" he offers with a shrug.

Rebecca grins flatly. "That's sweet, D. Much appreciated. Just try to keep it together tonight, all right? The sixties are over."

VII: Should I Be Frightened by Your Lack of Devotion?

After a clumsy presentation of corsages, the four of us head to the dining hall.

DePaul does keep it together, as much as he can. He only stops twice during the walk to gape at the moon. (In all fairness, it's full.) But when we arrive, my depression sinks to a new low. Marci was on the Spring Ball decorations committee, and it shows. The dining hall is bedecked with streamers and balloons. The scuffed-up wooden tables are shrouded with white linens and set with genuine napkins and silverware; they're even festooned with plastic floral arrangements.

"Real flowers attract too many bugs," Marci explains to me in a stage whisper.

My God. Who is this girl? Okay. I have to admit: The streamers look nice. Still, even with rented napkins, you can't fool me. This is the dining hall. This is the same stuffy cafeteria where we eat every single meal every day of our goddamn lives — meals like "Nantucket Canned Scrod." Marci and the rest of the decorations committee cannot magically transform this room, no matter how noble their intentions. This is not a prom. This is Dorchester's Spring Ball. This is a fraud.

"Whoa!" DePaul exclaims as the four of us sit down. "This place feels amazing. It's vibrating. It doesn't even feel like the dining hall. It feels like a . . . *prom*."

I bury my face in my hands.

"What's the matter?" Marci asks.

Before I can think of a lie, DePaul gasps, "Holy shit!"

I lift my head. DePaul jabs a finger at the stage — a makeshift wooden platform in an area normally reserved for garbage disposal.

"Check out Miss Wyatt," he says. "She's drunk. I heard she went to college with that band. Right, Marci? I think they're, like, an R.E.M. cover band . . ."

For once, DePaul isn't seeing things. Miss Wyatt *is* drunk, staggering amid an array of amps and drums, slurping some kind of suspiciously clear liquid from a Styrofoam cup. It's a cruel irony. The Spring Ball is *the* night when the faculty is supposed to be on high alert for student drinking, an offense punishable by suspension, yet she's wasted, while the four of us haven't imbibed a single drop. (Aside from DePaul, we haven't ingested anything more potent than breath mints.) On the other hand, who can blame Miss Wyatt? She's young. She's trapped here, like the rest of us. So what the hell? Bottoms up! Her musician friends sip from identical cups as they adjust their instruments, pedals, and microphones. . . . They are a bunch of underfed artist types, much like Miss Wyatt herself. I'm very worried they'll suck.

"So, you guys?" Marci prompts. "We should all get up and dance as soon as —"

Without warning, the band bursts into Peter Gabriel's "Sledgehammer." Miss Wyatt stumbles offstage. My ears perk up. They don't suck. They're *good*, even. The sound is bass-heavy and metronome-steady. My fingers drum the tablecloth.

"OH MY GOD!" Marci shrieks. "I love this song! Miss Wyatt said these guys only did college rock." She casts a sidelong glance at me and starts to fidget in time to the music, the universal sign language for: *This is your last chance. I've asked you to dance, so please dance with me, unless you truly are the biggest asshole on the planet.*

I peer around the dining hall. It's packed with fellow seniors, most in rented tuxes and formal dresses like Marci and me. (DePaul and Rebecca are pretty much the only couple in exception to the rented-tux-and-formal-dress rule.) All are as antsy and deserving of fun as Marci. Several leap to their feet and sweep their dates onto the floor.

I turn away from Marci. I can't help it. I *am* that big an asshole.

VIII: Should I?

DePaul scoots toward me. "Hoop earrings, Mom," he breathes in my ear. "Dig Marci's hoop earrings. Chicks who wear earrings like that . . . it's a sign. They're saying they want to get freaky. That's why I should bang her."

"Excuse me?" I whisper back. I know I should be offended, or at least *act* offended. But all I can do is laugh.

"What kind of sign are you talking about? You want to bang my girlfriend because of her hoop earrings?"

"It's obvious you don't want to bang her."

I swallow. "It is?"

"Mom," DePaul chides, "when Marci and Rebecca first came in tonight, you looked Rebecca from the bottom up. But you looked Marci from the top down —"

"Will you guys stop whispering to each other?" Marci interrupts. Her glossy lips curl in a frigid smile. "It's not very polite. Can we either get up and dance, or can we all have a conversation?"

"Sorry!" I push away from DePaul. "What do you want to talk about?"

"That's a very good question, Zack," Marci replies curtly. "I want to find out, once and for all, why DePaul calls you Mom. I want to know why you let him do it."

"Because I breast-feed him?" I joke.

Rebecca slaps a hand over her mouth to keep from cracking up.

Marci doesn't so much as blink. Her face is an ice sculpture.

"Hey, Marci, Zack's just kidding," DePaul says. "Come on, let's dance. I love this song, too." He throws out a hand to Marci — surprisingly steady, considering his condition — and whisks her out onto the floor with the rest of the couples.

I sag back in my chair.

"You handled that very well," Rebecca remarks.

"I thought so."

"Can I ask you something?"

"Sure."

Rebecca leans across the table. "How did you and Marci get together anyway? I mean, really."

I think for a minute. "Because you and DePaul started going out. And she was pretty aggressive. I mean, she let me know she had a crush on me. . . . I was just flattered. Plus she's sort of hot, and she's your roommate — also, she has a last name that starts with *W*. We sit near each other at Chapel and stuff. It worked out."

"Very romantic," Rebecca snorts. "'She's sort of hot.' I have a *W* name, too, Zack. I sit closer to you than Marci does. I sat closer to you yesterday."

"But you're going out with DePaul," I hear myself mumble.

Rebecca doesn't respond. I stare at Marci as she clings to DePaul and tries to follow his crazed moves. He's far surpassed Deadheads and *Beat Street*; he's in shaman trance territory. Then again, "Sledgehammer" is a great song.

"You know what, Zack?" Rebecca says. "You should either break up with Marci this second, or go out there and cut in on that dance. Because Marci wants something to happen with you tonight."

IX: Should I???

Everything freezes. I stop breathing. My fake bow tie threatens to cut off the oxygen to my brain. "Something to happen? Like what?"

"Oh, come on. Don't play dumb. Marci thinks the Spring Ball is a 'huge rite of passage,' and she isn't talking about the fake prom vibe." Rebecca sighs. "I just wish DePaul wanted something to happen tonight, too. That's why I'm in a pissy mood. Not because I'm going to NYU. I'm psyched to go to NYU. *You're* gonna be there."

"Yeah. I am." The plastic flowers on our table spin as if *I've* just dropped Daffy Duck Blotter. "But you're in a pissy mood because . . . ?" I leave the question hanging.

Rebecca looks straight into my eyes and smirks. "Surprise, surprise. Yes, Zack, I am a virgin —" She stares down into her lap. "I'm probably going to regret saying that. Whatever. The cat is out of the bag. So I might as well finish. I don't want to lose my virginity to DePaul. I just wish he wanted to lose his virginity to me." She lifts her head. "You know what I'm saying?"

I nod, biting my lip. "Actually, I do. Can I ask you something now?"

"Of course. Please take your cat out of *your* bag."

"What is it that you like about Marci? I mean, why are you guys best friends?"

Rebecca frowns. "That's not a very nice thing to ask about your girlfriend."

"I know. But I'm not in the mood to be nice. I'm in the mood to be honest. Like you're being."

A smile flits across her face. "You want to know what I like about Marci, Zack? What I love about her? *She's* honest. She is the most honest, unpretentious person I know. She buys into the whole romantic notion of a prom. And she's proud of it. By the way, that dress she's wearing? It's the same dress her own mother wore to *her* prom. Marci did this all for you." Her hazel eyes bore into my own. "For you, Zack."

I'm not sure how to respond to that. I feel sick. My eyes flicker toward Marci as the song ends. She and DePaul pull apart, hooting and clapping — and the band immediately launches into R.E.M.'s "Radio Free Europe." In a flash, DePaul and Marci are back in each other's arms, whooping it up.

"What are you thinking?" Rebecca asks.

"That I'm happy Marci seems to be having fun right now," I murmur — and I am telling the truth. "And that I want to get out of here. I want to go throw out D's stash of acid. I know some uptight asshole teachers are gonna be checking our rooms and trolling our mini fridges for booze tonight, and I don't want them to stumble on . . . you know."

Rebecca nods. "Yeah. I do know," she says with a rueful smile. "Hey, I'll come with you if you want. I don't really feel like hanging out here, either."

"You don't? What about —"

"Mr. Tambourine Man? Seeing as he's going to finish up the night on Pluto, I don't see much point in sticking around." She brushes a red curl behind an ear and fixes me with another intense stare. "That leaves the question of Marci, though."

My mind whirls. *I can either stay here or go back to my room alone with Rebecca. I can either stay here or go back to my room alone with . . .*

I jump out of my chair and hurry across the dance floor. The song is blaring full force; DePaul's face is soaked with sweat. He's grinning crazily. His eyes catch mine.

"I'm gonna go get some punch," he gasps over the music. He stares at one of the balloons on the ceiling, and then lurches away.

Marci is breathless, too. Her lungs heave beneath her strapless pink gown.

99

"Marci, I'm sorry I've been such an asshole to you," I confess. "I really am."

She sniffs. "You're not *that* sorry."

"Can we . . . I don't know — talk? Can we —"

"How about we talk tomorrow?" she interrupts, following DePaul. "I want to have fun tonight. It's the Spring Ball. I've put too much time and energy into this night not to have fun."

X: Oh, You Better Be Good to Me

Rebecca tries to console me on the walk back to my dorm. I'm not quite sure what to make of her behavior. I've been an asshole to her best friend. She should be *telling* me that. But instead she loops her arm in mine and snuggles close, making it impossible to concentrate on a word she's saying.

The halls are eerily quiet. There are no faculty prowlers, looking to bust illicit drinkers. With silent and professional detachment, Rebecca and I remove the sheets of Daffy Duck Blotter from the mini fridge and open DePaul's desk, to slip them inside a porn magazine or whatever he has hidden in there (more LSD?). And the whole time, I'm wondering, *Did Rebecca just agree to come back here because she wants to hook up?* I don't trust myself to speak —

And then our eyes come to rest upon the sole contents of DePaul's drawer: an unsealed envelope with Rebecca's name on it. There's a date scrawled on it, too, at the top. A future date: June 11, 1986. The day of our graduation.

For what seems like a long time, we both stare at DePaul's sloppy handwriting.

Honestly, I'm surprised that there's anything in the desk at all. I've never actually seen DePaul *open* the desk. Besides, he keeps his porn magazines very publicly strewn on the trunk by his bed. Come to think of it, I've never seen him open one of those, either. As far as I can tell, he only buys porn to piss off Rebecca and to screw with the heads of the teachers who inspect our rooms.

Rebecca turns to me. It's my decision. My pulse picks up a notch. I nod.

She opens the envelope as delicately as she can. I read over her shoulder.

Dear Rebecca,

Whew. We are finally OUT OF HERE! I would say congratulations, but I've already congratulated you in our caps and dresses. I mean, gowns. And just so you know, I am not tripping right now. But you might be wondering why I decided to write you a letter. How to phrase this? I am figuring things out. I am.............. Shit, this is harder than I thought!

Okay. So. You know me, and I think you love me — as a person, that is. A very flawed person, of course. Zack knows me and loves me, too, I think. But there's something neither of you knows and it's been driving me crazy because I want to tell you both because when I said it to myself in the mirror just now, it felt really good. Except, here's the problem:

I think I may be gay.

Hmm. It definitely felt better to say it out loud than to write it. Looking at these words on the paper, they just seem so.......... GAY.

Ha! Sorry. Lame attempt at comedy. All right,

so part of the reason I'm writing this letter, too, is to clear up one matter once and for all: You and Zack. You know what? Nothing would make me happier than you and Zack. No joke. Maybe something will happen this summer with you guys, away from school. He's a total dick to Marci, and I'm a total dick to you, and even though my reasons for being a dick are different — and I apologize for them — I know why Zack is a dick. He's just as into you as you are into him.

Want to hear something <u>really</u> funny? I've spent a lot of time driving myself crazy trying to make up some BS about how I want to hook up with Marci, just to piss Zack off and send him running into your arms. How fucked up is that? But the truth is, I love you, Rebecca. And I love Zack, too. I'm on your side, both of your sides! I just don't <u>love</u> love you. I don't love anyone that way yet. I never have, but I want the space to find that person. I don't want to lose you, either. Or Zack. I don't even know if I'm going to give you this letter. Maybe I'll reread it after I drop a tab later. Yeah I think that's a good idea. Shit.

Love, DePaul

Rebecca glances at me upon finishing. Neither of us says a word. She neatly folds the letter and replaces it in the envelope, then drops the envelope on top of the sheets of Daffy Duck Blotter — and closes the drawer.

I sit on my bed. She sits beside me.

"So he *is* gay," I hear myself announce after a while. "I thought he was . . . happy."

"You can't be both?" Rebecca asks in a faraway voice.

"At this school? Are you kidding?"

"So does that bother you? That he's gay?"

"No — what bothers me is that he didn't tell me," I mutter. For the first time in my life, I'm annoyed with her. She knows better. I shake my head, running over a thousand different memories and scenarios — some of which fall into place like easy fly balls, others of which bounce out of the glove without any explanation. (And why am I thinking in terms of baseball metaphors? I don't give a shit about baseball.) "He could have told me," I finish. "He *should* have. He's my best friend. Why didn't he?"

"He was scared," Rebecca soothes. "You said it yourself. You know how this school is. He was worried you'd get freaked out."

I turn to her. "How about you? You seem to be taking this remarkably well."

"To be honest, I'm relieved."

"Relieved? How?"

"Because DePaul is right. Not just about him. About you and me."

I open my mouth. It falls shut.

"Aren't you into me, Zack?" she asks, so quietly I can barely hear her.

"Yeah, of course. I mean, I almost told you once. . . ." I fight off the dizziness. "Remember that night we all got drunk on DePaul's boat, and he passed out? But I can't tell you now. I have a zit on my nose. I'm wearing a fucking rented tuxedo."

She kisses me once, very softly, on the lips. "I don't

care that you have a zit on your nose. And you can take your tuxedo off. Tonight can still be amazing. I want it to be amazing. Don't you? It's the Spring Ball."

It is indeed the Spring Ball. So we talk about that for a little bit. We talk about how we're going to explain everything to Marci, and to DePaul, too. We talk about a lot of things, but the talk eventually grows fuzzy and pointless and peters out.

I stand and turn off DePaul's desk lamp. My knees are shaking. I know we're done with conversation for the evening, DePaul's desk lamp included; I know because my heart is thumping too hard to do anything but let Rebecca take control.

And when I return to the bed, she fumbles in the darkness, reaching into the pockets of her skirt — and I hear a soft plastic crinkling. And in that instant, I am both more frightened and more elated than I've ever been in my life, and she knows it, because her fingers intertwine with mine, reassuring me. And I don't have to lie or put on an act. I don't have to speak. I can be honest. DePaul *is* on our side.

THE END (CUT TO THE FULL CHORUS)

GLOSSARY

Randy: An adjective meaning excessively and inappropriately horny.

Bang and Olufsen: A sleek brand of stereo, very popular in the eighties.

DePaul Adams: Best friend, best man at our wedding; renounced hallucinogens and came out of the closet freshman year at Princeton; he and his partner, Norm (music professor at Columbia, sick piano player, disagrees with my classic rock musical tastes but whatever, jerk) are godparents to Harper.

Marci Wolf: Ex-girlfriend, wife's best friend, maid of honor at our wedding, married a Kansas City weatherman who shares her penchant for heavy makeup.

Timothy Leary: Deceased Harvard professor who believed that LSD was the key to salvation. Advised the sixties generation to "Tune in, Turn on, and Drop Out."

AC/DC to ZZ Top: Two grizzled bands (and every grizzled band in between) who wrote kick-ass guitar-driven classic rock songs, and who don't wear cover-up to this day. At least Rebecca and I hope they don't. But we know they do.

MTV: Up until 1986, MTV *was* music television: no commercials, no "reality" programming, and no self-congratulatory awards shows. The downside was that they mostly played videos by bands like The Thompson Twins.

The Thompson Twins: Google them. I won't go there. I still have some dignity.

Looking-Glass Porters and Marmalade Skies: References to lyrics from the Beatles' psychedelic classic "**L**ucy in the **S**ky with **D**iamonds."

Deadhead: Fan of the Grateful Dead; a smelly hippie who is often annoying or high.

Beat Street: Break-dancing movie. Funny.

Sammy Hagar: Replaced Van Halen singer/icon/legend "Diamond" David Lee Roth in 1985. Should be shot. (Original Van Halen = *ONLY* Van Halen.)

College Rock: The 1980s term for "alternative rock." Is "alternative rock" even a term anymore???

Mr. Tambourine Man: A Bob Dylan song, rumored to be about a proselytizing, pied piper druggie type (see **DePaul Adams**).

"Better Be Good to Me": Okay, it's not that horrendous a song. Listen to the lyrics if you ever read this story a second time. It grows on you. (The song, not the story.) Screw it; the song rocks, not that I'd ever admit that to anyone. DePaul insists on blasting it at every one of our anniversary parties — in front of *you*, Harper. Jerk.

Three Fates

by Aimee Friedman

I think I've made a mistake.

A month ago, in May, I was sitting in calculus class, scribbling a poem in the margin of my tattered notebook, when Pete DeSilva passed me a note that said: *You + me = Prom?* Because Pete writes in equations, and because he laughs like a coyote, and because I've known him all my eighteen years, the thought of him tying a sweaty corsage onto my sweaty wrist and leading me in a slow dance made me just this side of nauseous. So I bent over the sliver of paper and wrote *I'm sorry, but that would be mathematically impossible.* I knew Pete didn't have a crush on me — most likely his pushy mom had volunteered me while he was eating his oatmeal that morning — so I didn't feel the need to sugarcoat.

But now it's June, prom is two weeks away, and karma has not been kind to me: I don't have a date. All my girl-friends have theirs lined up, practically tuxedoed already, a row of eager penguins. And Pete DeSilva, who I clearly should have said yes to that day, has somehow lassoed the long-lashed Michele Martin into going with him. Everybody is pairing off, wearing the panicked look of third graders choosing partners on a field trip. And I'm the lame runty kid, the one with the shoelaces forever untied and the nose forever running, left partnerless. Alone.

"You'd better do something, Abigael — and fast," my best friend, Iris, advises me as we walk home from school, book bags low on our backs and flip-flops slapping the sidewalk. I can tell she is serious by the way she uses my full name. The sunlight glinting off the flat surface of Lake Serene momentarily blinds us, and we squint at each other.

"Why can't I just go stag?" I argue, even though I hate that expression. I picture myself leaping like a horned antelope through a forest of girls in pink taffeta.

Iris groans as we turn onto Main Street, passing the bait and tackle shop her parents own, the bookstore *my* parents own, and the ice-cream parlor where her boyfriend, Ted, pours sprinkles onto cones. Growing up in a small upstate New York town can feel like a choke hold when you think about it too much. Thankfully, college — Boston, September, so close yet so far — hovers on the horizon.

"In an ideal universe — where, say, unicorns exist — it would be cool for you to go alone," Iris declares, stopping in front of Serenity Ice Cream and crossing her tan arms over her chest. Iris is lucky; with her dark hair and complexion, she turns the color of whole-wheat toast the minute the sun comes out. I'm blond, curly-haired, pale-eyed, and freckled, so my skin goes straight to lobster. "But as you and I know," Iris continues as she opens the door and lets out a gust of cold, conditioned air, "dear old Lake Serene High is not an ideal universe. Not even close."

"Tell me about it," I grumble, stuffing my hands in the pockets of my carpenter capris and trudging inside after her. "I knew I shouldn't have turned down Pete." It had become my mantra of the past week. At our pom-poms-and-pride high school, even the stodgy chaperones raise their eyebrows if you don't have someone to grope you during the last song.

And the thing is, I don't *want* to go alone. I don't want my *mom* to pin the corsage on the strapless green dress I bought ages ago, or my dad to walk me out to the waiting limo, all teary-eyed. I don't want to squish myself into a corner of that limo and pretend not to watch as Iris and Ted play competitive tonsil hockey on our drive to the country club. And I don't want to dance in a lame-ass circle with the two other dateless girls, shimmying our hips as the sadistic DJ blasts "It's Raining Men." I want, at the very least, a passably attractive boy who will lend me his tuxedo jacket when my shoulders get cold, who'll chuckle at my jokes about the way certain people dance, who'll — is it too much to hope for? — kiss me when the night is over.

But I don't even have a current crush on whom to focus my hopes. I absolutely cannot be into a boy who's dumped sandbox sand onto my head, like Archie Jong did when we were six. Archie himself moved to New York City in the fifth grade, but because most Lake Serene kids travel in straight lines from kindergarten to our high school's loving arms, I look at nearly all the boys in my class that way. My one boyfriend so far, Lyle Jamison, was a mop-headed, smiley college kid from Buffalo who worked part-time at my parents' bookstore. Our not-quite-burning romance ended the day my dad found

Lyle rolling a joint in, fittingly, the Plant & Garden section. Since then, my luck with the opposite sex has been the kind that puts fortune-tellers out of business.

The ice-cream parlor is crammed with loud ten-year-olds hopped up on sugar. The instant we enter, Ted, who has been scooping out a curl of blackberry chip for a scowling little boy, leans over the counter to kiss Iris. The sullen boy and I exchange eye rolls.

"Baby, do you know anyone Abby can go to the prom with?" Iris asks as we sit on the two free stools. She keeps her voice low and discreet, as if I have a highly contagious disease.

"Hmm," Ted says, tapping a finger on his stubbly chin. Despite his pink apron and the matching cap on his black-and-purple-dyed head, Ted still manages to pull off his hard-core look nicely. "How about Elijah Hayes?" he suggests after a minute. "He doesn't have a date yet."

"He *doesn't*?" Iris and I ask at the same time, wide-eyed.

I'd considered Elijah — who moved to Lake Serene in the seventh grade, thus missing the sandbox stigma — as potential crush material, but he'd struck me as too aloof. He lives on my street, and I've seen him peeling down Wildwood Lane in his beat-up vintage car. He's also in my AP English class, where he sits in the back, shaggy brown hair falling into his smoldering brown eyes, strong jaw set, his long fingers twitching as if he is going through nicotine withdrawal — which he probably is. He hardly ever speaks, except to murmur some hit-the-nail-on-the-head comment in his scratchy voice. It was Elijah who pointed out that the green light in *The*

110

Great Gatsby meant money, and that Edgar Allan Poe must have been smoking something while writing "The Raven." Hot, smart, mysterious Elijah — it was no wonder that I'd assumed he had a serious girlfriend with red Botticelli curls who'd be flying in from, like, Paris for the prom.

Ted shakes his head, reaching under the counter for a waffle cone for Iris. "Today in gym, Cody asked him, point-blank, and Elijah said he didn't give a shit about the prom, which — duh — means he's been too chicken to ask anyone."

At this, Iris nods wisely and shoots me an excited grin. "Go get him, Abby," she urges.

I rest my elbows on the counter, pondering the matter. I've never officially asked a guy out, but the idea doesn't make me *too* nervous. It's just a matter of holding your nose and taking the plunge, feet-first-into-the-pool style. And now — with the prom clock tick-tocking — is the time for risks, desperate measures, and all those things that brave, stupid people do.

It's when Ted hands Iris her cone and she leans forward to kiss him on the lips that I make up my mind. No more of this watching-from-the-sidelines stuff. I'm going to take the steering wheel of my destiny and find myself a prom date.

The next day, in last-period English class, all those notions of me not being nervous fly out the window. My stomach is twisted into Boy Scout knots as I chew on my pen cap. Elijah Hayes is hunched over his desk in the back of the room, oblivious to the fact that when the bell rings, his life will be forever altered. Mine, too.

Our teacher, Ms. Tannen of the frumpy black suits, kneesocks, and lofty literary aspirations, writes the William Ernest Henley poem "Invictus," on the blackboard. I focus on the words, realizing that they're weirdly timely — for me, in any case. "I am the master of my fate: I am the captain of my soul," I recite under my breath, ignoring the odd look that Iris shoots me over her shoulder.

When the bell rings, I'm up out of my seat so fast that I knock my knee into my desk and wince in pain. Uncharacteristically, I've worn a skirt today — a white skirt, a black tank, and my trusty flip-flops. Tossing back my hair, which I tried to tame with extra conditioner and a blow-dryer that morning, I hobble over to Elijah's desk. He is reclining in his seat, one arm flung over the back of his chair, and his free hand holding a copy of *No Exit* by Sartre over his face. It's obvious he thinks himself far beyond this class — beyond this *town* — and for some reason this gets me kind of hot and bothered. In a good way.

"Are you okay?" he asks without lowering the book.

"Yeah, why?" I put one hand on my hip as streams of classmates, smug and secure in their future prom dates, flow past me.

"You were limping," Elijah replies, snapping the book shut and piercing me with his dark eyes. Clearly, he's got bionic powers. I like him even more now.

"I'm fine," I assure him, even though my twisty-turny heart tells me otherwise. I can practically feel Iris sending me goodwill vibes from where she is waiting in the hallway. By now, the big, sunny classroom is empty; even Ms. Tannen has departed. "Listen, I was thinking, or, rather, wondering" — at this point I am realizing that I should have prepared a script — "what you think about the prom," I finish, then bite my lip. It's as good a start as any, I suppose.

"The prom?" Elijah repeats slowly, slipping his Sartre into his book bag. I have his full attention. "You mean that despicable 1950s-style conspiracy designed to brainwash the youth of America into buying overpriced formal wear, renting gas-guzzling limousines, and dancing to soul-deadening songs like 'I Believe I Can Fly'?" He coughs into his fist. "I think that anyone who willingly attends prom is no better than a calf being led to slaughter." Finished, he drums his fingers on his desk and stares up at me.

". . . Right," I say, my hands falling to my sides as my stomach drops with an almost audible *clunk*. But I can't back out now. *Master of my fate*, I remind myself firmly. "So," I add, holding Elijah's fiery gaze as my face burns, "I'm guessing that means you wouldn't be, you know, interested in going with . . . me?" I'm cringing before the sentence is even out.

"Oh." Elijah gives a start, as if someone has poked him in the back. His brown eyes seem to mellow as he studies me. "I didn't, um, know that's what you were . . ." He passes a hand over his face, looking as close to embarrassed as someone like Elijah Hayes can get. "See, it's not you, Abby, you're really nice and all —"

I've heard enough. "Gotcha," I say, backing up in a hurry. "Thanks." I wheel around, strap my book bag on over my shaking shoulders, and flee the classroom, amazed that it's possible to feel like you've been dumped by someone you've never even dated.

"Don't," I mutter to Iris as she bounds toward me, all hopeful exuberance. "Disaster."

113

"How bad?" she asks, wrapping an arm around my shoulder as I stumble down the hallway, still in shock. Above our heads, the purple banner reading SENIORS: BUY YOUR PROM TICKETS NOW! taunts me.

"Like, apocalypse," I elaborate as we near our lockers. Our friend Gloria is waiting for us there, her face glowing and her golden ponytail swinging as she hops from foot to foot, kind of like a third grader who needs to pee.

"Abby, Iris — look!" she exclaims, holding up a thick, shiny violet sash. Iris squeals but I raise my eyebrows in confusion. "It's a cummerbund," Gloria explains, giving me a get-with-it look. "Cody's cummerbund. He got one to match my dress exactly. So now everything, including my shoes and his boutonniere, will be violet." She sighs happily. I don't even know what a boutonniere is.

Gloria is the kind of a girl who keeps a binder filled with magazine clippings of what she wants her wedding dress to look like. And she doesn't have a boyfriend, let alone a fiancé. Cody was her lab partner in chemistry and randomly asked her to the prom one day when they both had their goggles on. Now poor, unsuspecting Cody has been sucked into her whirlpool of *Teen People* prom issues and violet cummerbunds. Obviously, Gloria is the last person I want to be around right now, so I grab my hoodie from my locker, tell a worried-looking Iris that I'll talk to her later, and beat a hasty retreat for home, trying my best not to cry on the way.

Since bad things happen in threes — first Elijah, then Gloria — my twenty-year-old brother, Brian, is in the kitchen when I get home. As I storm in, he's pawing through the fridge and humming "Pour Some Sugar on Me". He straightens up, a slice of cheese in his fist, and his mouth full, ready to look guilty.

"Oh. It's just you," he grunts.

"Love you, too," I spit, dropping my book bag on the floor while our beagle, Franklin, trots in, whining. "Did you come for the food, or to mooch cash off Mom and Dad?"

Brian is what I like to call the brown sheep of the Cooper family; he was enough of a smart-ass growing up to warrant being shipped off to military school, but he's never done anything truly criminal. With his blond buzz cut, delicate features, and big blue eyes, he can almost pull off looking angelic — "Ab, your brother's *hot*," Iris informs me on a regular basis while I pretend to hurl — but my parents and I know better. He just moved back to Lake Serene and is living with his bossy girl-friend, Nadine, who supports him while he writes his never-ending screenplay. Needless to say, the fact that I'm headed to college in the fall with good grades and no tattoos is a point of tension between us.

"You look like a truck ran you over," Brian says sweetly. "What's wrong?" He shuts the refrigerator and watches me, chewing steadily. I roll my eyes. I hate it when my lunkhead brother pretends to be all "insightful."

I kneel down to scratch Franklin behind the ears, planning to ignore Brian's question. But something in me is itching to complain, to finally spill my sorrows to someone who isn't obsessed with cummerbunds and stretch limos. I glance up at my brother, who is regarding

115

me from the fridge with a genuinely interested expression. Sighing, and not wanting to divulge too many dirty details, I say: "I asked this guy to the prom; he said no; now I'll never find a date. Happy?"

I feel as if I have just recited a haiku. On loserdom.

As predicted, the corner of Brian's mouth curls up in a wry smile. "Oh, shut up," I say, before he can even speak. "I know, I know — lame Abby strikes again." Brian spent his teen years vandalizing mailboxes and trying to sweet-talk girls into bed, so he thinks an adolescence spent any other way — say, going to the movies with friends, or actually attending school — is wasted.

"That's not what I was going to say!" Brian protests, knitting his brow, as if I have deeply offended him.

I let Franklin lick my hand; after all, he appears to be my only ally right now. "So what, then?" I ask Brian. "Do *you* know where I can get myself a date at the last minute?"

Brian grins, crossing his arms and leaning against the fridge. "*I* can go with you."

I snort, and Franklin looks up at me, startled. "Uh-huh, Brian. That would be perfect, wouldn't it? 'Oh, hey, everyone. Yeah, my prom date and I kind of look alike — so what of it?'" I shake my head, getting to my feet. "Great joke," I tell my brother.

"Well, we don't look *that* much alike," Brian says teasingly.

I tilt my head, studying his face; he's right — to a casual stranger, our resemblance might not even be noticeable. Especially not under the dim lights of the town country club. Suddenly, a flush spreads through my body. *Wait a minute.* I'm realizing that hardly anyone in Lake Serene even knows what Brian looks like now, because of his time away at military school. Only Iris has seen him in recent weeks, and I could swear her to secrecy —

Stop, I tell myself. *What are you thinking? Are you really going to ask your older brother to the prom?*

But as I stand there facing him in the kitchen, it appears that, yes, I am.

"Brian," I say slowly, resting my elbows on the counter. "What if . . . what if it wasn't such a joke?"

Brian blinks. "What if *what* wasn't a joke, Abby?"

"What if . . ." I pause, weighing the situation. It wouldn't be so bad, I tell myself. I can say he's a friend from out of town, and even let him take off before the slow dances if he wants to. All I really need to do is show up with a male in tow, and silence the likes of Gloria. "What if you *did* take me to the prom?" I finish, flashing my brother a hopeful smile before I explain the whole crazy plan.

Brian appears to think it over, first with a frown, and then with a smirk. "What would be in it for me?" he asks, thinking like a true petty criminal.

I clasp my hands together, rising up on my toes. "Brian, *please*," I say. My brother knows how much I detest begging, so he has to realize how important this is to me. "You don't know what it's been like . . . all my friends . . . I'll . . ." — inspiration strikes and I catch my breath — "I'll pay you," I whisper.

So it's come to this. Abigael Cooper is bribing her brother to take her to the prom.

Brian hooks his fingers through the belt loops of his battered jeans and leans against the fridge, twisting his mouth in thought. "How much are we talking here?"

"Two months' allowance," I offer, trying not to think about all the new clothes, sheets, and cute fringed lamps I want to buy for college. "And I'll cover the cost of your tux."

Brian nods slowly, clearly digesting the deal. "When is it?" he asks, scratching the cobra tattoo on his wrist.

"June nineteenth," I reply, feeling a tremor of panic as I realize how close the date is. "Saturday night. Seven o'clock."

"Ooh." Brian shakes his head from side to side, letting out a low whistle. "Sorry, Ab. Nadine's sister's getting married that night, and we've already R.S.V.P.'d and shit. Nadine will, like, cut off my privates if I bail."

"Okay, gross and unnecessary," I reply, shuddering.

"Look, maybe I can ask one of my friends —" Brian begins, taking a step toward me, but I move out of the way, balling my hands into fists. I know Brian's friends, and I can just imagine the toothless perv who'll pull up on his motorcycle and then try to cop a feel during the prim and proper dinner hour.

"Forget it, Brian," I bark, and Franklin punctuates my statement with a growl of his own. "Just take all the food you want and leave me alone." As I tear out of the kitchen and up the stairs, Franklin is on my heels, and though a part of me wants nothing more than to curl up with him on my bed and sob, I slam my door in his face the minute I get to my bedroom. Which makes me feel even worse.

"Why me?" I groan, collapsing into the butterfly chair in front of my computer. I gaze up above my desk at my neat, orderly bookshelves — Brian always mocks me for being the anal one — and study the spine of a Greek

118

mythology text. I think of the three Fates: Clotho, Lachesis, and Atropos, who spin, measure, and snip the thread of life. They control it all. So then is everything — prom dates and colleges and the colors of cummerbunds — out of our hands? Somehow this idea depresses me even more. I allow a few tears to leak out and slip down the sides of my face, but then I blow my nose and switch on the computer. I've never seen the point in crying, and I feel a little ridiculous getting all existential over what is essentially an overblown school event.

Knowing I owe Iris more of an explanation about Elijah, I log on to MySpace, which is our favorite means of communication. Iris is even more obsessed with MySpace than I am; her profile page is decorated with crazy pink and orange swirls and drawings of Ted, she updates her song daily, and she always has a new picture of herself displayed. Meanwhile, my page is pretty basic: no song, plain blue background, and a black-and-white photo of myself, standing on the shore of Lake Serene and laughing as I shield my eyes from the sun. Iris took it last summer, way before prom was something either of us cared about.

I quickly check out my page, then click on Iris's picture — she's the first of my friends in my Top Eight — and send her a message describing the Elijah horror in detail. When I'm done, I idly scroll through Iris's friends, mostly Lake Serene High kids, and then click on Pete DeSilva's picture, feeling my typical pang of regret about him.

One of Pete's friends, I notice, is a semi-cute Asian guy named Archie. When I click on his picture, I realize it's Archie Jong — the sandbox fiend from grade school.

I smile for the first time that afternoon, feeling a flood of nostalgia. I haven't seen Archie in, like, eight years, and it's funny to study his photos, like the one where he's leaning against the deck of a boat, the wind messing up his black hair. He looks all chill, and confident, and . . . grown-up. I skim his list of favorites, impressed by his music choices — I, too, have the Subways and Death Cab on my page — and I'm about to survey his book selections when I notice the flashing orange icon telling me that Archie's online. I picture him sitting in a room in New York City, his windows looking out on tall buildings and taxicabs. Feeling spontaneous, I decide to send an Instant Message. I *never* do stuff like this. But whatever; it's just Archie.

Hey, I type. *Remember me?*

I wait, nibbling on my bottom lip and feeling stupid until Archie's response finally pops up.

Abby Cooper! I grin and, for no reason, feel my face turn warm. *What's up, girl? Have u forgiven me?*

For what? I type back, enjoying the sound of my fingers clicking along the keys.

For being a beast back in the 1st grade, Archie writes. *I have some memory of sandbox showdowns. . . .*

I send back a smiley face. *All is forgiven,* I write, because suddenly it's true. And, suddenly, I know what I have to do. It's like MySpace is the portal to my fate, and somehow it's led me to Archie. Not in a true-love sense, of course — Archie still feels like a second, much-less-messed-up brother — but in a this-is-right way. Archie seems charming and presentable, and he'd probably be up for a trip back to his hometown.

I know this is going to sound weird, I began, typing more

120

cautiously now. *But any chance you'd want to experience the Lake Serene High prom?* I squeeze my eyes shut, press SEND, and then jump to my feet. I can't sit still while I wait, so I pace the length of my room, praying to the poster of Emily Dickinson above my wooden dresser. When I hear the small *ding* of Archie's response, I race back to my computer, breathless.

Would love to. Know it's the 19th, though, and I have something in the city that day. Bummer.

Damn June 19th! Who got together and decided to schedule every freaking world event that day? I let out a huge sigh and write back that I understand.

And I do, I realize as I sink deeper into my chair, sadness welling up inside me. Things couldn't be clearer. I've struck out three times in one day. If the fates exist, they are definitely telling me that it's time to pack it in. Give up. I'm meant to hit the prom alone.

Maybe another time, Archie writes back, and this makes my throat ache even deeper.

Maybe, I write back, grateful that Archie cannot see my teary-eyed expression. Then I log off and shut down. Game over.

Despite it all, I boldly purchase a prom ticket at school that week. "Just one?" Michele Martin, our class president and Pete DeSilva's unlikely date, asks, her voice breathy and incredulous. We're standing in the student council office, which is decorated with another purple banner that reads JUNE 19TH: THE NIGHT OF YOUR LIFE! Michele is behind the desk, holding a slim stack of tickets in one hand, while the other falters over the money I am handing her.

"One," I assure her. "You know? *Uno?* The number that comes after zero? The loneliest number you ever knew?" My voice breaks a little on the word *loneliest* but hopefully Michele is too dense to notice.

She flutters her caterpillar lashes. "Abigael, I don't know how to break this to you, but . . ." She drops her head for a minute, her silky red hair falling over her cheek, and then stoically lifts her gaze, acting like a doctor who's about to tell me that the X-ray doesn't look good. "You're the only person who's bought a single ticket so far," she whispers.

I hate the fact that these words make my heart sink. Hard.

"That's cool," I bluff. *You will not make me crack, bitch.* "Thought I'd keep my options open on prom night, maybe play the field a little. . . ." I grin to show her how funny I find myself, but Michele only shakes her head grimly.

"Tell you what," she says, finally accepting my money. "Don't say *anything*, because I could get in serious trouble, but I'm going to give you two tickets for the price of one."

"It's not a money issue —" I begin, even though the price *is* way too high for a night of what is likely to be crappy food and worse music.

Michele hands me the two tickets, discussion over. "Abigael," she says sternly. "Take both. You never know — you could still —" She pauses, but her meaning is clear. *You could still find a date.*

Right. And balloons filled with diamonds could come pouring down on my head the minute I step out of the office.

I thank Michele for the secret ticket, walk outside, and realize that people only give you stuff for free when they pity you. I've become a prom charity case. I'm surprised random girls I pass in the hall aren't handing me extra dresses and shoes, their eyes wide and concerned.

But I already have a dress and shoes, which are two of the reasons I feel obliged to attend the whole mess in the first place. Over the next week, I am forced into that dress and those shoes many times, for what Iris calls "rehearsals." There are three types of rehearsals: body (keeping the dress from slipping off my boobs, even when I move), face (Iris testing out different and equally garish shades of shadow on my lids), and attitude (sashaying in the strappy gold sandals as if I do it all the time). To keep me sane, I think, Iris comes over almost every day for these rehearsals. And when we're collapsed on my bedroom floor from laughter, our dresses pooling around us, I can almost forget the way Michele asked *Just one?* or Elijah (who I've been studiously avoiding all week) said it wasn't me. I am determined to walk into the country club on Saturday alone, head high and heels click-clacking in triumph. I am Abby, hear me roar.

By the time June 19th arrives, I'm feeling rather upbeat. The day is sun-drenched and breezy, and the thicket of trees outside my window are lit up emerald green to match my dress. There is something freeing and luxurious about getting ready with no one in mind. I eat a big lunch with my parents (who, aware of my dateless status, have been tiptoeing around me for the past two weeks), take a long, steamy shower, and start changing. I turn on Marshall Crenshaw as loud as he'll go, spray a cloud of Happy in the air, and spring through it as Iris taught me. I end up with a mouthful of perfume, but I'm feeling content as I cough. Lip gloss, liner, and shadow are all applied — sloppily, but still. Damp blond hair is brushed, then piled atop my head and secured with pins. A few tendrils escape onto my neck, but, hey, they look kind of alluring. Step into satin dress, zip it up, let it swish around my knees, reach for shoes, and —

"Abby!" my mom hollers from downstairs. Franklin is barking like crazy.

"I'm not ready yet!" I shout back over Marshall singing "*My cynical girl . . .*" I know she's waiting at the foot of the stairs with the corsage in hand while my dad lurks in the corner, digital camera at the ready. But I still have a good twenty minutes before the limo shows up.

"Your brother's here!" my mom calls, sounding equal parts confused and amused.

Ugh. Anger swells inside me. How dare he? It's obvious that Brian, who I haven't seen since our nasty confrontation in the kitchen, has dropped by to mock me on his way to Nadine's sister's wedding. Fine. Whatever. Suddenly, I *want* him to see me all decked out and fashiony, not in my carpenter capris for once.

It's not my mom but Brian who's waiting at the foot of the stairs, holding a bright red rose corsage. He's wearing a tux, and even I have to admit that he cleans up nice.

"Check you out," Brian says, grinning up at me as I descend, barefoot and frowning.

"Check *you* out," I retort, stopping short on the last step. "Nadine must have really cracked the whip to get you into that tux."

Brian accepts the compliment with a hammy little bow, then straightens up and adds, "Oh, yeah, I didn't tell you guys. Nadine has cracked her last whip. We're not together anymore."

"What?" I jerk back, surprised. "Since when?"

"Since, like, a week ago," Brian replies lazily, running a hand over his bristly golden head. "I got fed up with her constant nagging and controlling. I realized that it's high time for me to be a man, you know? Stand on my own two —"

"She caught you with another girl, huh?" I ask, folding my arms over my chest.

Brian sighs, lifting his shoulders. "Her best friend." As I bury my face in my hands, he adds, "It's cool, though. Nadine kicked me out, but I'm living with Marissa now."

"So let me get this straight," I say, checking the hall clock, because Iris will shoot me if I'm not waiting outside when the limo comes. "Nadine dumped you, you're shacked up with her best friend, and you're *still* going to her sister's wedding?"

Brian blinks at me like I've just spoken Sanskrit. "I'm not going to her sister's wedding," he replies. "I'm taking you to the prom."

"You . . . what?" I whisper, unsure which direction to burst in — laughter or tears.

Beaming, Brian extends the dewy-petaled corsage toward me, his smile toothy and proud.

Shock and relief and disbelief all hit me at once, like a wall of water, and before I can absorb any of it, the doorbell rings.

"God, the limo's probably early!" I gasp, skirting

around Brian and darting past my bewildered-looking parents as Franklin barks and bounds after me. Flustered, I open the door, ready to ask Iris for a few more minutes to gather my wits and put on my shoes.

Only Iris isn't in the doorway.

Elijah Hayes is.

"Hey," Elijah says with a sheepish grin. His shaggy hair is tucked back in a low ponytail, and he's wearing a '70s-style burgundy tuxedo, complete with bell-bottom legs and a wide collar. He's *almost* sexy enough to make it work. I notice he's holding a baby-blue corsage in a small frosted box, and he reaches out to offer it to me. "Happy prom," he adds. "Are you surprised?"

"Uh, a tad," I stammer. "See — I —" I glance over my shoulder to see Brian and my parents gathering, all of them eyeing Elijah suspiciously. *I already have a date*, I want to say, but my tongue doesn't appear to be functioning.

"I know I acted like a jerk," Elijah is saying as I turn back to him, stunned. "I felt really bad afterward, Abby. And seeing everyone getting all hyped up for the prom, I realized —" His face breaks into another adorable smile. "Maybe I needed to be brainwashed, too."

"Look, Elijah —" I decide not to remind him of the calf-being-led-to-slaughter comment. Keeping the door open, I glance back again to see Brian advancing toward us. "There's something I need to explain. . . . When you said you didn't want to go with me, I —" What can I say? I don't want to admit that I asked my brother. But I can't shoo Brian off; he may not ever do anything this sweet for me again. And I can't send Elijah away, either, not

126

when he's gone to all the trouble with the corsage and the tacky retro tuxedo. . . .

"Is there a problem here?" Brian interrupts in his best drop-and-give-me-fifty voice, sizing Elijah up. Elijah sizes him up right back, but he looks vaguely intimidated. I truly hope Brian won't try to kick his ass.

A horn beeps from the street, and I see a sleek black limousine pulling up. The moonroof slides back and Iris emerges in her flowy pale pink dress, waving her arms above her head. "Abby Cooper, I love you!" she hollers. Clearly, she's had some champagne on the way over.

I wave back, but it's a wave of distress. Iris doesn't notice. What she does notice are the two tuxedoed guys standing in my doorway. Her eyes go wide and I see her duck her head down and say something to someone in the limo. I know Ted, Gloria, and Cody are ensconced in there, and I can imagine their buzzing and whispering: "Who?" "*Two*?" "How?"

"Damn, we've got a dope ride," Brian notes appreciatively, nodding toward the limo with a satisfied grin.

"*We*?" Elijah repeats, glancing from me to Brian and back again, narrowing his brown eyes in confusion. "You mean . . . we're all going together?"

At the moment, I see no other recourse. "Listen, guys," I begin, trying not to get overwhelmed. I take a deep breath. "I only have one extra ticket —"

"Well, I bought two," Elijah says, still wearing a half-dazed, shell-shocked expression. He reaches into the pocket of his bell-bottoms and displays the tickets in his palm.

"Okay." Through my dizziness, I'm somehow able to

make sense of things. "Elijah, you can give Brian the other ticket. I'll use one of mine."

"Your name's Brian?" Elijah asks my brother, and sticks his hand out. "Just trying to keep things straight. Nice to meet you."

"Hey, thanks for the ticket, bro," Brian says warmly, pumping Elijah's hand, as if they're two buddies meeting up for a baseball game. How do boys have the ability to bond in the middle of lunatic situations? I watch them in near awe.

The limo driver honks the horn again, and my parents bustle into the foyer behind us, clucking about pictures. My mom, having rescued my shoes, sheer green wrap, and green beaded clutch from upstairs, is holding them out to me, and my dad is brandishing the camera. It's clear that neither one of them is going to ask any questions at this point. My dad motions us into the living room, and, dazedly, we gather on the colorful area rug. When my mom inquires about a corsage, I glance in panic from Brian's rose to Elijah's blue monstrosity. Neither remotely matches my dress, but beggars with two prom dates can't be choosers. Elijah pins his flower to my dress, so Brian slips his rose on over my wrist. Corsages in place, I stand between my brother and the best-looking boy in my grade. As the flash flickers like lightning, I'm not sure if I'm smiling or grimacing. All I know is that I'm extremely grateful that this moment has been captured, that evidence will exist. No one would believe it otherwise. I'm not sure *I* believe it.

"Hey, Abby," Brian remarks in his wryest voice as the dots dance before our eyes. "You didn't get me a boutonniere." Hearing that French word emanate from my brother's lips is as absurd as his being here at all. "You know, a flower for my buttonhole?" He gestures to his tux.

"I wasn't exactly expecting you," I say through gritted teeth, giving my brother a death glare. "Or you," I add, turning my head to Elijah, who shrugs apologetically.

"My little girl — so beautiful," my dad chokes out, lowering the camera and dabbing at his eyes while my mom hands him a pack of Kleenex and shakes her head at me, grinning. For a second, I feel a rush of gladness that I'm able to share this moment with them, crazy as it is.

"Dad, you're killing me," Brian groans as my dad continues to sniffle.

"Dad?" Elijah echoes, furrowing his brow.

Oh, God . . .

"We should go!" I announce, tottering to the door in my skinny heels, my wrap and clutch tucked under my arm. I quickly kiss my parents and lead Brian and Elijah out onto the front path. The evening air is cool and scented with honeysuckle and I take big calming gulps of it. I am reaching for the handle on the limo when I hear another car come to a screeching stop on our street. I look up to see a flashy silver Audi — "a city-slicker car," my dad would call it — and when its driver-side door opens, I freeze. My already shaky feet almost give way underneath me. It can't be — no — it is —

A tall, slim Asian guy steps out. He's wearing a black tuxedo with a dark green vest and green cummerbund, and he's holding a tasteful white-and-green corsage. He has straight black hair combed away from his face, sharp cheekbones, light-filled dark eyes, and an easy smile.

"Archie," I whisper. "Archie Jong."

I recognize him from his MySpace photos, of course, but it's more than that — I remember him from grade school, too. The mischief in his expression, the slight crookedness of his front tooth, even the confidence of his gait as he walks toward me. And something about that familiarity, instead of turning me off, makes my heart expand like a bubble.

"I thought you were busy in New York," I say matter-of-factly. Suddenly, it feels like nothing in the world can surprise me anymore. I'm half-expecting a Martian date to land his spaceship on my roof.

"I was," Archie says, stopping in front of me and then leaning forward to kiss my cheek. "But when I woke up this morning," he continues, pulling back and smiling at me, "I realized I couldn't miss an opportunity to see the old neighborhood." He pauses, his eyes resting on my face for a beat. "Or Abby Cooper."

I smile back at him, feeling my face flush in the most pleasant way.

"This is a joke, right?" I hear Elijah asking Brian.

"I'm glad I caught you," Archie is saying, checking his wristwatch. "I got stuck in major traffic around Albany and then I realized" — he laughs and taps the flat of his palm against his forehead — "I never even bought a ticket. I'm screwed, right?"

"Nope," I say, patting my clutch. "I am the proud owner of one additional ticket." *Thanks, Michele Martin.* Then I glance over at a disgruntled-looking Brian and Elijah, who are obviously feeling neglected. "Oh," I add, still a little flustered, "Archie, these are my two other dates. Elijah, Brian, meet Archie. I guess you guys will be spending some time together tonight."

"Um . . . okay," Archie says, knitting his brow, but I can tell, from the way his mouth twitches, that he also finds the situation supremely funny. He, Brian, and Elijah exchange awkward hellos. I want to take another picture.

"Abby, what the *hell* is going on?" Iris gasps the second I open the door. I realize I never once told her about asking Brian and Archie. I can only pray that she won't give Brian away.

"I know that kid from elementary school," Ted, freshly purpled hair incongruous with his natty tux, announces, leaning over Iris to peer up at Archie. It's obvious that, for once, Ted and Iris will be too distracted to even consider making out.

And Gloria and Cody, festooned in violet, immobile in their seats, merely gape up at me. Wonder and confusion race across Gloria's meticulously made-up face, followed almost instantly by . . . jealousy? Yes, unmistakably jealousy; her heavily lined eyes narrow and practically switch from brown to green. And then it hits me:

Gloria wants three prom dates, too.

Wouldn't anyone?

Suddenly, I understand Archie's earlier impulse. I, too, am dying to laugh.

"Abby?" Iris prompts, reaching up to tug on my wrist corsage.

"Well," I reply at last, lifting my heavy skirt so I can slide inside. "I decided not to go stag after all."

By the time we join the fleet of other limos outside the sprawling white country club, which is turning rose pink in the darkening twilight, everyone's shock has faded a little. Ted and Archie are reminiscing about grade

131

school, Brian and Elijah are debating classic rock bands, and Iris has managed to greet Brian without revealing his true identity. Only Gloria and Cody remain silent, jaws slack. As for me, I'm staring out the window, still trying to digest the dizzying fact that I have somehow wound up with a triple threat.

It's a fact that fully hits home when the limo door opens, and Elijah takes my hand to help me out. Immediately, Archie is on my right, offering his arm, and Brian is behind me, smoothing out the wrinkles in my skirt, just as our mom taught him. We head up the paved, flower-lined path like that — Elijah, Archie, and I walking three abreast and Brian bringing up the rear like a bodyguard. The rest of our limo crew trail behind us, still murmuring over my scandal.

When my dates and I enter the grand foyer of the country club, where girls in floor-length pastel gowns and their black-and-white dates are sipping flutes of fruit punch and handing their tickets to the chaperones, an actual hush falls over the crowd. Heads swivel, mouths open, elbows nudge ribs, and Michele Martin's furry eyelashes blink like mad. Normally, a mass of my classmates gawking at me would make me fidgety and uncomfortable. Tonight, instead, a wave of pride washes over me. *Three dates.* It's nutty and over the top and unbelievable. But here it is. Here *they* are. I tighten my grip on Elijah's and Archie's arms and smile at Brian over my shoulder. Let everyone — especially Michele — stare. I'm here to have the night of my life.

Besides, I'm too busy keeping track of my dates to notice the stares or the whispers, such as "Who's the hot blond guy?" and "Is that really Archie Jong?" In the foyer, I sip sweet punch and talk literature with Elijah, discovering a shared passion for Emily Dickinson. We vow to e-mail each other our poet preferences when we're in college. Over dinner at the candlelit table to which we've had to pull up extra chairs, Brian steals half the filet mignon off my plate, causing me to poke him with my fork and wonder how the others *don't* realize we're related. Then, after some sweaty fast-dancing in the purple-streamered ballroom, Brian ducks out to smoke a cigarette and call his new girlfriend, and Elijah ends up chatting with a surprisingly coiffed Ms. Tannen, who is one of the chaperones, so I'm left alone with Archie.

They're playing a slow song, so Archie and I decide to head off the dance floor. On our way, we pass Iris and Ted, who are wrapped around each other, swaying in time to the music, and even I have to admit they look adorable together. Iris glances at me over Ted's shoulder — we haven't had a chance to talk yet tonight — and she grins, indicating that we'll make up for it tomorrow, and I grin back. When we pass Michele and Peter, who are holding each other at arm's length and moving like petrified robots, I shoot Peter a look of gratitude. Had I not turned him down that day, I would never be where I am right now. Which is with Archie, who is making me laugh and think as we wander out onto the back terrace, talking about books and music and growing up in Lake Serene.

"Wow," Archie sighs, taking in the sky above us, which is sprinkled liberally with huge, nearly tangible, sparkling stars. "Unbelievable."

I huddle into my wrap, sucking in the fresh night air. Even for a native like me, it *is* a sight; Lake Serene shimmers in the moonlight, and the shadowy outlines of the mountains are visible in the distance, but the stars eclipse almost everything. "It's only unbelievable for you because there are no stars in the city, Mr. Sophisticate," I reply, shivering a little.

Archie laughs, slipping off his tuxedo jacket and resting it on my shoulders. My heart jumps. "That's true, but there are other things to see in cities," he says thoughtfully. "You'll find out soon enough."

I'm mulling over what Archie has said and putting my hands in the pockets of his jacket when my fingers brush something. I pull out a slightly crumpled white-and-green corsage.

"Oh, no," Archie says, shaking his head. "I forgot to give that to you before."

I gesture down to my multiple corsage action. "I think I'm covered," I tell him. But then I notice how perfectly Archie's corsage matches my dress. And then I glance at his cummerbund — it, too, is green, the exact same shade.

"That's so weird," I say. That Archie knows what I mean makes my pulse quicken.

"Green suits you, I believe," he says, his voice half-teasing, and with warm, steady hands, takes the corsage from me and slides it onto my free wrist. But instead of letting go, Archie moves his hand down my wrist, slowly and steadily, and then takes hold of my hand entirely. My skin tingles as our fingers intertwine. I can't believe I am holding hands with Archie Jong, who I knew when I was six years old. But his nearness, the warmth of him, feels natural and exciting all at once. I meet Archie's dark, shining eyes and hold my breath. I forget all about my brother, who has probably left the prom by now, and about Elijah, who may be sweet and smoldering but will never make my heart leap as it's leaping now.

"Abigael Cooper," Archie muses aloud, taking a step closer to me. "You know I had the biggest crush on you back in grade school, right?" When I shake my head, truly baffled, he adds, "Why else do you think I was always tormenting you?"

I shrug, but I'm still holding his hand. "Your pure innate evil?"

Archie laughs, and then leans close. "Can I apologize in person, then?" he asks, and there's no laughter behind his words now. I swallow hard and think about how my night could have gone in so many directions — from Brian to Elijah to alone — but somehow it's led me here, to Archie. To this breathless instant under the enormous sky as he cups my face in his hands and kisses me on the lips, soft and sweet. When he pulls back, we're both twinkly-eyed and giddy. Apology accepted.

I want to ask him how he knew I'd be wearing green tonight. And why he changed his mind when he woke up this morning. And what made him log onto MySpace at that particular minute on that June afternoon. But I don't want to mar the moment with questions. By not asking too much, you can believe in almost anything. Like a single girl with three prom dates, or a starry night in the mountains, or even the existence of fate.

The Question

A Play in One Act

by Brent Hartinger

SETTING: A teenage boy's bedroom, with a bed, desk, and dresser. The room's clutter is an illustration of a life in transition from child to adult: a smattering of toys (albeit ones with high teen appeal), an accumulation of sports equipment, and a dressertop of colognes and hair gel, along with a tie or two sticking out of a drawer. A Slinky rests on the bed.

AT RISE: Two boys, Eric and Allen, enter. Both are eighteen and, like the bedroom itself, there is an unfinished, contradictory quality about each of them. Allen is the trendier, better dressed of the two, but nothing quite fits; there's a sense that he's trying too hard. Eric, meanwhile, has an athlete's size and grace, not to mention a clueless disregard of his own good looks; still, something is making him guarded and edgy. Nonetheless, the boys have natural, easy rapport with each other. They're right in the middle of an energetic conversation. Clearly, they're both very smart and, now that they're away from school and alone in Eric's bedroom, they no longer have to hide it.

ALLEN: (impatiently) <u>So?</u> Did you ask the question?

ERIC: What question?

ALLEN: What do you mean <u>what question</u>? What other question is there? "Do you want to go to the prom?"

ERIC: No, I didn't ask her if she wanted to go to the prom! I can't ask her! I don't even <u>know</u> her!

(Eric picks the Slinky up off the bed and begins playing with it nervously.)

ALLEN: Of course you <u>know</u> her. You just spent the last twelve years going to school with her.

ERIC: Yeah, and in all that time, I've probably spoken to her a grand total of six times.

ALLEN: So you've got six whole encounters to talk about over dinner!

ERIC: Not really. In five of those times, she didn't say anything back. (beat) Allen, I can't do this! What if she turns me down?

ALLEN: (almost gleeful) I already told you, she <u>won't</u> turn you down! That's the beauty of this. I know for a fact she thinks you're cute, and that she wants to go to the prom with you. She just doesn't have the nerve to ask you.

ERIC: <u>How</u> do you know?

ALLEN: I already <u>told</u> you! She told Jessica.

ERIC: That's only one source. No reputable newspaper would print a story with only one source.

ALLEN: Eric, you're asking a girl out on a date, not vying for the Pulitzer Prize.

ERIC: Okay, okay. I'll ask her tomorrow.

ALLEN: Call her tonight. Call her now. (He turns for the door.) I'll dial.

ERIC: (stopping him) Allen! What difference does it make when I ask her?

ALLEN: Because if you don't do it tonight, you won't ever do it. Maybe we should get you drunk first, like right before they amputate a leg.

ERIC: You don't need to get me drunk! And so what if I don't ever do it? I don't see what the big deal is.

ALLEN: The big deal is that this is your senior prom! If you don't go to your senior prom, you'll regret it. Maybe not now, maybe not tomorrow, but soon, and for the rest of your life.

ERIC: So I regret it. When I'm lying on my deathbed, you'll be able to flash me your dried, withered boutonniere and say, "See? I told you so."

ALLEN: Just call her.

ERIC: Why do you want me to ask her so bad? Oh, I get it. You're ashamed of me.

ALLEN: Eric, I couldn't care less what other people think of you.

ERIC: (pouncing) Ha! So people <u>do</u> think I'm strange!

ALLEN: Eric, no one thinks you're strange. They <u>should</u>, but they don't.

ERIC: I just don't see why you're so determined —

ALLEN: Because I don't wanna be alone with Jessica all night long, okay?

ERIC: Then <u>you</u> ask Brittany to the prom.

ALLEN: I don't wanna be alone with Brittany, either.

ERIC: Then who — ?

ALLEN: You, you idiot! I want to go to the prom with <u>you</u>.

(There is a pause. Holding one end of the Slinky, Eric drops the other end; it falls down against the floor with a thud.)

ALLEN: Wait. That didn't come out right. I mean I want you and Brittany to come to the prom with Jessica and me.

ERIC: (turning away) Oh.

ALLEN: I want someone to talk to during dinner.

ERIC: Okay, okay. I'll <u>call</u> her.

ALLEN: Now?

(He tosses the Slinky back on the bed and turns for the door.)

ERIC: (irritated) Yes, now! You're obviously not going to stop bugging me until I do.

ALLEN: Wait!

ERIC: Now what?

ALLEN: Let's practice first. (He picks up the Slinky.) Here, take one end.

(Allen gives Eric one end of the Slinky; Allen holds it up to his ear like a tin-can phone.)

ERIC: Oh, brother.

ALLEN: Come on. Just do it. (Eric does.) Okay, I'll pretend to be Brittany. You pretend to be you. You've just called me. (He clears his throat; in a female voice, he "answers" the Slinky.) Hello?

(Eric stares at him drolly.)

140

ERIC: Is this really necessary?

ALLEN: With anyone else, probably not. ("Brittany's" voice again) Hello? Is anyone there?

ERIC: (bored) Hi, Brittany. I wanted to know if you wanted to go to the prom with me.

(beat)

ALLEN: ("Brittany" voice) Who is this?

(Eric lets go of his end of the Slinky; it retracts and hits Allen.)

ERIC: (annoyed) Allen!

ALLEN: Come on, that was funny! I'm just trying to get you to relax a little.

ERIC: (very tense) I'm relaxed, okay? I'm perfectly relaxed.

ALLEN: I don't get it. Didn't you go to the prom before you met me? Last year? Or the year before?

ERIC: No. (quietly) I've never been to a dance, okay?

ALLEN: What? Never?

ERIC: Never! Do I have to wear it on a sign around my neck? (quietly) I'm . . . not sure I even know how to dance.

141

ALLEN: (gleeful again) Really?

ERIC: Allen!

ALLEN: (reassuringly) Okay, okay. There's nothing to it. You just sort of . . . (He begins to sway.) Move to the music. That's the great thing about danc- ing — it's impossible to do it wrong. Do you have, like, a radio or something? Turn on some music.

ERIC: Yeah, sure.

(Eric turns the radio to some up-tempo song.)

ALLEN: Okay, just sort of . . . go with the flow.

(ALLEN begins to dance. He's clearly practiced for hours in front of a mirror, but he's actually pretty good.)

ALLEN: Now you try.

(Eric looks to see what Allen is doing, tries to mimic his moves.)

ALLEN: No, don't look at me. Just do whatever feels right.

(Eric tries again. He is embarrassingly awkward.)

ALLEN: You're too stiff. Try to loosen up.

ERIC: I thought you said it was impossible to do it wrong!

ALLEN: I was wrong, okay? I'd never seen you dance. (watching Eric) That's better.

(They continue to dance. Eric is still awkward, but in an endearing, big lug kind of way.)

ALLEN: That's it! That's it. That's all you do.

(The song comes to an end. A slow song starts. There is an awkward pause.)

ERIC: What if Brittany wants to . . . slow dance?

ALLEN: What?

ERIC: Slow dance. What if Brittany wants to slow dance?

ALLEN: (hesitantly) Well . . . it's sort of just the same thing, only you do it a lot slower, and you do it while holding on to someone else.

(They stare at each other for a second; the slow music continues to play.)

ALLEN: Oh, what the hell!

(Allen steps forward and takes Eric in his arms. Still, they stay at least a foot apart.)

ALLEN: Okay, pretend I'm you, and you be Brittany. I put my hands on your waist. You put your hands on my shoulders.

ERIC: Like this?

ALLEN: Close enough. Now we just sort of . . . sway back
and forth. I'll lead and you — Brittany — follow.

(They dance away.)

ALLEN: You know, there's not another guy on this
planet that I'd do this with.

(They continue to dance. Eric is getting into it now — far
better than before.)

ALLEN: Say, you're not bad. You're actually a lot better
than Jessica.

ERIC: Come on.

ALLEN: It's true! She dances like Frankenstein walks.

(Eric has obviously gotten the hang of it, yet still they
dance on, comfortable and intimate. It is Eric who finally
puts an end to it by stepping away from Allen.)

ERIC: Anyway . . .

(There is another awkward silence. When Allen speaks,
he is much less enthusiastic than before.)

ALLEN: Well . . . I suppose we should call her now.

ERIC: (quietly, head down) Yeah, okay.

(Allen starts for the door. Eric speaks, stopping him.)

ERIC: Well, actually . . . there is one more thing.

ALLEN: Yeah?

(There is another pause. Allen looks at Eric in confusion. Something is happening here that he doesn't quite understand. But Eric is suddenly nervous, avoiding his gaze.)

ERIC: Nothing. Never mind.

ALLEN: No. Tell me.

ERIC: (dismissively) No, really. It's stupid.

ALLEN: Come on.

ERIC: Well . . . it's just that I . . .

ALLEN: Yeah?

ERIC: (embarrassed, awkwardly) Well, what if she wants me to . . . kiss her good night?

ALLEN: Huh?

ERIC: It's just that I've never actually kissed anybody before.

(Allen stares at Eric again, still puzzled. But this time, Eric stares back. It is as if Allen is seeing Eric for the very first time.)

ALLEN: (quietly) Oh.

ERIC: (turning away) You probably think I'm an idiot asking all these stupid questions.

ALLEN: No! No. There are no stupid questions. Well, I don't believe that anymore — not after world history with Wanda Vandersol. But these aren't stupid questions. Not at all.

ERIC: So, um . . . how do you do it?

ALLEN: Well, there's nothing to it, really. You just sort of stand together, really close.

ERIC: Stand together close. Okay.

(Eric and Allen step closer together. They stare at each other. It feels like there is something coming, but neither is exactly sure what it is.)

ALLEN: Don't pucker. That's what everyone thinks at first, but it's not true.

ERIC: (nodding) Don't pucker. Okay, got it.

(They keep facing each other.)

ALLEN: (almost a whisper) And you probably shouldn't bother with tongues. At least not at first.

ERIC: No tongues. Okay, got that, too.

ALLEN: Then you just . . . press your lips together.

ERIC: Press lips.

ALLEN: And hold them there.

ERIC: Hold them there. (beat) How will I know when to stop?

ALLEN: You just sort of . . . know.

(Still, they face each other. The tension is incredible; someone simply has to act.)

ERIC: Allen?

ALLEN: Yeah?

ERIC: Do you ever think . . .

(Suddenly, someone pounds on the door to Eric's bedroom. Both Eric and Allen start in alarm, then scatter like cockroaches to opposite sides of the room. The knock comes again. Eric turns to face the door.)

ERIC: What is it?

(A woman enters, Mrs. Sloan, Eric's mother. She is a hard, tightly clenched woman; it is as if even the loosening of her hair will cause her to fly apart into a million pieces. By interrupting, she has completely sucked the oxygen out of the room; even the light seems brighter now, and harsher.)

MRS. SLOAN: Eric, your father needs to see you in the garage. Is it true you loaned the Gordons his power saw?

ERIC: Mom, I've kind of got company right now. Can you tell him I've got company?

MRS. SLOAN: Oh, hello, Allen. I didn't know you were here.

ALLEN: Hello, Mrs. Sloan.

(She notices the fact that they are on opposites sides of the room.)

MRS. SLOAN: What are you boys doing?

ERIC: (simultaneously with Allen) Reading comic books!

ALLEN: (simultaneously with Eric) Playing a game!

ERIC: We're just hanging out! Tell Dad I'll come down after Allen leaves.

(Mrs. Sloan lingers, staring at them suspiciously.)

148

ERIC: Anything else?

MRS. SLOAN: No. No, I guess not. But we're having dinner in an hour. Oh, and make your bed.

(With another lingering look, she leaves, pointedly not closing the door behind her. Eric turns to Allen, but it is, of course, impossible to pick up where they left off. There is an awkward silence as they continue to face away from each other.)

ERIC: (quietly) So I guess I should call Brittany now, huh?

ALLEN: (quietly) Yeah, I guess you should.

(beat)

ERIC: Okay, then.

(He starts for the door.)

ALLEN: Hey, maybe after the prom, we can drive up to the lake.

ERIC: With the girls?

ALLEN: With 'em. Or without. Either way.

(They exit.)

(BLACKOUT)

(END OF PLAY)

Shutter

by Will Leitch

It occurred to Joe, in a way that depressed him in a way he couldn't put a finger on, that Andrea seemed awfully relaxed for someone preparing for her senior prom. When he had gone to his prom, thirty years earlier, he spent a good fifteen minutes sitting in his car, idling, just around the corner from Jennie Dooley's parents' house. Fidgeting with the cross hanging from the dashboard mirror of his father's Buick. Staring straight forward.

He remembered sweating a lot then, scratching at his cummerbund, doing everything he could to talk himself out of putting the car back in first and heading right back home. It would look bad. It would look very bad. Eventually, he made it to the Dooley front door and, after a few minutes of bringing his finger to the buzzer and pulling it back, he finally pushed it. There was no reason for him to be nervous; he'd met Jennie's parents (her dad had even been his American Legion baseball coach), and Joe was charming, quick, the type of guy parents loved. But still. Something was making him sweat.

He found himself sweating more now, more than his daughter, so much so that she frowned and asked him if

150

he'd taken his blood pressure medication. (She was always bothering him about this. He found it both sweet and annoying.) It was unlike him to be nervous these days; with her college applications, her scholarship rejections, his own endless nights out restoring power to the dark homes for the electric company, he hadn't much time for nervousness these days. Too much happening, with Andrea, with all of it, to sweat. But there he was, anyway. *Like a stuck pig*, his father used to say. *You're sweating like a stuck pig*. Joe had never understood this expression — wasn't it *bleeding* like a stuck pig? But there was no doubt about it: Joe was sweating like a stuck pig.

It was impossible, Joe felt, that it could have been four years since Andrea had enrolled at St. Anthony, a Catholic high school about twenty miles up I-70 in Effingham, since life suddenly became so *serious*, since Joan had left. One day, Joe was the type of guy who drank Natural Lights with the guys from the shop at the V.F.W. until dinner was ready; the next, he was an expert in toasted cheese, permission slips, and feminine hygiene. There were no Cliffs Notes or study guides. He just bolted into doing it all, immediately, and that was that.

He knew it was going to happen; he knew from the minute he checked his voice mail and heard the message that he'd be lying to himself to pretend otherwise. Joan had been spending too many hours with the other teachers after class ended, much more than she ever had before. At first she pretended that she was just readying herself for Andrea to arrive next fall — their only child needed to know that the same rules applied at school, too — but her distance, from him, from Andrea, was palpable and obvious. She and Andrea had never quite connected, Joe thought, the way a mother and daughter were supposed to, whatever that was. Andrea went to Joe when she had problems with math, or boys — or, more often toward the end, Joan. Joan had always been different from Joe, more yearning, more restless. She had always seen their family life as a defeat somehow, a confession that she wasn't what she had always wanted to be. Whatever that was. Whatever the hell that was.

His name was Harold. Joe had known him for many years. He had been divorced twice, had a broad laugh, and wore a bushy, thick mustache that Joe couldn't have pulled off if he had tried. Joe had liked him once. That was a long, long time ago.

Joe didn't need Joan to lie about staying late after school. He had known, he had always known. And the worst part was that Andrea had always known, too. But maybe that wasn't so bad, either.

"We're gone, Joe," she said, her voice pixilated and furry. She sounded like she was ordering a pizza. "I had to make my choice. That's what you said, right? I needed to make a choice. So I have. This is my choice. Tell Andrea I'm sorry." He had come home that night and discovered that Joan's belongings were already out of the house. Thing was: It didn't look that much emptier than it had in the morning.

It was inconceivable to everyone but Joe and his daughter. Andrea cried for a while, but then she stopped, and then she just never cried anymore. One late night, a few weeks after Joan left, Andrea came to Joe's room hours after she was supposed to have been asleep, lights out.

"I don't miss her, Dad," she said.

Joe told her that was wrong, that she should miss her mother.

"I know I should, Dad, but I don't." Andrea's eyes were clear and hard. Joe thought she looked like her mother right then. "And I don't think you should miss her, either."

Joe told her to go back to bed, and they'd talk about it later. But she didn't, and they didn't. That night, they fell asleep watching *Singin' in the Rain*, humming a happy song, "*Good morning, good MORning! It's great to stay up late. . . .*"

Then a funny thing happened: Andrea, who had always been a listless, bored student, became a book monster. Halfway through her freshman year, her counselor called Joe at home and said Andrea needed to be moved to the honors classes, that she had "earned the opportunity." She joined the volleyball team, volunteered for St. Anthony's eco-squad, and even ran for student council. Joe had been worried Andrea would feel out of place at St. Anthony's as one of the few non-Catholic students. But she never did. She just decided that she was going to take over the school, and nothing was going to stand in her way. And, as far as Joe could tell, she had.

It had been surprisingly easy, these last four years. Andrea had done much of the heavy lifting; he had never had to deal with any rebellion. No clandestine parties, no smell of alcohol, no boys calling at all hours of the night. In fact, from what Joe could remember, there had never been any boys at all. The four years had passed in a blur of practices and math meets and car pools and the occasional all-night study session, which usually consisted of Joe quizzing Andrea from a textbook and her answering every question correctly until Joe fell asleep. He felt he'd done a pretty good job with her, if he'd actually done much at all. But the boys-thing was odd, he thought. Weren't teenage girls supposed to be obsessed with boys? Wasn't he supposed to be throwing them intimidating glances and "you be careful with my daughter"? There had been none of that. Not that he minded — he knew he wasn't particularly intimidating — but it still was peculiar. He also didn't understand why Andrea's friends, the fat one and the Asian one with braces, talked about boys whenever they were over, while Andrea usually just nodded blankly. She was so much prettier than they were, prettier than any teenage girl had any right to be. Where were the boys?

He asked her about it once — only once — about a year ago. She had been watching the History Channel; it always unsettled him that she watched the History Channel, and he did whatever he could to discourage it, though he wasn't sure why.

"Hey, An, did some guy call here the other night for you? I thought I heard the phone ring," he said, knowing it hadn't.

"I don't think so, Daddy," she said, bored, not really listening.

Joe sat next to her on the couch. It was an old couch and always smelled of Cheetos. He told himself to be as casual as possible. "So, uh, are there any boys out there I should know about?" he asked, lightly punching her in the shoulder, just joshing, ha ha ha.

She changed the channel to a program where people

were trying to cook really fast. "No, I don't like the boys at school," she said. "They're all immature." She flipped to a music video with a teenage girl writhing on the ground with a snake. "God, she's so awful," she grumbled. "Don't you think she's awful? I think she's awful."

And that had been the end of it, all of it, until a week ago. Andrea walked into the kitchen, where Joe was trying to fish the remnants of a Pop-Tart out of the toaster, and, as briskly as if she were mentioning that she needed money for a class trip, said she was going to prom. "So I guess I'm going to need a dress or something," she told him.

Joe dropped the Pop-Tart. "You are? Really? Uh . . . when is it?"

"Next week," she said, pouring a glass of some syrupy orange beverage she inexplicably liked. "It's a guy, Paul, from the scholastic bowl team. He's, uh, really nice. We really can't wait." She then kissed Joe on the cheek and went up to her room. He had left $100 on the kitchen table, and then it was gone, and then it was today, and then she had come out of her room in the dress, a black strapless thing, and she was the most incredible creature he had ever seen. This made him sweat.

Paul, whoever he was, was late. The Jenkins family (all two of them) sat uncomfortably in the living room, like there was something they were supposed to be doing but neither knew quite what it was. Joe looked at his daughter. She was wearing makeup — too much, frankly. He didn't know whether he'd ever seen her in makeup before. Surely she had worn some at least once, right? He also noticed, with considerable alarm, that she had sprouted cleavage. Joan had wondrous breasts — large, full, obnoxious — but Andrea didn't have that gene. She'd always been flat-chested, or so Joe had believed. But maybe he simply hadn't noticed? Not for the first time, he looked at a woman in his home with confusion, as if he had just realized she was there and couldn't figure out how she'd gotten in the house.

He went to the fridge and popped open a beer. He only drank at home these days, and not very often. This time was as good as any, though, and he had a sudden insane inclination to offer one to Andrea. He resisted.

"So, uh, this Paul guy —"

Andrea interrupted him with words that sounded like they were being read off a teleprompter.

"His name is Paul Sarker, and he's the captain of our scholastic bowl team. He earned all-conference honors and is trying to get on *College Jeopardy*. His parents both work at the Donnelly's plant in Mattoon, and he's going to Millikin next fall to study economics. He is very excited to meet you." She said the words way too fast, like a dog drinking from a bowl, lap lap lap.

"Sarker," he said. "I think I knew a Sarker once."

"His aunt," she said. Joe realized she'd prepared an internal dossier for his benefit. "She graduated with you. She's a nurse out at the hospital. She took care of Grandpa for a while after he had his first heart attack."

"Yes," he said. Had he really drunk that beer so fast? Time for another.

They sat back down, and Joe attempted to fill the air with questions about application deadlines and upcoming finals. They had tickets for a Cardinals game in St. Louis in a few weeks, with Joe's brother Hal, his wife, and their son, Gene. Andrea had never liked Gene — and, frankly, Joe didn't like him much, either. They had been privately making fun of Gene for years, and Joe hoped a mention of him would bring the conversation back to a safe, familiar level. But Andrea just nodded and said she'd make sure to have the car's oil changed by then.

More waiting. Joe wanted to strangle this Paul character, with his "scholastic bowl" team and his economics major and his sudden, perplexing entrance into his and his daughter's life. Andrea turned on the television; dolphins were trying to avoid a shark.

"So, are you and this Paul, like, boyfriends or something?"

"I'm not a boy, Dad," she said, annoyed and dismissive, like Joe had said something wrong. "And, well, it's kind of a long story. It's not a big thing, it's just that —"

The doorbell rang. Andrea's head twisted around the room like she was looking for a place to hide. She stood up, finally, and walked to the door. Joe, feeling a sudden urge to do something that a normal dad would do, cut her off and answered it himself. He practiced the suspicious sneer he imagined dads were supposed to have when their daughter's prom dates showed up twenty minutes late.

He opened the screen door to . . . Paul. Joe wasn't sure what he was expecting, but it wasn't quite this. Paul looked like he was about thirteen years old, with a barrage of zits, a cowlick, and, even though he seemed skinny, a preponderance of chins. His tuxedo looked to be about four sizes too large.

"Oh, hello, Mr. Jenkins," Paul lisped. Joe thought

this was the type of guy who would have been really good friends with that boy from *Napoleon Dynamite.*

Joe snapped to. "Yes, you must be Paul," he said. "Come in, come in." He opened the screen door and tripped on the rug as he stepped backward, almost falling over. Not something a normal dad would do, he thought, angry with himself.

Andrea straightened up and walked through the room like she was trying very hard to look like a movie star. Strange thing was, Joe noticed, she appeared to want him to be the audience more than she wanted Paul to be. Paul seemed as confused as Joe.

"Hi, Andrea," he sputtered lamely. "You, uh, look great."

"You, too," she said. "Though your hair, it's . . . well, here." She licked her palm and went to work on his cowlick, tensely, her eyes shifting back and forth between her father and her date. She didn't have much luck; it actually looked worse than it did before she started messing with it.

Everyone stood around for a moment, awkwardly, waiting for something else to happen. For a second, they looked at the television and stared blankly. The shark caught the dolphin.

"Oh, I guess I need to give you this," Paul piped up, bringing a white box out of a strange man bag he was carrying with him. It was an odd shade of purple. He took out a wrist corsage with white roses. Joe figured they were white roses; they looked like roses painted white. Did they make white roses?

Paul tried to put it on Andrea's wrist but missed,

hanging it on her thumb and then dropping it alto-gether. She picked it up quickly and put it on correctly, blushing. And then everyone stood around again. It suddenly struck Joe that he had a couch.

"Paul, would you like to sit?"

Before Paul even had a chance to move, Andrea grabbed his arm. "No, no, Daddy, we're late already, we don't have much time, we have to go. Come on, Paul, we have to *go*." Paul looked alarmed, and his body went limp, causing Andrea to drag him for a second, like a cop hauling away a protestor who has turned himself into dead weight. And then he came to and remembered something.

"Wait, my mother asked me to get pictures," he said. "She can't believe I'm going to prom, and she wants to have some physical documentation." Paul was squinting and his eyes were watering, like he usually wore glasses but had received some poor advice to forgo them tonight. "I even brought my camera."

From the man bag, he whipped out an enormous, unnecessarily complicated camera with more dials on the back than the cockpit of an airplane. He handed it to Joe and turned to Andrea.

"So, where?" Andrea frowned, and for a brief moment, Joe thought, *She's going to leave. She's going to tell him right now to go home, and she's going to leave all of us.*

"Oh, over here," she said, directing him in front of the fireplace where she had burned her hand a few years earlier on some smoldering kindling. She hadn't cried; she just turned to her father and said, "I think I have to go to the hospital. I burned my hand a bit."

"Stand up straight," she commanded now, and Paul complied, stiffening himself up the best he could. Joe looked at the camera and tried to find the largest button. That had to be the "Take Picture" button.

He looked through the viewfinder.

Somehow, his daughter's and his eyes locked.

Look, Daddy. I'm going to prom. I'm completely normal. We're completely normal. This is what you wanted, right?

I just wanted you to be happy.

I am happy enough. Look. It's a date. I'm going to prom.

Paul seems gay to me.

He is. Obviously.

Are you happy, An?

I am happy enough. We have done well. We are completely normal.

Joe shook his head sharply, realizing it was probably impossible to lock eyes with your daughter through a viewfinder.

"Say cheese," he said, and *clicked.*

Geechee Girls Dancin', 1955

by Jacqueline Woodson

Geechee girl. Gullah land. The way the sunlight beats down and down and down on a body. Sea sounds always but the sun so hot how do you move? The women fan. Sit on their porches. Fan and fan. *Child*, they say. *It too hot today*. And it is. So they sit.

Just gotta set, they say. Just set and set and set. And if you not from here, how you gonna speak a word to them dem will understand. No way. Oy. No way. Ay.

Night fall down. Moon go high. Waves come in. Go out. Whistle come. Drum too. Soft. Quiet the land. Soothe the heat.

Rice and okra, shark meat, dem eat. The ocean brought them here — many years ago. Slaves then. Proud. From so many West African countries nobody speak the other man's language. So they work. Bump backs. Carry cotton. Plow fields. Bring Master and Mistress water. Brown breast in white baby mouth. She suckles. Grow strong. Say Mama to the black woman. Her own mama cry. Her own mama slap the black woman. Hard. *You stay away. You come here. You stay away. You come here.*

Time moves on. The land grow up. The babies become mama. Some mix but nobody want to say — Him daddy. They all know. Nobody say. Nobody want the white hot of whip against back. Nobody want the slow burn of sores in Gullah heat. Press poultice. Press prayer. Scars heal over. Numb now. Souls heal over. Numb too. Many die. Graveyards spread across the land. People go and press hands against ancestors. Heat come up. Strength too.

Gullah land gets passed on.

Geechee girl Rue-Jean born on a Sunday — pretty eyes from long, long time ago — some spirit coming back through this child. Old folks look down on the baby. Hit the mama hard. Cry now, they say. Real tears coming later with this one. Rue-Jean looks from blue black granny to blue black granny. Red and yellow grannies too. All bending down. Dem see in she something different. Old. Something inside she already running. Pulling spirits. Pulling people. Them see a Next Place in she. Scare some bad. Other grannies look down at she and know. Remember the Running Spirit got killed in them own selves. She coming now again. Rue-Jean.

Girl grows tall. Drum beats. She moves pretty. Boys think: One day Rue-Jean be all mine. Gullah land sun drops down — bright yellow, red, gold against the moss. Trees weep. Water come in high — always singing. Gullah men pull in fishes. Live on land them own now. Masters and Mistresses gone long, long time ago. Graveyards tell the stories. How many generations of Gullah people come before them. Make this land fertile.

Teachers say, *Time we celebrated these young ones.* Look over the shining faces, proud. How deep and strong that blood in them go back. Tall, muscled. Cheekbones cut high. Skirts cut tight. Girls laugh. Boys know where to touch them. At night. So many willow branches. Pine and oak. Magnolia. Hands still cut from cotton but healed over — numb. Touch and the touching tells stories people came before them could never tell.

Stories bounce back here then there again — dem know to talk like books talk. Slowly forget their mama's tongue. Hold on, the spirits say. Day heat and love sometimes be pulling their tongues back. Dem. They. She. Her. Words be like braids in dem mouths some days — over and over, this way and that.

At night they call *Rue-Jean. Rue-Jean. You gonna be mine, Rue-Jean.*

And from her window, Rue-Jean looks down. Sees the boys and on beyond.

Rue-Jean, her mama says. *You almost seventeen now. Time you start thinking about settling down. Miz Wright's boy . . . and Ernesto. Gannar getting good grades. His mama say he'll be going off to college too.*

Already May and all around town, the stores getting ready. School dance coming and the girls move through town, thick as gumbo. Gullah heat all the way to their bones.

Rue-Jean, you need be thinking about telling Miz Wright's boy . . .

Big day come and she walk along the water and the sun setting down. White dress to her ankles — linen and cotton, bare foot. Then running. There, with the sun near gone, Rue-Jean dances. And from the water, it feels like from the water, the girl joins her, a slow dance, salt air thick between them until there is no room for the salt. No room for the air.

Dem dancing . . . ! the spirits call out. *Dem dancing . . . !*

And Rue-Jean takes her hand. The old folks knew this was coming. The other a Geechee girl too. Quiet though. Her family not churchgoing but everyone know her mama.

I know she mama. Don't think me no tell she mama! This thing so nasty! Rue-Jean's own mama's voice slipping into the old language.

School dance at the old barn. Still smell of horses. Something else too. Young people with dem bodies pressing out hard against their skin. They don't know past this hunger. Deep history of water and whips, this dancing moves it through them and on out to the other side.

Rue-Jean come in with the girl some people be knowing from she mama, they say. Way back, she mama's mama clean for the white woman long passed on. She mama's mama in the graveyard with dem own peoples — side by side like this now.

Rue-Jean takes the girl's hand. It's like the spirits done rose up and covered the girls over. Schoolteachers look on. Fried okra stop midway to dem mouths. Rue-Jean with the eyes so bright and the questions in class coming dem got have answers for. She off next year to study on the mainland, they say. All the schools out there calling she name.

The old people come up by the barn door. Watch the girls move over the floor. Drums. Kora too. Tide breaking deep out. Breeze coming through.

Lord, they say. *Lord, we knew.*

This child. This child.

Soon, the other young people crowd back in. Surround the girls. Hold their honey-sweets tight. Song of the kora moves toward the ocean, back over it. Keeps going. Tell the ones not sold across the water this story. This girl. These girls. Dem dancing. Dem dancing. Dem dancing . . .

How I Wrote to Toby

by E. Lockhart

19 days before prom

Paul Bader catches me after French (he is bad at French, but manages to make it seem like it would be stupid to be good at French), and the two of us talk about nothing while he walks me to class. Nothing being like, "You didn't go to Steve's party Saturday, did you? I didn't see you there," and me saying, "No, I was busy," meaning busy watching DVDs with my parents, because I only got here in March and my social life is still limited to lunch in the cafeteria with Ling and Joelle, two girls I met in homeroom.

I look at Paul's smooth neck, his wide mouth, and his slightly-too-big ears and think:

Paul Bader,

Paul Bader,

Paul Bader is talking to me.

I wonder why, because I'm reasonably pretty but not enormously, and my clothes are wrong for this new school, and Joelle and Ling are nice to me but it's not like I'm popular. Yet here is this soccer captain guy — talking and laughing.

"Are you going to the cafeteria dance tomorrow?" Paul asks.

It's not the prom. It's a food-drive thing. You have to bring a can of food to get in.

"I hadn't thought about it. Are they fun?" I say.

He grins and answers, "Yeah. They can be."

My little brother is in rehab.

My little brother is in rehab.

I feel like those words are written on my arms whenever I push up my sleeves, written on my cheeks whenever they relax out of my fake smile. They want to come out of my mouth, all the time. When I am called upon in class, or when someone says, "Hey, what's up?" — that's what I want to answer. "My little brother is in rehab." But I never do.

The clinic said he'd be in for a month, but it wasn't a month like they said. It wasn't another month like they said, either.

Now they don't know how long.

Toby is having episodes, like maybe the junk did something to his brain, or maybe his brain was turning on him and so he was self-medicating with the junk. We don't know. My dad got a leave of absence from work, and my mom got permission to work from home, and we moved up here, where the treatment center is.

I've been foggy, generally.

The world doesn't seem real. Like I woke up from a nap and can't really understand everything yet because I'm still halfway asleep. But it's been like that for months now.

My little brother is in rehab.

"Paul Bader asked me if I was going to the cafeteria dance," I say as Joelle and Ling make room for me at a table in the cafeteria.

Ling nods seriously and says, "We wondered who would pounce first."

What?

Joelle says, "He's pounced."

Oh.

Ling says, "Don't you know they've been circling you?"

No.

"Well, they've been circling you."

Joelle shoves a fry into her mouth. "I made out with him last year at some party. What was it, Kerr's party? I think it was Kerr's party. You'll have a good time."

Ling nods. "I went with him freshman year, four months."

"Maybe only three and a half," Joelle says.

"Yeah. I was rounding up. He's all right," says Ling.

I must look baffled, because Joelle leans forward as if explaining something to a small child. "Look at us," she says. "We've been in school together since kindergarten. All of us. There are only sixty people in each grade. There's not a lot of choice going on."

"It's a long and sordid history," adds Ling. "You probably don't want to hear."

"Now do you see why they're circling you?"

Who?

"The boys."

"Listen, Paige," Ling says, standing up to bus her tray. "By the time you get to the end of junior year, this school is an arid desert of old plants. Everyone is starving and dehydrated, romantically speaking. And you — you're fresh meat."

"Don't worry," says Joelle. "We're both so over him."

"Oh yeah," says Ling. "Paul Bader is like a dried-up bit of cactus to me now."

18 days before prom

Ling and Joelle pick me up for the cafeteria dance. I get in the backseat with my can of green beans. "Oh, bleh," says Ling. "I forgot my can. We have to stop at Cumberland."

"God," moans Joelle. "I almost brought a can for you, but then I didn't. I knew you'd forget."

So we stop at Cumberland. Ling buys a can of pre-cooked spaghetti and I get mints.

Back in the car, Joelle and Ling are talking about prom. Ling has a date with Kerr, and Joelle thinks Rory might ask her. The night seems dark to me after the bright lights inside Cumberland, and the world is suddenly bleak.

My little brother is in rehab.

What am I doing in this car, going to a dance, when people are so sad? When my parents are home, sad? When Toby is locked up, sad? When people need a food drive of canned green beans and precooked spaghetti?

"Wake up, Paige," says Ling. The car has stopped.

It is hot at the dance. All the lights are off. I hand my green beans to a teacher at the door and in two seconds Ling and Joelle are gone. Disappeared into the dark. I shove my jacket under one of the tables, which is pushed up against the wall.

The music is crazy loud and people are not so much dancing as jumping up and down. In the dark, it's impossible to tell who anyone is, and anyway, I don't know that many people.

I haven't danced since —

But now, Paul Bader is standing in front of me. He yanks my hand and pulls me to the center of the crowd, and we start jump-dancing dance-jumping like everyone else, and he is sweating and we aren't really dancing together so much as jumping while aware of each other. But the point is, I'm doing it.

17 days before prom

Rory, one of Paul's friends who is on the staff of *The Eagle Eye* (school paper), comes up to me in the cafeteria during lunch. "Are you Paige?" he asks.

"She's Paige," says Ling.

"Paige with an *i*?"

"Paige with an *i*."

"Just checking my facts," says Rory. And he goes away.

Joelle leans forward in her chair. "What was that about?"

Ling shakes her head. "Don't ask me."

"He's *your* prom date," I say.

"That's my point," says Joelle, pointing her finger at me. "He already knows your name."

"Oh."

"He's gotta be up to something. But what?"

Ling nods. "They all know your name already, Paige."

16 days before prom

After French, Paul suggests we drive off campus and buy licorice at Cumberland during the free period. He says he's in dire need of licorice because it keeps him awake through calculus.

We get in the car.

"So. Ah," he says, starting to drive.

"So, yeah," I say.

"God, French is boring."

"Uh-huh."

"What?"

"Sorry, I was thinking about something else," I say.

My little brother is in rehab.

My little brother is —

"Would you want to go to prom with me?" he asks, still driving, but looking over.

"I thought you were taking Maria Rivington," I say, because Joelle told me he was.

"Nah, that was just a rumor."

I'm surprised because Joelle heard it from Maria herself during track practice, but something must have happened.

Yes. I'll go to prom.

When we get to Cumberland, Paul turns off the car and kisses me. I haven't kissed anyone in months and months, and there's too much spit, and his hands are roaming, but instead of pulling back, I decide to go with it — just go, and not be half-living anymore.

I find it's not too hard, actually. We have a pretty good time.

Then we go buy licorice. He says, "Paige with an *i*, let me call you. Give me your number."

So I do.

14 days before prom

Ling and Joelle take me shopping for a dress.

Ling is going with Kerr. Joelle is going with Rory. "Cacti, they're nothing but cacti," says Ling. "But at least we're going."

They insist that full skirts are back. They talk about tulle and candy colors. Joelle bosses salesladies around. We are all squashed into one dressing room, the floor draped with piles of lace and chiffon and fluff. Ling makes me try on a strapless dress and at first it looks okay, but when I put my arms over my head, my boobs pop out like they're escaping from prison.

We become hysterical in the dressing room.

I am laughing on the carpeted floor, leaning against the mirror with my boobs hanging over the edge of this flouncy dress, and I haven't laughed so hard since long before I came here, and for a second I feel guilty, because how can I laugh when the world is like it is? When Toby is locked up.

But later, I think: It doesn't help Toby for me not to ever laugh.

13 days before prom

Paul Bader calls my house and says he misses me. He wishes we'd made plans for the weekend, and now the

172

weekend is almost over, and he misses me. He just had to call and tell me that.

I say, "Have you been drinking?"

His parents went away for the weekend, and Kerr is over and they only had a bottle of wine, but yes.

I think it's bad that he was drinking. And then I think I'd like to have a drink myself.

We hang up, and he rings me back, ten minutes later. "I missed you again," he says.

"Get to school early and meet me on the steps. It'll be like a rendezvous," I say.

"Definitely," he tells me, and hangs up.

12 days before prom

Paul Bader finds me on the steps and puts his arm around me, and I give him the licorice I bought him. We go driving in the free period, with his hand on my knee. His fingers feel hot, and he strokes the edge of my skirt as he drives. We are listening to the radio, and it's so loud I don't think. About anything.

10 days before prom

Ling finds a new dress and makes me come with her to return the old one. We try on makeup at the counter and buy glitter eye shadow — silver for her, green for me. She tells me she's going to rush sororities in August at the U.

"Don't," I say. "Won't they make you run across campus naked? Won't they make you drink pig's blood? Because that's what I heard."

She says, "Pig's blood, my ass. My sister already told me it's cranberry juice."

"You mean they really make you drink some blood thing?" I bark. "I was making that up!"

"What? Yes, at Kappa Phi whatever, the one she switched out of after freshman year. But not anywhere else, I don't think."

"I was making that up!" I cry again.

"There's no pig's blood at Kappa Kappa Gamma," says Ling. "And anyway, it's cranberry."

"Will you run naked if they make you?"

"Sure," she says. "It'll be August. Totally warm."

"Hello? Naked!"

"The body is a natural thing, Paige. Be mature."

"Do they let you wear running shoes? What if you step on glass?"

"You worry too much," says Ling.

Yes, I do.

9 days before prom

We go to Joelle's house and watch movies after school. There are four dogs and smells of cooking, people going in and out and yelling about where is my soccer shirt and don't be home later than seven and don't forget I have to bring in two zucchini for school tomorrow morning.

No one is injecting anything behind closed doors. No one is gone when he used to be here.

At night I go out with Paul. We sit in the movies holding hands. He strokes the inside of my arm. I look at his profile, lit up by the flicker of the screen and think:

I didn't know I could feel this way, how did it happen?

He is so beautiful. He is touching my arm.

8 days before prom

I write a letter to Toby, which I haven't done before. I do write "hi" and "get well soon!" on my mother's letters, but I've never written him on my own until now.

I see him when we all go visiting. Visiting is why we moved here. I am required to visit almost every weekend. But I never know what to say.

You stupid idiot, how could you do this to us?

Why can't you get hold of yourself?

Did something awful happen, once?

What?

What?

Do you know how messed up we all are, because of you?

Do you know I left everything behind?

Do you ever think of anyone besides yourself? Because it doesn't seem like you do, Toby.

We all revolve around you. Our every thought, every day, revolves around you. All our money goes to making you better, all our weekends go to visiting you, all our meals are ruined by what you've done. And you give us nothing back.

So. Since that's what I felt like saying to him, I didn't talk much. And since that's what I felt like writing, I never wrote.

But today I've got something else I feel like writing,

and because I suddenly remember how I used to be able to make Toby laugh. I used to make him laugh so hard he'd spit soup across the table or snort milk out his nose.

I write about how I have a red dress with black lace over the skirt, and how Joelle's little brother is doing a three-week study of the zucchini in second grade, and the thing about no pig blood at Kappa Kappa Gamma, and how Paul, my boyfriend (or at least my prom date), likes licorice, and then the plot of the movie I've seen.

Toby used to always want me to tell him the plots of movies my parents wouldn't let him watch.

I put the letter in the mail.

Maybe he'll hate me for telling him about my silly life when he's locked up in a clinic. Maybe he'll think I'm stupid and callous. And maybe I am.

Or maybe he'll laugh and be glad he hasn't completely ruined everything for everyone.

Maybe.

6 days before prom

I go to Paul's in the afternoon and we make out in his bedroom for nearly an hour with the radio playing.

At some point, I think both of us feel like it's gone on too long and we don't know how to be finished and go do something else. I am relieved when his little sister bangs on his door and tells him he has to drive her to soccer practice. "Dad's not home yet so you have to do it. Mom said so."

Paul throws a pillow at her and says no way, and she

says, "Who's your friend, you moron?" and so I meet her, and her name is Rosie.

"Come on, Paul, let's drive her," I say.

We drop her off at the soccer field. I watch her run toward her friends, not even saying thanks to Paul, pulling off her sweatshirt and dropping it on the bleachers.

"My little brother is in rehab," I say.

"Harsh." Paul is looking for a CD in the glove compartment. "What for?"

"Heroin."

"Harsh," he says again.

"His name is Toby," I tell him.

Then I tell him everything else. How I knew but didn't know. How we'd stopped talking. How it had been before, how he'd snorted milk out his nose and played soccer, like Rosie. How he got sent away. How he never came back, and it was always one more month, one more month, and we came up here.

How very thin Toby is now. How very blank. How I finally wrote to him, and how I picture, over and over, a smile flickering across his face when he reads my letter.

5 days before prom
Paul runs off after French class. I don't see him all day.

4 days before prom
He won't look me in the eye. At lunch he sits with his friends.

I call him after school, but his mom says he's out and takes a message.

He never calls back.

At nine o'clock I call Ling.

"Don't feel bad," she says. "It's not you. He's just white chocolate."

"What?"

"Joelle came up with it."

"Explain."

"White chocolate. Intense, sweet. But not deep. Okay for prom dates or flings, but not to get serious."

"Oh."

"Milk chocolates are guys you could date for like a few months, and dark chocolates are for love."

"Oh."

"What, you thought he was dark chocolate? Paul Bader?"

"I don't know. I like white chocolate best, actually. For eating."

"Wait," says Ling. "Did something happen? Did something go weird?"

I tell her I told Paul about Toby.

Then I tell her about Toby.

All the same stuff. We talk so long, I lie down on the kitchen floor and put my feet up on a chair.

"Oh my god," Ling says, "that is so, so sad. You must be so sad. I am so sorry."

"It's okay," I say. "I'm okay, at least."

3 days before prom

The Eagle Eye prints a Senior Gift List every year, around graduation time. The staff gives every senior an imaginary gift.

For Joelle, who's going to Penn on a fencing scholarship, it says, "To Joelle Glasser we bequeath . . . a spot on the Olympic team."

To Ling, the editors give a "sock to stuff in it" — because she talks so much. To me they give "a mystery gift," because no one knows me well enough to think of anything personal.

To Paul Bader, the staff of *The Eagle Eye* bequeaths . . . me. Paige.

That's what it says.

All day long, people are coming up to me — people I don't know — and making sweet jokes about me and Paul. How gorgeous we'll look at prom together. How adorable it was for the staff of the paper to do that. How romantic. How cute.

And all morning long, Paul can't look at me. He doesn't kiss me. He doesn't smile.

"What do you think about the paper?" I ask as we leave French class.

"The what?"

"What they wrote in the paper. Should we talk about it?"

"You're big on talking, aren't you?" he says.

Which is funny. Because I only just started talking. "I thought . . ."

"Rory's a good friend of mine," says Paul. "But he doesn't always . . ."

"Oh."

"They wrote that list up a long time ago."

"Oh. Yeah."

"Don't take it seriously. Rory's a goof."

I shouldn't have forced it. Because now it's brutally evident that Paul hasn't been busy, hasn't been preoccupied, nothing like that — he's lost interest.

He lost interest the minute I opened my mouth about Toby. The minute I opened my mouth, really.

Now we have prom in three days and I'll have to go and fake smile and pretend to be happy with a broken heart and a boy who doesn't want to be there with me but doesn't have the guts to tell me so. And though I want Paul's face to soften, and I want to hear his brash laugh and taste his licorice lips and have him be my boyfriend — though I want all that, I say, "I need to tell you something."

His eyes glance up at the clock. It is almost time for fourth period. "Lay it on me." He is disingenuous. He thinks I'm going to keep talking about the Senior Gifts.

"I can't go to prom with you," I say. "I don't want to go."

He breathes in quickly, as if he's going to speak, but stays silent. "Fair enough," he says eventually. "I was going to take you even though things were —"

"Yeah," I say. "But I don't want to go."

He laughs, a little disbelieving. "I'm going to end up going stag to my senior prom."

"Sorry," I say, though I am not.

"Think nothing of it," he says, and walks away down the hall.

2 days before prom

Toby hasn't written back to my first letter, but I didn't think he would anyhow.

After school, I put on my prom dress and invite Joelle over to do my hair. I wear heels and stockings and jewelry. Joelle uses Toby's Polaroid camera to take a picture of me in the dress. *I dumped my prom date!* I scrawl across the white space on the bottom. *But this is what I would have worn.*

Then I put the picture in an envelope and write the address of the clinic.

1 day before prom

I return the red-and-black dress. Walk out of the shop with a palm full of cash.

Prom day

I go with Mom and Dad to visit Toby at the clinic. We walk around the grounds, all of us pretty silent.

We get cups of coffee and sit in the television room for about an hour. Toby is thin. He looks vacant. Like he's grateful for the stupid television show, filling up his head and blocking out his thoughts.

Mom chatters on about her garden, the way she always does, and Toby's not listening. I used to wish she'd shut up about her plants, because nobody cares — and certainly not Toby — but now I understand. She is letting him into her world, as much as she can. The little bit that she can.

We get more coffee in the dim cafeteria, between meals. Just to have something to do. Toby keeps rubbing his jaw, like he can't help it. Like he can't stop.

"I mailed you something," I tell him. "A stupid little thing, but it should get here soon."

He nods, but doesn't answer me. Only at the end of the visit do we go up to his room.

It must have just come this morning, in the mail: My prom picture is stuck to Toby's wall with sticky tape.

The day after

Joelle says it was magical. Ling says it was full of white chocolate cacti. Paul ended up taking Maria Rivington to the prom.

I bring Toby's Polaroid with me to the public pool the next day and shoot pictures of Ling and Joelle, vamping around in bikinis. Ling threatens to sue if I ever take them public.

"Can I mail one to my brother in rehab?" I ask her.

"Sure, whatever," she tells me. "Give the kid a thrill."

And so I do. *My girlfriends*, I write on the bottom of the picture. *I wish you could meet them.*

A Six-pack of Bud, a Fifth of Whiskey, and Me

by Melissa de la Cruz

It was a month before the Senior Prom, and I had just taken a huge bite out of my tuna salad sandwich when I saw the Trio — the three most popular girls in our class — approach, their faces set in grim lines of determination. Sitting slumped against the wall of lockers, I felt trapped — cornered. There was no way out — I had to face them. I knew what they were up to, and part of me was elated, part of me was terrified, and part of me was humiliated knowing what was about to happen.

"Melissa," said the tallest one, Luna.* She was one of the prettiest girls in our class — but odd, so odd that even her friends called her "Loony" behind her back. (It was rumored she'd once farted at a party in front of all the hottest guys at St. Ignatius.) Her face was a grimace of concern and pity. "Do you have a date for the prom?"

I chewed for as long as I could, swallowing that lump of tuna and forcing it down my suddenly dry throat. "Nuh . . ." I managed to choke out.

I didn't have a date for the prom. I would never, in a

*Names have been changed to protect the popular.

183

million years, have a date for the prom. I went to an all-girl private school in San Francisco, and there were only thirty-nine girls in my class. More than half of them were debutantes from the city's wealthiest, most prestigious families. And then there was *us* — the misfits and losers — scholarship kids, metalheads, foreign students, the scarily anorexic girls. I was one of the immigrant scholarship kids and hence a member of two overlapping loser groups.

Some of us in this unfortunate bunch had lives outside of our little private hell. They had boyfriends stowed away in Oakland, San Jose, or San Mateo. They had lives full of all the normal teenage fun — bonfires on Stinson Beach, double-dating at the movies, "ragers" at their homes when their parents went on vacation. *Those* girls had dates for the prom.

But not me.

I had heard that the Trio of Caring Popular Girls had made it their mission to make sure every girl in our class would attend the Senior Prom. This was part of their outreach — an act of charity on their part. They were Giving Back to the Community. Real bleeding hearts, *they only thought of those less fortunate*! So, one by one, they interviewed us losers to make sure that we had a date for the evening and that we would attend the dance.

Their thinking was that since this was our "last" year together (sniff! sniff!) they wanted to make it a "class bonding" experience as reparation for all the mean, cliquey things they'd done over the past four years, so we could all sing the class song (the theme from *St. Elmo's Fire*, with the lyric "we laughed until we had to cry, we loved until we said good-bye") with a clear conscience on Commencement Day. Their plan: renting buses instead of limos so that no one would feel left out when their date pulled up in a twelve-year-old Honda, and having a formal catered dinner hosted by one of the popular girls' families in their Pacific Heights mansion so that we poor ones wouldn't have to worry about shelling out for a hundred-dollar dinner at the Fairmont Hotel. The bonus: Everyone was invited to the after-party at some other rich girl's beach house in Marin.

"Do you want to go to the prom?" Luna asked gently.

I felt like a paraplegic. I wanted to say, I'm not disabled, just unpopular. As far as I could tell, that was not yet a disease.

"Yeah, I guess." I shrugged.

"WE NEED TO GET MELISSA A DATE TO THE PROM!!!!" she suddenly yelled across the entire locker room, her voice echoing like a bullhorn.

Lord, kill me now.

A week later they gave me the good news. They had managed to scrounge up one Patrick O'Shanahan, a half-Filipino, half-Irish Joaquin Phoenix look-alike, a skater guy with an asymmetrical haircut and a sullen expression on his handsome face. Patrick was a junior at St. Ignatius and an ex-boyfriend to several of the girls in the popular clique — he was secondhand goods, but with a reputation as being a "great friend" and "the life of the party."

Patrick checked me out at the Senior Luncheon that Saturday, when we girls got all dolled up in our white gloves and white tea dresses (hemlines mid-calf, no cleavage, sleeves). I had my hair pulled up in a chignon, with curls cascading down my forehead, and I wore a white lace dress with stiff butterfly sleeves my aunt had especially made in the Philippines — the whole outfit made me look like Imelda Marcos Junior. I still cringe at the photos. But apparently Patrick wasn't completely repulsed. He agreed to be my date.

Against my skeptical nature, I was actually pretty excited. I had spent four years of my life wishing high school over, and now that it was almost coming true (I had my escape ticket — an acceptance to Columbia University in New York City), I wanted to experience what having a social life was like for once instead of just sitting at home hanging out with my parents and younger siblings, watching *SNL*.

My mom and I bought my dress from JC Penney. Don't laugh — it was actually quite stylish, and I still remember it was $75, which seemed knee-shakingly expensive then. It was a sleeveless black silk dress with a drop waist and three tiers of ruffles — very 1920s flapper, which I wore with my mom's old Ferragamo heels (hey, we were rich once) and a black lace shawl that my mother made on her Singer sewing machine. Plus, my date was actually really cute, popular, and all mine. All I thought about was how Patrick was going to fall deeply, totally in love with me at the prom and give me my first kiss.

You can imagine my surprise when Luna delivered a message from him the week before the prom. "Here's a list of alcohol Patrick wants you to get for him for the night." Apparently, as payment to be my date, I had to provide him with two six-packs of Bud and a fifth of Jim Beam. As my mind raced with the thought of how I would ever be able to ante up the desired bounty while being underage, Luna dismissed my concerns. "Don't worry, my maid is hooking us all up. You just need to pay me back."

Sweet relief, and back to my daydreams once again . . .

Since we were all taking the same bus to the prom, it was agreed that Patrick would just meet me at the house where the dinner was being held. Stepping inside the bus was like making an entrance in a fashion show; everyone's date and dress were scrutinized upon arrival. I was thrilled when Caitlin Reardon, one of the popular girls, stepped in wearing a dress shockingly similar to mine — black silk, drop waist, tiers of ruffles. She even commented on it later at the party, complimenting me on my good taste. She told me hers was from Saks Fifth Avenue. Was mine? I shook my head demurely and gave her a vague answer. It was the first time I realized what *knockoff* meant.

When we finally arrived at the dinner party, I saw Patrick standing by the foyer, and my first thought was disappointment that he wasn't wearing a black tuxedo — he'd cheaped out and rented a blue smoking jacket instead. (It only cost $40, he told me later, rather than the $100 for the tuxedo, and he had the decency to apologize.) The second thought was that he looked even cuter than I'd remembered — like a rockabilly star, with his floppy black hair and bright blue eyes.

I handed him his carnation boutonniere and pinned it on his lapel. Then I waited expectantly. All around me, all the other girls were sporting monstrously large flower arrangements on their wrists.

"Oh shit." He grinned sheepishly. "I forgot your corsage at home," he said, smacking his forehead with fake disgust. I knew he'd never even bought it. He'd agreed to be my date, but that was as far as it was going to go.

Still, I was elated. I was dressed up, I was out on a weekend night, I was going to the prom! I was with a date — he'd have to dance with me, right? He'd have to talk to me . . . right?

Wrong.

Patrick ignored me throughout dinner, asked *several times* if the booze he'd ordered was secured, and flirted with all the popular girls in the room.

He also spent the entire evening taking sips from a silver flask in his pocket, so that by the time we arrived at the prom, he was completely plastered, slurring his words and smelling like a liquor distillery.

But ever the romantic, I found all this extremely exotic and charming. I kept thinking, *When is he going to kiss me? Maybe when we say good-bye tomorrow morning? I can't wait!*

Our prom was held in the ballroom at our school. It used to be the mansion of some rich oil family, and the public spaces were routinely rented out for weddings and fashionable society events. We were supposed to feel privileged that we didn't have to rent out some dumb hotel room for the event, but all I could think about was how we were "partying" in the same place where we had

188

principal's meetings. Still, the marble floors shone, and it did look very elegant.

Patrick danced with me for a few songs and proved a capable and very suave dancer — he had a repertoire of 1950s Jerry Lee Lewis moves. I was starting to relax and think it wasn't turning out to be such a huge disaster after all, but when the DJ put on a slow song, Patrick decided he wanted to hang out outside in the cortile where the cool kids were hiding and smoking.

I sat next to him on the edge of the fountain for a while, watching as he said hello to everyone in his popular clique, feeling more and more like a useless appendage. It soon dawned on me that they had given me Patrick as a date simply to get him an in to the party. Everyone went back inside, and Patrick and I were all alone. I thought we would finally get a chance to talk to each other, get to know each other more.

And that's when he threw up on my dress.

Bleeuggh.

And I shook it off, disturbed but also kind of elated. He'd liked me enough to try not to get most of it on the skirt hem! He'd even turned his head and everything, when he saw what was happening.

I helped him to his feet and practically carried him back on the bus, wondering once more, *Does this mean he's going to kiss me tomorrow morning?*

When we arrived at the after-party in Marin, Patrick proceeded to drink all twelve cans of Bud and the fifth of whiskey I'd bought him, laid down on the carpet, and promptly passed out. I sat next to him the entire evening, nursing my two wine coolers (you also had to put an alcohol order for yourself at the party) while the popular girls played a game of sticking beer bottle caps up their butt and attempting to see who could release them daintily on the empty beer bottles. Sphincter control — entertainment for all! I still remember one of the girls pretending to be drunk by walking around with a lampshade over her head. Seriously. She was stone-cold sober but just didn't want to be left out of the fun.

The party was the first time I got buzzed, and I was relishing my position as date to Totally Passed-Out Boy. I had to hold his head up to make sure he didn't choke on his vomit, and I felt like a true heroine — I had to keep my date alive!

The next day, my dad picked me up from the afterparty. I had changed into jeans, and Patrick was still asleep. He was going to hang out for a while with all the other popular kids, but I didn't want to take any chances, I was ready to go home. I was still reeling from my first brush with teenage debauchery — The drinking! The vomiting! The butt-clenching! And I wanted to go home to be alone and think about everything in the privacy of my own room.

But I wasn't going home without getting THAT KISS.

"Hey," I said, tapping him on the shoulder. "Thanks so much for taking me to the prom."

"No problem." He smiled, bleary-eyed. In the morning light, he already had a five-o'-clock shadow and his breath stank faintly of alcohol and puke. He obviously wanted nothing more than to continue to sleep, yet he lifted himself up on his elbows like a gentleman to say good-bye. I was touched. Even looking totally wasted, he was still a hottie.

He was about to close his eyes again and that's when I did it. I just leaned over and kissed him on the lips.

It was just a simple peck, but it mattered to me.

My lips had brushed the lips of an attractive boy. It wasn't a real kiss at all — but it was *contact*.

And to this day, I don't regret attending the Senior Prom for one second. I even proudly displayed Patrick's picture on my dorm room mantle and called him "my boyfriend." If I saw Patrick today, I'd thank him again and present him with another six-pack of Bud for his troubles.

Primate the Prom
by Libba Bray

It was going to take a lot of work to get the gorilla to go to the prom. I'd been at it for a month now. I'd had us both measured for tuxes, "just in case." I posted a prom flyer inside his locker. When we'd pass the mall florist shop, I'd point to the yellow rose boutonnieres and say, "Hey, that's nice. Just like a banana." Nothing worked. The gorilla was not going public with our status. We were not out and that was that. After all, he argued, things were good with us. Why rock the boat? Why look for trouble?

We'd been keeping a low profile for the whole six months we'd been together. When we passed in the halls, I'd say, "Hey, bro," and he'd grunt and bump his fist against mine. Simple. Sweet. Not at all suspicious. No one would know we were dating. But that was the point — I was tired of hiding. This was my senior prom. Last dance of my high school career. And I was not going to sit it out watching *Mighty Joe Young* reruns on the Primarily Primates! Channel. About a week before prom, I couldn't take it anymore. We were at his house playing *King Kong Road Rage III*. He'd won as usual. I consoled myself with a bag of Cheetos and started the prom argument again.

"Come on. You never want to go anywhere," I said.

He scratched his privates and sniffed his fingers. It was a nervous habit. Sometimes I found it charming. Sometimes.

"We could rent a limo. Stock it with a little contraband. Some champagne. In-N-Out Burgers. Banana extract."

He pounded his chest, screeching loudly, then took his meaty paws to a papier-mâché replica of the Empire State Building. The Barbie Fay Wray flew off, ass over teakettle, and stuck fast in the wall-to-wall carpeting.

I rolled my eyes. "That's not impressing anybody, you know."

This made him sulk. He took the TV remote, manipulating the buttons with his toes. It was something I found unbearably cute when we first started dating. But now, I could only think about what it would be like to watch him do that on prom night, and I was pissed. A traffic jam of afternoon talk shows blared and snapped from the screen. He settled on *Judge Justice*, pretending to watch intently as the ex-Marine-turned-TV-guru dispensed quick sound bites like "Do the crime, do the time" and "If you sue, you might boo-hoo" and, worst of all, "Apes and Man — that ain't the plan."

"I thought we were going to make a statement," I said. He grunted in response. "Fine. Stay home. I'll go stag."

With a toe, he changed the channel to music videos. I had one card left and I put it on the table.

"They'll play The Smiths."

He looked at me longingly, and for a second I wanted to say, fine, you know what? Who cares about the stupid prom? Let them keep it to themselves. We won't go where we aren't wanted. But I couldn't do that. Not this time. And if the gorilla wouldn't go with me, well, maybe he wasn't the ape I thought he was. So I left. The next day, I put a box of his stuff on the front porch — some Smiths CDs, a small beanie chimp, a banana pillow that read SOMEBODY AT THE PORTLAND ZOO IS APE FOR ME, and a British import punk magazine he'd given me on our first date. He watched me from the window. As I left, I heard him trashing the living room and howling like an animal.

Here's how the gorilla and I met. It was a Monday afternoon in November. My refusal to join in organized extracurricular activities, i.e., sports for Dad or band for Mom, had resulted in my being banished to the thankless world of after-school minimum-wage slaving. "If you're not going to be part of a team, son," Dad had said over some barely nuked takeout being passed off as dinner, "you can earn an honest buck." Dad was big on blowhard pronouncements. He liked to say things like, "There's no *I* in team." That's true, but there's no *I* in assholes, either, and I'd met plenty of those on various teams. And for the record, when did bucks become honest? But I digress.

Dad speared some soggy broccoli and pointed it at me. "Jim Brent needs an assistant at the Ye Olde Yogurt Shoppe. I told him you'd be there Monday after school."

Mom smiled. "Oh, I love their soft-serve. So good — and historical, too."

Ye Olde Yogurt Shoppe was one of those unfortunate marketing plans that assumed people wanted an Elizabethan experience when they ordered a frozen yogurt sundae. I guess if you can pretend that frozen chemical liquid doesn't taste like a Chernobyl-size mutation in your mouth, you can pretty much get down with anything, including employees dressed in tunics and tights, and walls adorned with posters of Queen Elizabeth I dipping into a waffle cone, the words *Forsooth, that's royally good!* in heavy script underneath. The pay was crap, but at least it got me out of the house. Plus — and this was the genius part — I got two fifteen-minute breaks a shift as mandated by law.

After I'd served my last customer a Sir Walter Raleigh — vanilla yogurt with a bloody cherry topping — I ripped off my tunic and skipped over to the potted plants to smoke a cigarette. That took all of about four minutes, leaving another glorious eleven minutes to fill. I spent it at MegaMusic — music, movies, books, and more, more, MORE! It was like a megalomaniac had gone into retail. I made my way past the headphone kiosks and countless bins of CDs to the magazines in the back. I liked to thumb through the import UK garage band reports without plunking down my life's savings in British sterling. I'd just picked up a slick pub on the British neopunk scene when I saw him, a big, hulking brute rocking a Morrissey T-shirt and a Kangol hat. His arms were about the size of my head and covered in silky black fur. I wished I didn't have on tights. It didn't make me feel manly. He caught me staring and I fumbled the magazine back into the stand, mumbled something about being late to work, and took off.

I came back on Tuesday, Friday, and Saturday. By the next week, I'd learned his name — Carter. I knew he was from Akron. His folks had just split and his dad was back at a nature preserve. He liked old '60s spy shows from the BBC and stylish, chronically depressed singers backed by a tsunami of guitar and drums. He worshipped, *worshipped*, The Smiths. I was hit hard. And the first time Carter kissed me out behind the Orange Julius garbage cans in back of the mall, I was gone. Sure, it was a hell of a kiss, but it was more than that. It was the kind of kiss that told me who I was and made me feel okay about it.

I suppose there had always been clues about me and my ape tendencies. There were the monkey pajamas I wore till they fell apart. The nature shows on a Friday night in the dark privacy of my own room. The time my mom caught me blowing kisses to my Curious George books. I watched the entire King Kong oeuvre millions of times. I'm talking stinkers like *King Kong versus the Backup Singers from Mars* and *It's a King Kong Fourth of July!* (That one was a variety show where Kong screeched and pounded his way through a bunch of comedy skits, a couple of patriotic songs, and one rap number with a big teen pop star named Justin Time. Kong wore a backwards cap and break-danced in front of a new theme park. It was Ape Old School, and the crowd dug it. They turned the fountains yellow just for the occasion. It was all cool till the fireworks went off and freaked Kong out. But truthfully, Justin Time was so over, and his CDs sold like crazy after they had to put him in that iron body cast thing that breathes for him.)

I never told anybody how I felt. When I turned eleven, my dad threw away my *National Geographic* collection and handed me a baseball glove in its place. That night, while my parents slept, I dug them out of the trash and stored them under my mattress. When the house was still, I'd pull them out and stare at those pictures of apes in the wild. I'd imagine myself with them, grunting and grooming, scurrying through thick jungle on leg-hands, banging my chest in defiance.

I suppose it would have been all right if I hadn't left the e-mail from Carter lying around. It was pretty innocent, really. Just a big Photoshopped picture of Carter and me hugging, with "Gorilla My Dreams" in the subject line. Of course, there was the fact that their son was cozily arm in arm with a primate. Any illusions my parents had about my "cute Curious George" obsession pretty much vanished then. They called me down for a family meeting. We sat around the kitchen table while Mom tried to run interference.

Mom: There are so many nice, um, *people* you could date, honey.

Dad stared at me, his fists balled up on his knees. I could hear his jaw clenching like bone machinery.

Mom: Sometimes kids go through a phase. It doesn't mean it's a life choice.

Dad's fingers uncurled, revealing themselves like the small animals that live inside shells. He gripped his knees. He looked pale and murderous.

Mom: I'm sure those magazines under your bed belonged to someone else. Just because you have (whisper) *National Geographic*s . . . doesn't mean you're . . .

She couldn't finish. Dad stood, his fingers balled again and hanging at his sides.

Dad: No son of mine is going to be a Gorilla Lover.

When I got up to my room, the magazines and e-mail were gone, and in their place was a book called *God Wants to Fix You*. It had testimonials from other people my age, about how they'd completely kicked their unnatural, ape-loving urges. There were glowing, happy pictures of them being all popular at school and shit, pictures of them dating the right species. They wore a lot of sweater vests. I thought they looked creepy and sad and terribly lost. I tore out the pages and used them to make chap books of poetry. Then I IM'd Carter. *Things suck here. Miss you.*

Twenty seconds later, he sent me back a photo of him in his jeans jacket that had HIGHLY EVOLVED across the back. *Miss you, too,* it said.

My parents made a date for me with a girl named Yvonne. She was the daughter of a neighbor's best friend's sister in Ottawa.

"Oh, she's a sweet girl," Mom chirped one morning while wiping the breakfast dishes clean with a cherry-print dish towel till they gleamed like a beauty queen contestant's runway smile. "She's got a little endocrine problem. Excess hair. You'll like her."

Yvonne and I met at the food court in the mall. She had on a KILL BARNEY T-shirt, camo pants, knee-high lace-up boots, and a large rhinestone clip in her dyed-black hair that made her look like one of the Seven Samurai with a secret obsession for Claire's Accessories. She also had a faint beard and mustache. I liked her instantly. She was funny and smart and she had an interesting theory about global warming being caused by an overabundance of pop stars singing bad songs. It was like an ecosystem gone wild. There needed to be a correction, like a giant squid that only ate people with hair extensions and pimp wannabe track suits. Yvonne was easy to be around, and I wondered if I could date her. I wondered if maybe I could be wrong about the whole ape attraction thing.

A crumb of moo shu pork landed in the tufts of fuzz on her chin. I went to wipe it off. She held my fingers playfully in hers. I swallowed hard and concentrated on her slightly furry forearms. They could be sort of ape-like. If I squinted.

"Something in your eye?" she asked.

"No," I said quickly.

She licked her lips. "Do you want to kiss me?"

I stared at her for a few tense seconds, trying to imagine her nose wide and hard, her body covered in soft, black fur, her forehead pronounced as the ridged plastic packaging that hold cheap toy cars in place.

"Um, I . . . sort of?" I said to be nice.

She grinned wide and licked the rest of the moo shu off her fingers. "Yeah, me neither."

And just like that, we were best friends.

It was Yvonne who talked me into going to prom. We were lying around in her room doing reader's theatre of bad song lyrics when the subject came up. Yvonne was taking a DJ named FlashGordonFive who only spun Queen songs from the movie *Flash Gordon*. Trust me, you have not lived till you've heard a camp classic aurally Benihanaed by a vinyl scratch master.

"Ryan, you so totally have to do this." She'd been babysitting two ten-year-olds down the street, and her language was becoming Tweener Than Thou by the day.

"So totally?" I mocked. "OhmiGOD, Yvonne!"

She threw a pillow at me. "Shut your piehole, shithead. Better?"

"Much."

"Flash told me about this movement. It's called Primate the Prom. It started in Kansas, after what happened to William Lamb."

William Lamb was a band-boy-cute seventeen-year-old from some small town in Kansas. He had a gorilla boyfriend named Johnny. The two of them tried to make a statement by crashing their prom. A mob of kids in tuxes and prom dresses beat them bloody and tied them to the flagpole. They shaved Johnny of all his fur. And William Lamb ended up with serious brain damage. He won't date another ape. He won't date at all.

Yvonne pulled her hair out of its clip. It stuck out in all directions. "This year, nobody's sitting it out. Every ape couple across America is suiting up. Nick and Chimp are so there. Sally Bowers? From Dayton Day School? She's been dating a baboon for like, forever, and they just bought matching prom gowns."

"I don't know," I said. "Sounds cheesy."

She slapped my arm. "It's social activism!"

"Okay, it's social activism cheesy."

"Come on! It'll be sooooo fun! I'll be your bodyguard. Anybody messes with you, I will so totally kick their asses."

I put a hand to my chest in mock horror. "The things they teach ten-year-olds to say these days."

Yvonne stared at me for a long, uncomfortable thirty seconds. She shook her head. "You can hide but you can't run, Ryan. Not forever."

Two days before prom, I left a size 82 tux on Carter's front porch with a note: *Screw the prom. Let's make our own.*

XO. Me. I didn't hear from him. I checked my IM every three minutes. Nothing. The morning of prom, a boutonniere arrived from the mall florist shop. It was yellow, the color of a banana, with a stamped reply: *8:00. Limo. Primate the Prom.*

He was there right on time. He wore the banana bow tie I'd given him as a gag gift for his last birthday. His fur shone. He looked gorgeous. I stood in the foyer in my own tux with the red Chuck Taylors.

Mom met him nervously at the door. She had a camera and was smiling like an actress who has wandered into the wrong movie but is determined to see it through. Dad had gone to a sudden Rotary meeting, which was bullshit, because Rotary was never on Saturday nights.

"You must be Carter," Mom said, extending her hand for a shake.

Carter wasn't having that. He pulled her into a big ape hug.

"Oh. My," she said, pulling back with a laugh. She patted her hair into place. "Well. How about some pictures of you two?"

Mom snapped some of us standing side by side, looking like bored groomsmen. At one point, the den door opened a crack, and I saw Dad peeking out. I thought maybe he'd come out and say hi after all, give me twenty bucks and a *don't stay out too late, you crazy kids* speech. But the door closed quietly and it stayed closed.

Carter grunted and bared his teeth. He picked something off my tux and ate it. Mom's camera faltered for a sec.

"It's an ape thing, Mom," I said. "Don't worry about it."

"Oh," she said, nodding like she understood, when I knew she didn't. But I appreciated the gesture.

Carter put his arm around me, and this time we both smiled big. Mom snapped more until we were flash-blind and begged for release.

They'd decorated the gymnasium to look like a space station. The walls had been painted with planets and moons, shooting stars, and something that I think was supposed to be the Milky Way but just looked like someone had puked in space. Don't ask me — I don't get the relevance of intergalactic travel and school dances, but as themes go, it could have been worse, I guess. The ceiling was pretty spectacular, though. Every inch had been wrapped in yards of plush black velvet so thick it looked like it went on forever. Tiny fiber optics inside made it glow like stars. I wished I could reach up and grab one and hand it to the gorilla.

We'd made a plan to come in separately and, when the music was cued, to make our entrance as a couple. Yvonne ran up to me. She had on a distressed pink gauze number that was very punk fairy princess. I dug it.

"Ryan! You came — I'm so, so happy!" She threw her arms around me and jumped up and down. I felt like I was being mauled by a pogo stick. "Where's Carter?"

"Over there," I said, pointing to the snack table. "Where are the other supposed Primate the Prommers?"

"Not here yet. But they will be." She took my lapels in her hands and stared at me meaningfully. I could smell the rum on her breath. "If you build it, they will come."

"Yvonne," I said, staring back into her eyes, "that is the stupidest fucking thing you have ever said to me. Let's dance."

A few minutes after ten, Carter gave me the signal. Heart hammering, I made my way to the DJ booth. FlashGordonFive had on his trademark wraparound shades and a sharkskin jacket. If the DJ thing didn't work out, he could be a bookie at OTB.

"Flash, could you play The Smiths?" I yelled over the din of Queen spliced to some weird Yoko Ono screaming shit. It made me want to spike the punch with Xanax.

"Sorry, man. This is my art, you know?"

I passed him a twenty. "One song."

He held the bill up to the light, peered at it, and shoved it into his pocket. "Can I add an intro?"

"Sure," I said.

Sweat trickled down the inside of my tux. I'd probably stain the shirt and not be able to return it to Bob's 12-Hour Tux. I'd worry about that later. The opening chords of The Smiths' "There Is a Light That Never Goes Out" kept time to my nerves. What would people say when they saw us on the dance floor together? Would we be kicked out? Beaten? Left tied to a flagpole?

DJ Flash purred into the mic. "Here's a little song for all you ape lovers out there."

Carter moved through the crowd, dragging his knuckles along the floor. God, he was one beautiful ape, and when he offered me his paw, I took it. There were some gasps and a few ohmigods. People moved away from us on the floor. But we stood our ground. It seemed like forever that we were out there alone, turning around to The Smiths under a glittering gym sky. But soon, others followed. Nick and his chimp boyfriend. Sally and her baboon girlfriend. There was an orangutan holding hands with a sweet-faced guy in a gray suit. I counted six couples, then eight, then ten. Ten. It was a start. Some guy stepped out of the shadows lining the dance floor. "Ape lovers, go home!" he shouted. He was joined by a few more red-faced guys.

Carter turned around to face them. He pounded his chest with both fists and roared. The guys ran back into the shadows, right into the punch bowl. And that was that. Nobody else said anything. DJ Flash spun our tune twice as a little shout-out. Pretty soon, the dance floor was half full, not just apes but everybody. Yvonne was there, dancing with the sophomore kid working the door. There was a constellation of girls who'd come stag and were tired of waiting to be asked, so they just danced with each other. There were couples and a few teachers and even Mr. Zwick, our vice principal, who was rumored to live with a gorilla himself.

I moved in closer to Carter. He smelled like the earth, rich and solid under my feet. The song floated over us, pulling us into that hypnotic state you can only feel on a dance floor full of possibility. Morrissey crooned about a light that never goes out, about not caring whether a double-decker bus crashed into him and killed him right then and there, because at least he could die happy, because he was in a car with someone else; he wasn't alone. It was a typical cheery Smiths song and I hated it. But Carter, that big ape, had this totally misty look in his big brown eyes. He had my hand cradled in his paw; his other paw rested just at my waist. We were slow-dancing at the prom. Our prom. Laughing, I leaned my head back while we twirled and watched the ceiling blur into one big ball of light.

Apology #1
by Ned Vizzini

I got invited to three proms. It's more than anyone I know, but it doesn't really count. Two of them were with the same girl at different schools — my girlfriend, for whom prom was an event not unlike Election Day: planned for months in advance and involving a war chest of funds. The third is the one I owe an apology for. It's the prom where I stood the girl up.

I didn't mean to do it. The invitation was such a kind, sweet gesture. It justified everything I was doing with myself at the time. It might have led to all sorts of opportunities for me, to a wonderful relationship or a different set of friends or entrance into a global elite, but I had to get stoned and miss it.

Here's how it worked: At seventeen, as my senior year wrapped up, I was writing small stories for a local alternative newspaper. A girl, whom we'll call Sarah, read the stories and liked them, and so she e-mailed me to invite me to her prom.

I'm not quite sure where Sarah got my e-mail address, but she was respectful and not at all crazy. She said she thought I was a cool guy; she really liked my writing;

she and her friends thought it would be fun if I went to prom with her. It wouldn't be a date, of course, and she understood that I had a girlfriend; it would just be something for her to talk about later. I accepted.

I told my father about it. He asked:

"Will she be able to fit through the door?"

He didn't need to be so mean. Sarah sent me a picture, and she wasn't fat — she wasn't particularly beautiful, either, but who is? — and our further correspondence revealed her to be an intelligent and penetrating young lady, as well as an attendee of the Fieldston School, an Ivy incubator that costs $26,800 a year plus $600 in books. It dawned on me that going to the prom with Sarah was going to be a dress-up, care-about-it kind of experience.

Unfortunately, I was a bit tapped out with regard to dressing up and caring due to my commitments with my girlfriend, who was meticulously planning her prom and meticulously planning my own planning of mine. I had to get a tux twice, find a corsage and boutonniere twice, and get myself into a limo — thankfully that was only once, since my girlfriend planned the limo trip at *her* prom. At my school I wasn't quite popular enough to be with the sort of people who were splitting limos, and so I would've had to beg and plead to get into one.

Communication dropped off with Sarah as we approached the date. In addition to my two proms, I had a then-promising future to think of, which included attending an Ivy League college (I never quite made it) and my writing career. But while I was ambitious, I devoted myself wholeheartedly, simultaneously, to things that would derail my ambitions, namely playing in a band and smoking pot. The two were pretty much synonymous.

I had been playing in the band for four years then (and smoking for two). I started with the band in freshman year, after I had traded saxophone for piano for bass, when I met a guitarist named Paul who could really shred. We found a drummer named Hector and went through a few singers, one of whom was opera-trained, before settling on my buddy Jackson. We called ourselves Hybrid.

In the band, aside from Jackson, I was supposed to be the ultimate girl magnet. Much more than writing, playing bass was rumored to bring the ladies a-callin', steadily and without me having to talk. The bass players are supposed to be the strong, silent types who have women waiting for them in the van, and while I talked a lot and did not have a van, I found that the stereotype held up. Playing bass in Hybrid put me in contact with artsy, crazy women who got me into all sorts of trouble.

Hybrid practiced in a rehearsal studio near Madison Square Garden, an expensive and well-appointed place run by a guy who used to know Johnny Thunders. (I hadn't heard of him, either; he's the sartorial forerunner to Axl Rose.) We didn't deserve as much. We would have done just as well practicing in a dump, garage, or squat, as all of our practices became alcohol-filled bacchanals in which more than a few people who weren't in the band found their way into a heap on the floor.

Hector lived close to me, and on a fine spring day I found myself walking to his house, my bass strapped to my back, looking to show him a song I wrote. When I arrived, we went up to his room and sat in his window, his girlfriend watching. We smoked a little and started practicing. I wasn't doing a whole lot for my future up there, I knew, but I was calm and happy.

I get worried when I'm calm and happy. It means I'm not doing something I should be doing.

At five o'clock I got a phone call. Sarah. I had forgotten several key things. Namely, (1) that it was the day of her prom, (2) that she had my cell phone number, and (3) that I had needed to keep that last tuxedo one extra week.

"Oh, yeah, of course," I told her. "I'll be there."

"You know where it is, right? The Plaza."

"Right, the Plaza. Like where Eloise lives. Like, the most expensive hotel in New York."

"Exactly. But don't be worried. It's going to be fun!"

"Yeah, uh, I know it will be."

"It's too bad you couldn't come with us. But you know we're not taking a limo. I'm just riding in my friends' car. It's really casual."

I looked down at my clothes. I was wearing khaki pants and a bright T-shirt.

"It's not casual enough for me to come in a T-shirt, right?"

She sounded confused. I think it was her first inkling that things were going to go horribly wrong. "No . . . it's not *that* casual."

"Okay, fine. No problem! I'll be there in, ah, in two hours?"

"You have to be here in one. How am I going to recognize you?"

"I'm ungainly, with a large head and dark hair?" I tried.

"That works!"

I hung up the phone.

"Hector!" I turned to him. "Quick! I need to go to a prom!"

His girlfriend threw her head back and laughed. "What? You're kidding, right?"

"I know, I know, it's stupid." I explained the whole story. "But I forgot about it, and now I have to go, and I have no tuxedo, and . . . look at my shoes!"

I displayed them to the group. They were New Balance, the choice of the homeless generation, and while I knew I had purchased them in the color blue, they now appeared mauve.

"I can help you," Hector said. He disappeared into his basement and returned, moments later, with the kind of jacket that really *is* only worn by used car sales-men — a checked khaki sport coat with burgundy lining.

I put it on and looked in the mirror.

"No. I can't wear this."

"Why not? You're, like, the edgy writer!"

"No, you have to be a lot more successful than me to pull that off. I need to go home and get nice shoes —" But I also needed to be at the prom. I stared at myself. There wasn't any choice.

"Thanks for the jacket, Hector," I said, hugging him and his girlfriend. I left the house into a perfect May evening and walked to the train, cursing myself.

It was not just a problem, me forgetting the prom; it was a *symptom* of problems. It confirmed my suspicions, as something did nearly every day, that happiness was dangerous. Anytime that you feel at peace, that you've reached a base in life, something you can lean off of and run back to if need be, you are most certainly neglecting an important responsibility that is going to come up and attempt to kill you. Relief is not the natural state of things. Competitors are always moving. If you are not, then what are you doing?

It's a sad, horrible way to live, and I wish I didn't think that way.

I arrived at the Plaza at 6:30 P.M., muttering. I was a half hour late. I was wearing sneakers and no suit. I didn't have a flower or an invitation or anything that my girlfriend made me get for her prom. I guess Sarah never got the memo that I don't act unless ordered.

A small placard outside the hotel said THE FIELDSTON SCHOOL. One of the famed Plaza doormen gave me a look but opened the door for me. Inside, directed by the signs, I trudged down a short hallway, which was padded with red velvet and flanked by lilies. I got about five feet when I saw it.

They had an ice sculpture.

It was a swan. Shimmering and producing vapor. With detailed ridges on its beak. Its eyes slowly melted into themselves. It was at least three feet tall. And underneath it was an arrow pointing to the ballroom. The prom.

I looked the swan in its face. I don't want to say it, but, yes, it had an icy glare.

"I'm sorry, I can't," I said to no one, passing the doorman as I left.

I entered Central Park and plopped down on a bench, next to a paper bag that a pigeon was investigating. I didn't deserve it. I didn't belong at the Fieldston prom. If I had prepared better, maybe. But I wasn't born into that sort of thing, and if you're not born into it, you

211

have to work your way into it, and I had chosen not to do the work. Now the only thing I could do was be the nutty outsider, and I was *sick* of being the nutty outsider; I had a suspicion, later confirmed, that they get lonely and tend toward the deranged. So I just sat on the bench and watched people pass by in the progressing evening.

My cell phone rang once but I couldn't answer her. I let it go to voice mail. It rang once more and then nothing.

After an hour I got up from the bench and left for home, knowing that the worst part was that I felt *free* to not go to the prom; I felt like I had won something. I felt like I was back to the version of me I really enjoyed, back to the one that didn't care about women or clothing in any capacity. The one that played in a rock band.

Maybe a week later, I got an e-mail from one of Sarah's male friends. He said I was a dick; she hadn't been devastated because she was too smart, but she wondered why I hadn't had the courtesy to call her and tell her I couldn't make it. I wanted to tell him that it was because of a clothing situation, but in the end there were no excuses — and there are none.

Sarah, you're the first of a long list of personal grievances I need to rectify. I'm sorry I never met you at that prom. Maybe, someday, you can get back in touch and tell me how I can make it up to you. I'm sure that, so far, living well has been your best revenge.

See Me

by Lisa Ann Sandell

"Ten for Matt Sarznick!"

"I have five more."

"So, that's eighty-three in all. And Biggest Party Animal goes to good ol' Matt Sarznick," Brian calls out.

The room lets out a breath. Everyone nervously starts fussing with the crinkly candy wrappers that litter the table, along with monstrous stacks of graph paper, ballots, rulers, pencils, and photos.

We're sitting in the yearbook room, which feels more like a very hot closet. By we, I mean the yearbook editors. And you would think, from the tense hush as the votes for senior superlatives were being called out, that we were hosting a UN summit. We've gotten through Best Eyes, Most Flirtatious, Biggest Kiss-up, and now Biggest Party Animal. I haven't gotten a single vote — not in any category.

I'm not sure why I'm invisible. Or how I got to be this way. I simply melt into the throngs of students in the hallway, the rows of bobbing heads in the classroom, the cheering fans in the bleachers — faceless and forgotten. My mother always tells me I'm pretty, though it's usually followed by a *you should cut your bangs, Katie, why do you always hide your face like that?* I know better than to take her at her word. I mean, she's my mom, after all. But the kids here at school, they just don't seem to notice me. Maybe it *is* my too-long bangs.

Now it's finally senior year. The end of everything familiar. The end of childhood, really. And all these kids I've been with for my entire life, well, suddenly the road is about to split, and everyone will go their separate ways. So senior year comes to be about remembering and being remembered — as the coolest, prettiest, cutest, funniest, smartest, baddest. . . .

We have the yearbook, pages of pictures with our names, so everyone can see one another in the days or years to come and remember. And we have the senior prank, senior superlatives, senior prom. The photos, the memories.

But to be remembered, you have to be noticed first, right?

A few hours ago, Brian Muller, one of my coeditors on the yearbook, asked my best friend, Melody Hines, to go to the prom with him. He asked her in the cafeteria. He got up real close to her — they were standing against the back wall — with his head bent down to hers. Mel was tugging at her fingers, twisting them so her knuckles turned white, twisting them like you wring the wet from laundry. It was clear he was asking her, because suddenly Mel's face lit up in this big, beautiful smile, and a big grin stretched across Brian's dopey face, and I was so happy for her.

Only there was this tiny gnawing voice scratching at the corner of my mind. *I'm happy for her. I am. It's just . . . who will go with me?* Melody is the only one who really sees me, hears me. Probably she wishes she didn't hear so much of me. She's the sounding board for my songs. No one else even knows that I write them.

After I watched Brian make his move, I looked around the noisy lunchroom; everyone was sitting in their usual spots, in their usual groups. Nerds with nerds, jocks with jocks, chic clique with chic clique, goths with goths, and so on. When you don't fit in with one of these boringly typical groups, how does anyone know who you are?

I spotted Dan Jacobs, sitting with his soccer team-mates, laughing at a joke, and stuffing Tater Tots in his mouth.

God, I wish he would ask me.

Ugh, I'm such a loser.

Not in my wildest dreams.

It will never happen.

He's in my calculus class, my physics class, and my world history class. He sits beside or behind me in all of them, because of the way our last names fall alphabetically. But he's never spoken to me. He's never even looked at me. And I'm sitting in the cafeteria, eating alone.

Back in the yearbook room, I'm sifting through photographs. I'm the editor of the senior section, which means that I am the one choosing which pictures will go where. I select who will be seen and remembered in the years to come. It's sort of ironic, since I'm not in any of the candid photos that our photographers took. I'm invisible even to my own staff.

This is making me depressed. So I go back to counting more votes for senior superlatives. Ninety-nine for Alissa Thompson, Most Likely to Succeed. The whole thing kind of makes me want to throw up. Why do we feel the need to categorize ourselves — are we talking about the past, describing the present, or is it a forecast of the future?

Mel leans over and whispers to me, "You should ask Jason. Brian thinks he'd definitely say yes."

"Jason? I don't think so," I say.

"Why not?" she asks, her voice rising a note.

"Because I don't know him, and I would rather not," I tell her. "Anyway, could you not scream it for everyone to hear? Come on, I'm going to lose count." I don't want to have this conversation again. I'm not asking Jason just because he's Brian's friend.

"Kate —" Mel's annoyed now. "If you wait forever, everyone will already have a date."

"Thanks for the vote of confidence," I snort.

"That's not what I meant. Ugh, you're so difficult!"

"Whatever. Anyway, I don't even know if I want to go. The prom is such a stupid cliché."

"What do you mean you don't know if you want to go?" she screeches. "Kate, *not* going to the prom is such a cliché. What's with you?"

"I just don't know if I want to go, that's all." I shake my head and keep tallying. One hundred and eight votes for Christine Clark, Most Artistic. No surprise there.

"Kate —" Mel takes a breath, pursing her lips in that *I don't know if she's crazy or just trying to make me miserable* way of hers. "You might really like Jason."

"And maybe I won't. Look, I'm fine. On my own. If someone asks me, great. Otherwise —"

"You mean if *Dan Jacobs* asks you," Melody interrupts. "Katie —"

"Please, can we talk about something else?" I just can't listen to her tell me that Dan Jacobs is never going to ask me to the prom, especially when she already has a date.

"Sure, whatever. I just wish you'd consider going with Jason. It won't be half as much fun for me if you're not there." Mel shakes her head and pulls over the yearbook spread she is working on. "Anyway, what do you think of this layout?" she asks. End of subject . . . but only for now.

As soon as I get home from the yearbook meeting that night, the phone is already ringing. I'm sure Mel wants to go back over all the details of Brian's proposal. I ignore the call, and help my mom make dinner instead.

"Who was that on the phone?" Mom asks.

"I think it was Mel . . . Brian asked her to the prom today."

"Oh, that's so nice. When are you going to get a date, Katie?"

"*Mo-om!* Why can't I tell you this without you bugging me? I'll get a date when someone asks me."

"If you just wait around, Katie, you'll end up sitting at home, alone. And then you'll regret it the rest of your life, like I do."

My mother brings up the prom on pretty much a nightly basis. She never went to *her* prom, and she still regrets it. Every weekend for the past two months, she's asked me if she could take me to the mall to shop for a dress. I keep reminding her that no one has asked me yet. But it's like talking back to the television set, so we're going to the mall on Sunday. I can't wait.

I excuse myself and go back to my room to work on my newest song.

> *If I wear pink lipstick*
> *and curl my hair,*
> *will you see me?*
> *If I wear this pink prom dress*
> *and powder my nose*
> *will you hear me?*

In this I find my voice.

At school the next day Melody finds me by my locker and asks where I was — why didn't I answer the phone?

"I must have been in the shower," I tell her, pulling out my books and slamming the locker shut.

My calculus notebook lies open on my desk. Formulas and equations are scrawled wildly across the page, framed by flower doodles, mindless scribbles, and snatches of verse. Mr. Cassian is giving a quiz next period, but I can't focus. The girls in front of me are whispering across the aisle to each other. Study hall is rarely used for studying.

Stacy sits directly in front of me, Tara to Stacy's right. Stacy and Tara are both in the Chic Clique. They don't know that *chic* is pronounced *sheek*. They say *chick clique*. No one has ever corrected them.

"I mean, he's the sweetest guy in the world, but he's positively clueless when it comes to colors! I'm sure he'll show up with red roses, but my dress is lavender!" Stacy whisper-wails plaintively.

"I know!" Tara whines softly, her voice dripping with sympathy. "Josh is, like, totally hopeless. He'll probably bring me spray roses."

"Eew." Stacy wrinkles her perfect pug nose, and the girls giggle.

A debate ensues: plum or rose-colored lip gloss? Hair up or down? Or both? False eyelashes or brown mascara? Liquid eyeliner or pencil? It makes my head swim.

I bet these girls have had dates for the prom since they were in their mothers' wombs. I'm pretty sure it's never crossed either of their minds to worry about not being asked. I just close my notebook, close my eyes, and wait for the bell to ring. I'll take my chances in calculus. Maybe Dan will notice me today.

The calculus quiz isn't too hard. I'll probably get a B. Once it's done, I quickly lean over to pull out my notebook from under my desk, so I can pretend to take notes while Mr. Cassian lectures. Before I can stop it, my pencil rolls off my desk and comes to a neat stop right next to Dan's soccer shoe.

Oh my gosh. What do I do?

Dan leans over and brushes at the pencil with his fingertips. It rolls a bit farther, then he grabs it. As he straightens and moves to hand the pencil to me, he smiles, his green eyes lighting into my own.

I feel my eyes widening and then a warm blush snaking its way up my neck and over my cheeks.

"Thanks," I whisper.

"No problem," he mouths.

I can't believe it. I can't believe it. Dan Jacobs *does* know I'm alive. He was forced to acknowledge it right here. Today. Here in this very mustard-yellow-painted calculus classroom.

Maybe he'll ask me to prom. . . .

"Did you hear?" Mel blabs embarrassingly loudly as soon as I see her in the halls. "Dan Jacobs asked Anne Croft to go to the prom!"

"What?" I can feel all the color drop from my face. I've been so busy replaying the pencil-returning incident that I think maybe I've missed what Mel just said.

"Katie, what's wrong with you? Dan Jacobs asked Anne Croft to go to the prom with him! So now will you ask Jason?"

All I can do is stare at her.

"Oh, Katie, come on. I know you have this big crush on Dan, but you've never even spoken to the boy. Did you really think . . ." Her voice trails off. I can feel her shock setting in. She's watching me and marveling at how pathetic I am. "Kate . . . I'm sorry," she says.

"It's okay." I sigh. "I'm just . . . never mind. I'm fine." The pencil exchange is private; it's mine. "I don't think I'm ready to ask Jason yet, okay?" I feel my eyes wander over to Jason Kemp. He was new to the school this year. I don't have any classes with him, so I've never really gotten to know him. I've never even spoken to him.

Could he like me?

Why doesn't he ask me himself?

Why do things have to be so complicated?

It's Sunday morning. The prom is four days away. My mom is waiting downstairs for me, the car engine running. It's PD Day — Prom Dress Day at the Weatherbrook Mall. When we arrive at the first of the two dress stores in town, my mom strides up to the clerk and says proudly, "My daughter needs a prom dress!"

She announces it like she's declaring peace in the Middle East. I want to die. Suddenly I'm in the center of a maelstrom of puffy dresses. Blue sequins, gold taffeta, red satin, Pepto-Bismol tulle. Ugh, it's too much!

"Mom, I think I'm done," I tell her, wiping my hand across my brow.

"What do you mean? You've only tried on four dresses. Here, try this one on." She thrusts a soft pink blush — *dusty rose,* Stacy Clark would probably call it — slip dress toward me. I finger the material; it slides through my hand like a whisper.

"Okay, I'll try this one on," I answer. "But that's it. Then I'm out of here."

As I pull on the dress, feeling it glide over my body, brushing my skin so lightly, suddenly I know what it means to *want* to look perfect.

"It's gorgeous," my mother breathes.

As I twirl in front of the mirror, I have to admit, I agree. It's stunning and totally me. Or the me I wish I were.

It's the day of the prom, and I don't have a date. I have shoes, a dress, even a handbag and a hairstyle picked out. But no date. And you'd better believe there's no chance I'm going stag. My mother seems to have convinced herself that I have a date. Even though I've told her no such thing. And every chance Melody has had this week, she's hissed that it's not too late to ask Jason.

Why doesn't he ask me? I keep wanting to growl. *Doesn't he know that I have a beautiful dress and it's just waiting for him to ask?*

Seniors don't have school today, because, even if we did, the girls would cut anyway so they could spend the day getting ready for prom. My mom made an appointment for me at her hair salon. I can't seem to get the words out of my mouth, *I don't have a date, Mom.* Rather, I let her lead me around like a show dog and try not to think about what will happen tonight when she realizes that I have nowhere to go.

As I sit under the stylist's deft fingers, letting her poke hairpins into the giant updo she convinced me I *had to have,* I thumb through our local paper. In the entertainment section, a listing catches my eye. Open mic night at the Red Beret, Weatherbrook's idea of a French café, starting at seven. I sigh — an actual full-fledged, romance-novel sigh — and look up at the mirror. I feel ridiculous. Who has their hair swept up into a cascading beehive when they don't have a date?

That night, my mom helps me get into my beautiful pink dress without mussing my hair. She tells me to look down and gently applies my eyeliner and watches as I brush on some mascara. Her eyes blink back tears, and she smiles at me. She takes some pictures — two rolls, actually — then drives me over to Melody's house. As her car pulls up to the curb, I lean over, kiss her on the cheek, and get out. I begin walking up the path to Mel's front door but stop halfway and wait for my mom's car to pull away.

Then I pick up the hem of my dress and hightail it back the way we came.

Running in pointy-toed high heels is not easy, but adrenaline is pumping and pushing me on. I've never done anything like this before.

When I get back home, my mother safely picking up dinner on the way home, I race around to the side of the house and pull out the guitar case I'd hidden beneath our blue spruce tree. I open it to make sure the overflowing folder stuffed with scraps of paper is still there. It was hard leaving this stuff outside in the open.

I replace the folder, sling the guitar case over my shoulder, and start walking.

White limousines seem to fill the streets tonight. Boys in tuxedos are standing up through the sun roofs, the wind blowing their hair, drowning their shouts. Girls giggle and scream from inside the cars. All the flowers in all the gardens are in bloom, and the air smells like one giant, universal corsage. In my pink dress, I feel like a petal of one of its roses.

This feels right.

Finally, I make my way into the dimly lit café. The Red Beret is only half full. I fall into a chair at an empty table, beads of sweat lining up on my forehead, on top of my lip. My heart starts to race. This is it. It's time.

When the first call for singers goes out, I find myself marching up the aisle to the spotlit stage. As I hang the guitar strap over my shoulder and begin to sing my first song, I hear my voice come out shaky. I look up and feel my eyes lock with — *can it be?* — Jason Kemp's. He smiles at me and nods, as though he's willing me to go on.

He sees me. Hears me.

What good is lipstick when
I'm not talking to you?
And I won't curl my hair for you,
Because I've got the Pink
Prom Dress Blues . . .

Only I don't feel so blue any longer.

Prom for Fat Girls
by Rachel Cohn

High school proms are all alike; every unhappy couple is unhappy in its own way.

The prom queen, Cherie, hadn't eaten for three days; damn if she wasn't going to show off a Scarlett O'Hara waist on her big night. She looked fabulous, it was true — except for the snarl that appeared on her lips every time she smiled for a camera and a flashbulb light transmitted hunger pangs to her stomach. Cherie couldn't wait to ditch Anthony, college boy (Delta Tau Delta) and February's *CosmoGirl!* Hot Zone Hunk pick, whose father made him take the bitch queen to prom because her dad was his dad's boss. After prom, Anthony would have to find another girl if he was on the hunt for sexual favors — Cherie planned a jaunt straight to In-N-Out for a double order of double cheeseburgers, thank you. Alex, the salutatorian, would be thanking his cousin Judy for agreeing to be his last-minute date; no girl would accept his invitation after that giant cold sore sprung on his lower lip. The respective presidents of the Spanish and Latin clubs, Nathaniel and Daryn, planned to celebrate the end of senior year and the culmination of prom by consummating their love. They'd sprung for a room at the Sheraton, executive level, naturally. Then Daryn discovered Nathan in a tryst with Darren (debate club captain) behind the giant SO LONG, FAREWELL photo banner. *Qui tacet consentit.* Damn right that silence implies consent, therefore Daryn had no choice but to tell Darren's date, Chad, the prom king, and now Chad wasn't speaking to Darren, either. So much for Chad and Darren's royal plans in the next room over at the Sheraton later that night.

The L-Name Club, of course, had boycotted prom. They'd also tried to boycott the school administration when it had demanded they change their club's name from the Fat Girl Club to the L-Name Club, but Lindsay, Lydia, and Liesel had wanted approval for their club's charter too much to get hung up over a silly name. Lindsay, Lydia, and Liesel weren't sellouts — there were college applications to consider, and forming your own club and writing a charter counted for something. Also, technically, Leander was not a girl, and though he'd wanted membership in their club, he hadn't been wedded to the original name choice. He was a fat *boy*, and while sociologically speaking, all members of the club recognized that a fat male was not generally considered an object of prom date nondesirability among the high school population, a fat gay boy totally was. So Leander was totally in.

Louella, strangely, was also in — that is, into prom. A fat girl who had infiltrated enemy camp, Louella (her real name forgotten sometime around homecoming dance junior year, when her amazing knack for harmful dissemination of gossip had won her admission outside of fat girl ranks and inside cheerleader territory) had dared to ask Aloysius "Scoop" Kwiatkowski, editor of the school newspaper, to be her prom date, and he'd dared to say yes. He might have said no if he'd known Louella would spend most of the prom relaying the night's events via cell phone back to the absent L-Name Club members hanging out in Liesel's basement.

Nobody knew what the deal was with Louella leaving prom so suddenly after Scoop's hands strayed too far down her back during "How Do I Live." (LeAnn Rimes version — who'd bother feeling up to the Trisha Yearwood version? *Please.*) What was *that* tantrum about? Wasn't it supposed to be a fat girl's secret dream — to get some play on her extended boo-tay? Whatever had happened between Louella and Scoop that had resulted in Louella suddenly smacking Scoop's cheek (face) *right under the disco ball* and then storming out of the ballroom, the promgoers left standing on the dance floor knew nonetheless that universal truth: There is no party better than a fat girl party.

Fuck the Sheraton. Follow Louella.

And so the L-Name Club, who had been riding out prom with a dazzling selection of party morsels that included bowls of M&M's and popcorn (mixed — so way better than Chex Party Mix), trays of Hostess and Little Debbie snack cakes (not mixed — the L-Name Club members were plump, not gross!), and Absolut absolutely! to chase down their Cokes, found their night's film festival (pre-1990 John Cusack; notable exception: *High Fidelity*) come to an abruptly premature end. They'd only just finished *One Crazy Summer* (one crazy mistake) and started *Tapeheads* (frickin' classic) when Chad, the prom king himself, burst into the basement and postured himself in front of the TV screen.

What. the. fuck.

"Dude, don't be messing with Cusack," Lydia said.

"You can't believe what Darren did . . ." Chad gasped.

"Yeah, with Nathaniel," Leander said. Beautiful thin boys. So caught up in their beauty, they couldn't see what was right in front of them. "We heard all about it. Louella hotline. Like you didn't see that one coming?"

No one had noticed Cherie coming into the basement. Light as a feather, that girl. Happy now, too — satiated on cheeseburgers. "Oooh, M&M's mix," she said, plopping herself onto the leather couch next to Lindsay.

Lindsay saw a musical emergency in the making. Fuck Cusack. This situation required the Godfather of Soul, James Brown. Lindsay pressed two remotes: TV off, stereo on. *Owwww, I got soul . . .*

"AND I'M SUPER BAD," the assembled group shouted out.

Tables were quickly re-situated, morsel bowls replenished, a keg produced (thanks, Anthony, college boy). Word spread fast. The L-Name Club gave great party, everyone knew that. Parties thrown by fat people involved great food in ample supply and nil expectation of hooking up. Do it if you want to but, hey, no pressure, and could you please pass the cheese dip? The crackers: *fabulous.* The music: even better — hot, loud, pulsing with sweetness and want just like the candy, and even a special dispensation granted to Fatboy Slim from Liesel. Good times, pure and simple. Just be cool. Be yourself.

Daryn discovered that *CosmoGirl!* boy Anthony went to 'SC, too. And she totally planned to go Tri Delta! Nathaniel who?

Chad, on his third beer (lightweight), finally nestled himself into the expanse that was Leander's comforting embrace. Ironing room. "Have you always been this hot, or is it just something about this magical night that's finally gotten me noticing?" Chad asked him.

Alex the salutatorian and his cousin Judy decided that second best was firstly good. Second cousins once removed with matching cold sores could totally make out. Nothin' wrong with that, unless they were too drunk or sugar-high, in which case they could just as easily write out lists of cousin movies: um, *Kissin' Cousins* (You love Elvis movies, too?!?!? No way!) and . . . were there any others?

Cherie and Lydia pored through Liesel's twelve-year-old sister's *Seventeen* magazine, prom edition, defacing the models' faces and groins with a Sharpie pen. Oughta teach that little twerp not to swipe Lydia's Anaïs Nin book and write annoying comments in the margins. ("Huh? Is this possible?")

Nathaniel and Darren never made it to the fat girl party. Tryst consummation, executive suite at the Sheraton. Nobody missed 'em. Two-timing dweebs is what Cusack might have called 'em.

"Why did you leave?" Scoop asked Louella when he'd finally cornered her at the basement fireplace. Louella was tough, and she really really didn't want to cry in such close proximity to Liesel's dad's oil-painting portrait of Kenny Rogers' "The Gambler" hanging directly behind the pool table. Instead, she reached for a Gobstopper from the bowl on the mantelpiece. "It's not nice to tease people like me," she said before popping a 'stopper. Mmmm, lime-flavored.

"What do you mean, 'people like me'?" Scoop asked. He reached for the bowl of Swedish Fish sitting on the fish tank table. He liked the green ones almost as much as he liked Louella.

"Big!" Louella burst out. Damn, it would take ten minutes to suck that sucker through to the center. She spit the 'stopper into a napkin. Don't cry, don't cry, it's the sour flavor.

She cried anyway, and Scoop had no choice but to reach out to her.

"But I like you," he said. "And size means nothing to me." He leaned in to kiss her, yet she recoiled.

"Well, it means a lot to me, bucko!" Louella said. But the crying instinct had transformed to laughter. The instinct was shared with Scoop, who laughed his way right into her arms.

Fat girl after-prom parties are all alike; any couple could be happy in its own way.

Chicken

by Jodi Lynn Anderson

Sometimes Elsie wondered how Ben had happened to
her at all. When they were crawling across the rooftops
of Annapolis, or when people were pointing at Ben's
chicken, she felt like a person with amnesia. *How did I get
here? Who is he? Who am I?*

If you stood facing the sun on redbricked Main
Street, Annapolis, Elsie and Ben were silhouettes flitting
back and forth between the shop windows, pushing each
other off the sidewalk or leaning against the windows or
eating Cadbury Flakes from the British Imports store
or trying to buy cigars. Occasionally Ben brought his
chicken on a leash, and it would be the three of them
silhouetted, Chicken picking spare gum wrappers off
the sidewalk. They were juniors.

In the store window reflections Elsie could see a
portrait of herself, framed by panes, and it was not
what she'd hoped for. Her face had hints of other
places she had never been, sandalwood, jasmine, roses,
cloves. Elsie looked little parts Japan, Morocco, India —
smoke-obscured, spicy. Her eyes swept out round like a
owl's, floating on high cheeks. Her hair was the color of
a November leaf. One time a group of German tourists

had approached her at Ego Alley and asked her directions in *Deutsch*. The Mexican cook at Fuddrucker's addressed her in Spanish all the time. It was like she was from everywhere. Elsie liked it, and didn't. She had always wanted to look as pure and bright and American as Ivory soap. Or was Ivory soap Irish?

By her side, Ben waved too big at people he knew, and they replied with the smallest slips of the hand, to compensate. A lot of times, it made Elsie want to be someone who was somewhere else. His lips were too wet, his hair was too curly, his elbows jutted out, tiny white specks formed at the corners of his mouth. Ben was always scraggle-haired, his body shaped in a wiggle — as if he couldn't quite straighten out all his long lines. He was made slightly crooked.

And then there was Chicken.

When Ben had introduced them, he'd promised Elsie that chickens had personalities. And, by God, it turned out to be true. Chicken could be inseparable from Ben's heels one minute and clucking off mysteriously the next. Without fail, she ran to the door to greet Elsie. If Noelle or one of Elsie's other friends came with her, Chicken grew shy and hid under the bed. Sometimes Chicken got moody and stared out the window with her beady little eyes, like she was thinking of something far away. Other times she looked you in the face, like she was trying to tell you about herself telepathically.

Ben used her to ask Elsie to prom, in a note tied around her neck with a red ribbon.

It had snowed earlier that day, and outside the yard was like the top of a fondant cake. Elsie stood in the foyer, cold air blowing on her calves through the cat door, which was supposed to be too small for Chicken. But sometimes it wasn't.

Her sweaty palms unfolded the note, knowing its contents and wishing she could back out the door: *Don't mind me, I was never here.* She knew by the way Ben stood there waiting, watching TV instead of watching her, all intent eyeballs and awkward waiting crook of the neck. He was afraid of too much, Elsie thought. He was afraid of girls — and also global warming, snakes, and swimming.

She took a long time to read the note, stalling. But since he had asked her, she said yes. "I'll be your prom buddy," she told him, letting him know what they were and what they weren't.

In Ben's house there were cabinets open everywhere, as if his family was too tired to close them. There was smoke hanging in the air from his mom's cigarettes and an empty dining room they had never decided to buy furniture for. Virginia Creeper, the cat, crept out from under the TV stand and took a swat at Chicken, who ducked between Elsie's feet. Elsie thought about leaving. And then they heard the *tickticktick* of the cat door, and Chicken was gone.

They spotted her puff of tail disappearing around the front of the house, going hell's bells like she was on a prison break. It wasn't the first time. Ben wrung his hands and breathed wispily as they ran across General's Highway, following her tracks now that they couldn't see her, looking wearily for splats of red. Eisenhower Golf Course rolled like vanilla taffy across the way, untouched except for two tiny triangular feet tracks.

By the time they saw her, she was a white flash hurtling away across the snow. Elsie watched, chewing her nails as Ben ducked and zigzagged after her. Finally he sprang, all power, but with soft arms designed for a Fabergé egg. He cupped Chicken between his elbows and stood to follow Elsie home.

Elsie watched her boots disappear into the snow and reappear again; the world was quiet and smelled white. When she turned, Ben had stopped, was sliding his feet through the snow. She pretended not to see what he was writing: *Elsie.*

In her bed that night, Elsie watched the lights of the occasional car cross the ceiling, heard them heading up the back alleys behind Main Street. With restless beating wrists and thin rib cage rising and falling, she thought that Ben was a thief, stealing a night in April with a note in March. She thought about Newley, who was true north and not all jangled up. Beside Ben in her head, Newley looked like a lion. Ben's eyes darted to the sides when he talked to you. He was cool like fluorescent lights at night. He burned with broad strokes. With Ben, Elsie always felt good. What she felt for Newley was too big to feel good. But she had thought at prom, if they were sliced neatly into a pair, she might feel something more.

Lying in the shadows, she saw shooting stars, red planets, nebulas in the dark ceiling. At Saint Judith's she kept her planets and stars and nebulas hidden under her plaid skirt. A cool draft brought up the musty smell of the basement. The house — historic, brick, connected to every other old house on the row — had been part of the Underground Railroad. Growing up, Elsie could feel the ghosts of people who had hidden there. She liked to imagine herself back there, offering shelter. Everyone *knew* they would have been that brave. But only a few people had been. So she wondered who was believing the truth.

On their way to school each morning, Elsie and Ben kept the windows rolled down. If it was cold, they turned the heat full blast. They whistled at construction workers and listened to Ben's mix CDs. His CDs were full of songs that didn't catch you at first, then crept into your head and curled up like a cat and stayed. Elsie's mixes caught you strong on the first few listens and then sagged like wet cardboard.

At her locker at Saint Judith's, Elsie dumped her stuff on Ben, making him a coatrack, a hat tree, a scarf hanger, a purse holder. It was a joke between them. She pretended not to notice him as she searched for her books. Their laughter echoed off the murmury marbled hallway, punctuated with slamming metal before third period AP English.

She felt a squeeze on her hip. "Else," someone said. She turned to look at Newley. When he said *Else* it sounded like part of *elsewhere*. He made her think the word *lover*. He was completely perpendicular with straight shoulders and straight brown hair, wide-open brown eyes, and skin soft as a nectarine. Atoms rearranged themselves to make room for him. He stretched life around him as a matter of fact. If he waved too big, the world would double in size to fit it — Elsie was sure of it. She had the urge to hitch a ride with him.

By this time everyone had dates. Newley and Noelle as pals. Elsie and Ben. Other couples for the limo.

Elsie and Newley walked to AP English with Ben flopping behind them like the tail of a tadpole.

They had to read the essays they'd done out loud. The topic was *something you've accomplished*. Elsie had written hers about how she accomplished procrastinating on her essay. She stuck a pencil in and out of her short russet ponytail, flopping her feet sideways as she read, and everyone laughed because she'd written it in a witty way.

Newley had written his about jumping into the ocean off a high cliff in Jamaica.

Ben read about the day he rescued Chicken.

He had stolen her from a Purdue truck parked at the BP. He said there were hundreds of chickens and he couldn't save them all but if he saved one it would be something. Elsie and Newley and Noelle looked hard at one another to communicate laughter, and not because it wasn't sad, but the earnestness was funny. Because *chickens* were funny. There was no getting around it. Ben read through the essay in a monotone. He didn't know how to dress his darkness up in dark humor, and it made Elsie embarrassed for him. Afterward, he soft-shoed back to his desk.

On the way out of class, Elsie walked with Newley, and thought of the night next week and what it could be. Ben was in the picture like a rip in a piece of silk.

Prom night was the first hot May night of spring. It made this wildness in the air. Elsie imagined the whole city turning pagan and dancing in their bedrooms.

They ate at Colonial House up General's Highway. Elsie hunched her thin shoulders in her strapless silver dress as they waited for their table, smoothing herself out, covered in a cool, thin, silver web that made her body feel divine. She knew what it was like to glow because she could feel sparkles shooting off her and drawing eyes to her from all over the restaurant.

Her shrimp came with the heads on, and looked to be climbing out of the bowl. Ben yelped but Newley popped the heads off and hid them. He had the chicken cordon bleu. During dessert Newley rubbed a pinky against Elsie's wrist where her hand held the cushion of her seat. With Newley touching her, even just lightly, Elsie felt *like* Newley — fearless, symmetrical, clean.

During dessert Newley made a still-life parade of the shrimp heads around a leg of the table.

"They're doing the cha-cha," one person at their table said.

"Somebody's going to have to clean that up," Ben muttered, but the others laughed.

The limo oozed through traffic like an oil slick. The girls made jokes and fiddled with the radio, singing along. Ben had gone shy in the corner seat and peered out the window. They had all voted for beers at Eisenhower Golf Course afterward. At the golf course Elsie and Newley could find themselves in a stand of dark trees, or slip away to talk. Elsie could feel Newley's stare like a second layer over her thin dress. She looked *sorries* at Ben. She fidgeted with the yellow carnation corsage he'd given her, glancing at Noelle's simple white rose.

*   *   *

On the dance floor she and Newley began gently, their bodies slowly pulled together in stages like two things melting — hands, chests, hips, stomachs. Elsie was sure it was love because it felt like there was something physical and soul-like shooting out of her fingertips where they touched his. No chandeliers or soaring ceilings above them, just a low boxy room with a Teflon surface for moving on. Ben sat at the round white table playing nickel basketball with himself. They were gone by twelve. In the limo again, they were wound up, wild, sticking their heads out of the sunroof. They collapsed, sweaty, into the leather seats, and Elsie let Newley pull off her strappy sandals and rub the soles of her feet. She leaned her forehead against the glass and watched the pagan moon following them to Bowie. Maybe following her. She was that full of bigness.

At Ben's, where their cars were parked, they tumbled in a gaggle across the street to the golf course, running after each other, tackling each other, howling, laughing, high with the spring heat and in the very center of the world.

Ben walked behind them like the zookeeper.

They found a hill and lay on top. Her ankles over Noelle's, Elsie wished the moon wasn't so bright, that she could sneak her fingers into Newley's on her other side. Her lips were dry but sweat misted her and the grass beneath her back.

In the distance they could hear others — guys, loud.

The voices wove closer and farther away, laughing and drunk. Then they were so close that everyone sat up to have a look. There were three of them, maybe a couple years older. Chasing after something under the bright moon, running like jungle kids.

As the picture came together, the night started to tumble inside Elsie.

The three were in pursuit. They were chasing what looked like a small, round white ghost stumbling across the grass ahead of them at top speed, butterball size.

One of them cocked his arm back, flung his arm forward, and something rocketed through the air. The white butterball, synchronized, bounced up into the air like it had stepped on a trampoline and landed in the grass, going still.

Elsie froze. There was the bigness of the guys. And then there was the naked act of saving. Ben was already on his feet, his arms and legs flying messy and ugly as he ran after them. An ugly scream came from his throat. The strangers turned and stopped, instantly sheepish and still.

Ben didn't chase them but slid onto the ground around where Chicken had disappeared. Elsie unfroze and stood, walking fast and softly toward Ben. She knelt beside him. Chicken lay on the ground, black eyes blinking at them. It crossed her mind that for all Chicken knew, they were the ones who'd thrown the rocks.

The strangers milled at the edge of the trees, watching. They moved with forced carelessness, hands in pockets, but Elsie could tell they were scared of Ben, of what he was willing to show them. Then they walked away slowly — in flight, even if they pretended not to be.

Elsie looked back for Newley and the others. They were making their way down the hill, suddenly awkward, not wild in their own skins. The boys had their hands in their pockets. Everyone looked away from Ben, because he was crying.

* * *

No one but Elsie came to the emergency vet. It was hours before they came out. They stood in the parking lot in the dark, listening to the cars rush by on Route 50, kicking feet at the curb. Ben had his shoulders hunched up and his head down, the bundle of Chicken in his arms.

"You wanna get out of here?" Elsie asked. He shrugged.

She drove to the docks. Annapolis was full of fingers of water stretching behind houses. They climbed into Ben's rowboat. The water slapped the sides as Elsie paddled. The front bench was missing so Ben sat on the metal floor, then lay back, laying the bundle beside him and looking at the sky.

Where the finger of water became the bay, Elsie pulled the paddles in and they drifted. She looked at the bundle. She'd never seen a chicken drugged before. Chicken would be bedridden for days, and maybe be okay. Or maybe not.

"Do you ever feel like you're living in a circle, instead of a line?" Ben asked. "Like, you never change?"

Elsie squinted at him, sleepy.

"Like, I'm me now," he went on, "but I'm also me on this big hike my dad and I took when I was ten, and I'm also me the first day of school freshman year. And I'm me in the future. It's like one of those wooden dolls. With all those smaller dolls inside." He blinked up at the sky. "Even when I'm surprised by how things turn out, deep down I'm never surprised, you know? Because it's all already there, and none of it disappears."

Elsie knew, and she didn't know. The boat drifted. She noticed the sky was a shade lighter than it had been.

241

"Have you ever stayed up for the morning?" Ben looked at her under heavy lids.

Elsie thought back to a weekend in Ocean City with her parents as a kid. Doing this was like picking up dragon scales: iridescent and ancient and not quite real. She remembered the orange tip of the sun rising over the sea. She remembered her dad's arms around her waist. She remembered being disappointed. She'd been expecting fireworks and all she got was a flat orange circle. Maybe she was the opposite of Ben. Maybe she was always surprised.

She started to say it to him, but his mouth hung open, asleep. Elsie yawned, then steadied the boat as she moved down on the other side of Chicken — beside him, still unwilling to touch him, but maybe just by the shoulder, just by the waist. Only like a friend. Like the word *only* applied to the word *friend*. She wanted to make it up to him, all her secret thoughts.

She had the momentary idea that if they floated for a few hours, just over to the other side of the bay, they would be in another country. Like France. Or Morocco. Or Japan. And, since they would only be strangers there, she would peel off her layers like heavy coats and be as naked as some people could be.

The Backup Date
by Leslie Margolis

"Lucy's behavior makes perfect sense, if you think about it. Since she can't use words, the only way she can communicate with you is by throwing up on your prom dress. Poor Lucy is trying to tell you something."

"That I shouldn't go to the prom?" I asked, somewhat hysterically.

"No, Jasmine." Dr. Kessler, Lucy's therapist, spoke in sweet, soothing tones — the kind that made me want to rip out her tonsils, and I am not even a violent person. "She's telling you she's stressed. She doesn't like these changes in her life, and she wishes you'd stick to her regular routine."

"Her regular routine involves shopping at Barney's, getting bows put in her hair, and sitting on my stepmother's lap while she gets pedicures at the Burke Williams Spa. That's not normal. All I wanted was for Lucy to have some fun."

"By taking her to the Laurel Canyon Dog Park, which is filled with animals ten times her size?"

"Look, how was I supposed to know they'd mistake Lucy for a chew toy? It wasn't my fault, and I got her away as quickly as I could."

"But not before that nasty English bulldog with a Napoleon complex ripped her favorite sweater."

I was dying to know how Dr. Kessler knew it was an English bulldog that attacked Lucy. And could a dog even have a Napoleon complex? I couldn't bring myself to ask.

"Lucy doesn't have a favorite sweater," I said. "Lucy is a dog."

"You shouldn't discriminate against small mammals, Jasmine. Lucy may not understand what you're saying but she certainly understands your implicit negative feelings toward her. She's acting out. Anyone would under these hostile circumstances."

"Look," I said, "I'm only the dog-sitter. This isn't my problem. My stepmom said to call you if there's an emergency. Lucy is a drooling, vomiting, trembling wreck, and I'm being picked up for the prom in two hours, so obviously, this is an emergency. I can't take Lucy with me and you're telling me I can't leave her home alone in this state, so will you please take her for the night?"

Dr. Kessler frowned. "I am a pet therapist, who specializes in communicating with hypoallergenic lapdogs residing in the West Los Angeles area. Boarding dogs is not what I do."

She handed me a card listing her services, in case I didn't believe her. It was pink with tiny paw prints in each corner. She was right. Boarding dogs wasn't on the list, but dog massage therapy, acupuncture, and reflexology were.

I tried pleading with her. "Can't you make an exception?"

"It's not healthy for Lucy to be out of her regular environment."

"Trust me. Right now, it's not healthy for Lucy to stay anywhere within kicking range of me."

Dr. Kessler recoiled, scooped Lucy into her arms, and headed out the door.

"Lucy's mother will be hearing about this. When does she return?"

"You mean Martha, Lucy's *owner*?" I asked. "In two days."

Lucy and Dr. Kessler left without saying good-bye. I was proud of myself for closing rather than slamming the front door behind them.

I would like to state for the record that I have never, ever kicked a dog or any other animal, small or large. Furthermore, although Lucy walks on four legs and has a tail, I am not fully convinced she is actually a living, breathing creature. It would make much more sense if she turned out to be some high-functioning windup toy designed for the sole purpose of annoying the crap out of me.

But don't worry. I don't kick windup toys, either.

Lucy belongs to Martha, my dad's fifth wife. She's a hypoallergenic cross between a toy poodle and a bichon frise. The dog, that is. My stepmom, Martha, is a hypochondriac cross between a trophy wife and a stylist to the star. She used to be a stylist to the stars but her second client dropped her.

Fortunately, the three of us (Martha, her star, and me) all wear the same dress size.

I headed for Martha's closet, which used to be the master bedroom, in search of a replacement outfit.

It's a good thing I didn't care about tonight. Otherwise, I might be upset that Lucy had ruined my dress.

But I understood the institution of prom for what it was: an artificial rite of passage that society has foisted upon innocent young people, to initiate them into a lifetime of loyal consumerhood. Between the dress, tux, shoes, hair, flowers, tickets, and limo, the average prom couple spends about a thousand bucks on the night. Then there's the prom committee, a bunch of misguided people who sacrifice precious hours of their lives decorating some stupid ballroom, as if anyone else cared. And don't even get me started on the whole prom court thing. It's so hypocritical, choosing a prom king and queen, and thereby celebrating rule by divine right, when we live in a democracy. I was shocked that so many otherwise intelligent-seeming people buy into the same bullshit, year after year after year.

And while it might seem as if I were buying into it as well, by going to the prom, I was actually only participating out of loyalty to my boyfriend, Austin Cooper. For some reason, he actually cared about that sort of thing.

I didn't, which is why I only spent three weeks shopping for my dress — a black-and-red sequined tank, which I'd planned to wear with combat boots. It's basically the anti-prom outfit. I would never, ever let myself become a walking cliché — one of those girls teetering on uncomfortable heels and squeezed into a wannabe-princess dress. You know the kind — all tight-bodiced, and strapless, and long, puffy-skirted.

It's silly how all that meaningless fluff can bring people joy. The only reason that I was happy about prom was because my entire family was in France, with no idea that I planned to go. And when I say "my entire family," I actually mean "my older brother, Jett," because he was the only one who would care.

My boyfriend happens to be his best friend. They're both seniors and I'm a freshman and if Jett had known that we'd been dating behind his back for two whole months, he would have freaked. It was okay, though. I didn't mind keeping it a secret. All that mattered was that Austin and I were finally together. I'd had a crush on him for years, since before I even knew what a crush was.

He was at our house all the time and it used to be that I'd think up any excuse to spend time with him: Austin, will you help me study for my math test? Austin, I just rented *Star Wars*. Do you want to watch it with me? Austin, I just hung this signed framed poster of Pavement above my bed. Will you come and see if it looks crooked? Oh, you love Pavement, too? I had no idea. . . .

About six months ago, Austin began throwing out excuses to hang with *me*: Jasmine, do you need help studying for your math test? Jasmine, Jett is going out tonight and I didn't realize and brought over *Say Anything*. Do you want to watch it with me? Jasmine, they gave me an extra Ultimo Burrito at Baja Fresh. Do you want it? Oh, you love Ultimo Burritos with savory pork carnitas, too? I had no idea. . . .

And the rest was history. Sometimes I felt like dating Austin propelled me to a higher stratosphere. Music sounded better, and colors seemed brighter, and we were going to the Bel Air Prep Senior Prom.

I mean we *had* to go to the prom. It was his idea, completely.

Well, he didn't ask me, exactly, but I knew he wanted to go and was just too shy to say so, which is why I invited him, and bought the tickets, and ordered my corsage and his boutonniere, and scheduled the limo.

It was a big inconvenience, although it could have been worse. Luckily I am NOT one of those girls who stresses about her appearance. I probably would have gotten a manicure and pedicure that morning, anyway. And as for having my hair blown out all slick and shiny and then twisted into an updo, with the ends curled, like that girl on the front cover of *CosmoGirl Prom!*? Well, I was just wondering what it would look like. It's not like I got my hair done *for* the prom.

Seriously. The only reason I was feeling giddy that night was because with my brother out of the country, Austin and I didn't have to sneak around. Jett got kicked out of our school three years ago. The only person he associated with there (besides Austin and me) is Lubna, his on-again/off-again girlfriend.

Lubna knew the truth but was sworn to secrecy. In fact, we were double-dating. (With Jett in France, Lubna was stuck taking her cousin, Adeel, but at least no one else knew they were related. She told everyone that she dumped my brother for a college guy who was flying down from Berkeley for the weekend.)

Anyway, Lubna was lucky that Jett was away because she was much too good for him. Basically, Lubna was everything that Jett was not: smart, sweet, thoughtful, and not inclined to set off bottle rockets on the school football field or streak naked across the stage during a U2 concert.

But back to my dress — before I could decide what was less typical prom-y, the black halter top with a knee-length flared skirt, or this long, turquoise, off-the-shoulder number, my cell phone sang from my back pocket.

It was Lubna. "Almost ready?" she asked.

"Not quite."

I launched into the backstory to explain why I was currently shopping in Martha's closet, but before I had a chance to ask her about dogs and Napoleon complexes, Lubna interrupted with, "Listen. I need to tell you something. Jett is on his way home."

"Very funny." It was a classic Lubna joke, and I wasn't falling for it.

"No, really. He called me from the airport. His plane just landed in LA."

She sounded serious. I felt a nervous fluttering in my stomach. "But they aren't supposed to be home for two more days."

"Something happened in France. Jett won't say what, but he'll be home any minute."

"He can't come here. You have to stall him. Please, Lubna. This can't happen tonight."

"Okay, don't hate me."

"Why would I hate you?" I asked carefully.

"You know how Adeel and I were both dreading going to the prom together? And how he only agreed to be my date because his parents made him? And honestly, I think my uncle actually paid him, too. Well, I was thinking, now that Jett is in town, since he is my boy-friend . . ."

"Ex-boyfriend."

"Actually, we got back together a couple of weeks ago. I didn't tell you because I knew you'd be mad. Anyway, Jett owns his own tux, so it only makes sense —"

"You can't invite him. Listen to me, Lubna. This cannot happen."

"It's too late. But I knew you'd understand."

I slunk down onto the floor. "How could you do this to me?"

"It's my senior prom. And don't worry. I've already got you covered. I told Jett that Austin was supposed to go to the prom with Jenna, but she got mono at the last minute, and you're filling in."

"You made me a *backup* date? I'm, like, second-string."

"But, Jasmine. You're only going because Austin wants to. You hate proms."

"I know. It's just, what happens when Jett sees Jenna there?"

"It'll be dark, so maybe he won't notice, and if he does, don't worry. He'll probably be too drunk to remember. Now relax. Oh, and you'd better call Austin to warn him. See you at eight."

"Wait!"

Lubna hung up on me.

Somehow, I managed to peel myself off the floor and turn back to the dresses.

I was so lucky that I didn't care about the prom, because if I had, I would have been crying. The only reason my eyes were tearing up was because I had really bad allergies.

Twenty minutes later, my family came home. Well, Martha and Jett did. My dad went straight to the office from the airport. No one would tell me what happened in France or why Jett had a black eye — only that it had something to do with a jealous investment banker and his girlfriend, and that the incident messed up a big deal for my dad. (He was in France for work. The trip was a graduation gift for my brother and I am not surprised that he found a way to ruin it for everyone.)

Just like he was going to ruin my prom. Austin's prom, I mean.

"I hear you're filling in for Jenna," Jett said as he walked in the door, with his duffel bag slung over one shoulder, and a mischievous grin on his face. "I can't believe Austin couldn't find a real date. I can't wait to give him shit about that!"

"The limo is coming at eight o'clock," I said. "And you'd better be ready because tonight is really important for Lubna and Austin."

"Where's my dog?" Martha wondered.

I told her the whole story and she was surprisingly understanding. Maybe she was still sedated from the flight. She even helped me pick out a new dress before she fetched Lucy from Dr. Kessler's.

It was floor length, emerald green, and gorgeous. (If you're into that kind of thing.) It had a few layers of crinoline under the skirt, so it was puffy, but luckily the tight, beaded bodice wasn't strapless. It had spaghetti straps, which meant it wasn't at all princesslike. Since my combat boots didn't go with the new dress, Martha lent me a pair of stilettos. They were only half a size too small.

The florist refused to change my corsage, regardless of how much I begged, so I was stuck wearing a red one. Austin's bow tie and cummerbund were also red, so standing next to each other we were completely mismatched, like Christmas in May. I felt so bad for Austin, because now the pictures wouldn't coordinate. He was sweet about it, though, and pretended like he didn't care.

The limo was twenty minutes late. We got stuck in traffic and I hated that we were going to miss the beginning of the prom, because Lubna was all dressed up and excited.

When we passed In-N-Out on Wilshire, Jett said, "Let's stop for burgers."

"We can't. They're serving dinner at the prom," I argued.

"It'll be rubber chicken and stringy beef," Austin said. "Your brother is right. We're better off here."

I turned to Lubna. "You don't want to eat greasy burgers, do you? What if you spill something on your dress?"

"Oh, I'm not worried," said Lubna. "And the food at the prom will be gross." She leaned forward and asked our driver to stop.

Poor Lubna! She was such a great sport, pretending like she didn't mind.

We ordered takeout. Before we headed back to the car, Jett poured out half of each of our sodas and filled them with the rum he'd swiped from Dad and Martha's liquor cabinet.

As we piled back into the limo, my hand brushed against Austin's leg. It was torture not being able to curl up in his lap. Too bad I wasn't drunk, because if I was, I'd have a great excuse to jump his bones. Jett always said that drunken hookups are meaningless. At least, that was the line he fed Lubna this one time she caught him making out with another girl at the Roxy.

I've never actually been drunk, and there was no way I'd let myself do so tonight. Getting drunk before the prom was the ultimate prom cliché.

But then something occurred to me. I could drink a little and just *pretend* to be drunk, and then hook up with Austin and blame it on the alcohol.

Sometimes I was so brilliant I surprised even myself.

After wolfing down my cheeseburger and fries (and half of Lubna's double double), I drained my Dr. Pepper and rum. Then I finished Austin's root beer and rum.

I pointed to Jett's soda, asking, "Are you going to finish that?"

He frowned at me. "Don't you think you've had enough?" he asked.

"Let her have it if she wants it," Lubna said.

Austin agreed. "Yeah, Jett. Stop being so overprotective."

Jett leaned over me and shoved Austin. "Dude, just because my sister agreed to be your backup date doesn't mean you have to be nice to her."

I screamed, "Careful of my dress, you asshole!" because he came so close to spilling his French fries on me.

Lubna and I locked eyes and I knew exactly what she was thinking: *Poor Austin's prom is ruined, and it's all my fault.*

She told me to chill and handed me her drink. Obviously, this was her way of apologizing.

By the time we made it to the Beverly Hilton, I was feeling so completely relaxed. (Not that I was nervous before.)

Since my shoes were pinching my toes, I decided to leave them in the limo.

"You're going barefoot?" asked Austin, frowning down at my feet.

"Sure." I wrapped my arms around his waist, but Austin pulled away, nodding to Jett, who was way ahead of us and not even looking back.

"It's okay because I'm drunk," I told him.

"No kidding," Austin mumbled. For some reason, he didn't seem all that excited about the prom, which was annoying, since we were only going because of him.

"No, it's okay," I whispered. "I'm only pretending."

Apparently, my brother has excellent hearing because he turned around and told me to shut up.

"I wasn't even talking to you, Mr. Jett!" I yelled. "And thank you for ruining the prom. For Austin."

Lubna glanced over her shoulder, worried. I waved and then stumbled. It was hard, walking in a straight line. I guess because I was barefoot. I held on to Austin's arm, glad I had the fake-drunk excuse, in case Jett decided to turn around again.

He didn't.

Walking inside, I was truly astounded. The prom was the single most beautiful thing I've ever seen. The theme was Las Vegas, and the ballroom was completely splashed out with roulette wheels, and giant playing cards, and neon signs that read CIRCUS, CIRCUS, CAESAR'S PALACE, and THE MIRAGE. Blinking, shiny slot machines lined one wall. There was even a fake fake Eiffel Tower in one corner, and a small volcano in another. A giant, shimmering disco ball hung from the ceiling. It didn't have anything to do with Vegas, but I suppose that a prom would not be a prom without a disco ball.

It was magical.

If you're into that sort of thing.

I grabbed Austin and pulled him onto the dance floor. My arms were around his neck and his arms were around my waist and we swayed back and forth to a slow song. And then when the DJ played a fast song, we continued to cling to each other. It was so romantic.

"You are the best dancer in the world," I said.

"Will you let go of me?" asked Austin.

"Sorry." I pulled away. "Hey, how do you think they managed to make this room so bright and so dark at the same time?"

My words sounded slurry, probably because we were standing so close to the speakers.

"I can't believe you're this drunk," he said.

It was just like Austin to go along with my plan even when Jett wasn't around. *He's so sweet!* I thought.

We danced for a few more songs, fast, without touching.

I was amazing, a dancing machine. It was as if the beats and rhythms inside the music were pulsing through my veins, causing my entire body to flail: arms, shoulders, fingertips, elbows, hips, legs, feet, even my head, all moving in different directions, yet at the same time, perfectly synchronized.

"Let's take a break," said Austin. "You're totally embarrassing me."

Poor guy was self-conscious that he couldn't keep up. "I think it's the sugar from all those sodas, giving me so much energy."

"Uh-huh." Austin nodded.

"Ooooh, let's play on the slot machines!" I darted toward the back of the room.

Turns out they were props and wouldn't accept real coins, not even after I tried jamming some into the slots really, really hard. Also, they weren't all that sturdy.

And yet, the prom was still the most fun I'd ever pretended to have.

Austin wanted to find me some water but I needed to pee, so I stumbled off to the bathroom, which wasn't tricked out Vegas-style at all. This sad fact made me want to cry. The committee could have decorated it a little, for all those people who cared about things like that. There was one empty corner, for instance, where they could have so easily constructed a miniature Hoover Dam. I went over to investigate, and then sat down because I felt tired.

A minute later Lubna burst into the room. "There you are!" she said. "I've been looking for you everywhere. We have to go." Her eyes were all squinty and red, like she'd just been crying.

"But we just got here," I argued.

"Jasmine, it's eleven-thirty. Austin hasn't seen you in over an hour, and Jett got kicked out of the prom."

"What?"

"He stole Marcy Calloway's tiara and she told one of the chaperones, who called security. Jett got frisked, and they found his flask, which was empty, but still smelled like booze."

So much information. But wait. "Marcy Calloway has a tiara?"

"Had. Jett threw it into the Hoover Dam."

"No one gave me a tiara. How come Marcy got a tiara?"

"She's Prom Queen."

I gasped. "Lubna, you were robbed!" I tried to stand up, using the wall to brace myself, but it was way too slippery.

Lubna shook her head. "You are so drunk, Jasmine. I wasn't even nominated. Now come on."

"I'm just pretending," I insisted as she pulled me up and half-carried me out of the bathroom and across the dance floor.

We were approaching the exit and I tried to stop her. "Wait! I still need to see the Hoover Dam."

Lubna ignored me, which was unfortunate because I had so many questions for her: How big is the dam and did they use blue construction paper and glitter, cellophane, or real water? Where did I leave my shoes? When are you going to wise up and dump my brother? Why does he always have to ruin everything? Don't you think Austin looks like James Bond in his tux? Do I look pretty with my updo? And who turned on the spinning?

Once outside, we made a beeline for Jett and Austin, who were both leaning against the limo.

As soon as Austin saw me he grabbed my shoulders and peered into my eyes. "Are you okay?"

"Fine, silly." Giggling, I tugged on his bow tie, because I didn't know if it was real or a clip-on.

"Stop it."

It was real.

The fresh air felt so fresh and the spinning had slowed considerably. I leaned into him. We were hugging and I was fake drunk and the way he stroked my hair made me not even care that his tux smelled like the mall.

"Someone had too much to drink," he whispered into my ear.

"Oh, I'm just dizzy." I buried my face in his neck.

"Next time you decide to get this dizzy, do you think you could warn me?" he asked. "Or maybe just not get quite this dizzy, and then disappear? I was really worried."

"You two should get a room," Jett said.

Austin's arms closed around me more tightly. "Shut up, dude."

"That's what you get for going out with a freshman," Jett said.

"What are you talking about?" I mumbled.

My brother laughed, asking, "What has it been, like two months now? You two must think I'm really dumb."

I glanced at Lubna, who threw up her hands and said, "I never said a word, I swear. I didn't even know he knew."

"How did you know?" asked Austin.

"You rented *Say Anything*. Why else would you bring over that dumb-ass movie, if not to try and impress my sister?"

"It's actually really good," said Austin.

I broke away from him and glared at Jett. "That was months ago," I shouted. "You knew this whole time? You knew and you didn't say anything? You ruined the prom for nothing?"

Jett grinned at me and pushed his hair out of his eyes. "Ruined the prom? What are you talking about? I'm having an excellent time."

Suddenly I felt all sweaty. My stomach churned. Then the slow spinning turned into a fast, dramatic tilting. I wondered if perhaps my body was pretending to be drunk, too. I was impressed with myself, thinking maybe this meant I'd make a good Method actor.

If only I could lie down.

I headed toward the limo, but Jett was blocking the door. If he and Austin and Lubna sat on one side, I could stretch out on the other and take a nap. . . .

When I stumbled, Jett reached out to steady me. "You okay?"

I wasn't, but I couldn't say so. I gagged and clapped both hands over my mouth. It happened so fast, before I could stop it, although I didn't actually want to stop it. It had to happen and I didn't want to mess up my manicure so I dropped my hands and then I, and then I, and then I . . .

I pulled a Lucy, all over my brother's tux.

Jett tried to jump out of the way, but he was too slow. "Ah, Jasmine! Shit, Jasmine. That's disgusting."

I wiped my mouth with the back of my hand. My stomach felt better but now my throat burned.

Austin and Lubna laughed and gave each other high fives. I don't know why.

"Wow, I feel so much better." Clutching my stomach, I sighed. "Must have been from the In-N-Out. I hope you guys don't get food poisoning, too."

But this just made them laugh harder. They were both red-faced, and Lubna was clapping and jumping up and down, happier than I'd seen her all night.

"I'll go get you some water," said Austin.

"Dude, forget it," Jett said, as he shrugged out of his jacket. "I'm taking it to the dry cleaners in the morning."

Austin patted Jett on the back. "I was talking to my girlfriend, dickhead." Then he headed toward the hotel.

I called out to him. "Austin, wait!"

He turned around, and there was so much I wanted to say: Actually, you're hotter than James Bond. I'm so glad we don't have to pretend anymore. And isn't it kind of funny that I threw up? Because now I'm your real date *and* your backup date, in the sense that my dinner came back . . . no, that wasn't it.

I lost my train of thought. It was all too complicated, and late, and I was tired, so instead I took a deep breath and yelled, "I love the prom!" Then I pitched my whole body forward, hoping to land in Austin's arms rather than on my face.

I think I succeeded but I'm not sure, because that was the last thing I remembered before I fell asleep.

Funny how everyone insists that I passed out. As if I could pass out when I wasn't even drunk.

When I woke up the next morning, I had a massive headache. My throat was parched, and my tongue felt too thick for my mouth. It's a good thing I hadn't gotten drunk, because a hangover on top of this flu would have been a nightmare.

Not to mention the fact that getting drunk and puking on prom night was the biggest cliché of all.

I am so lucky I didn't fall into that trap.

Lost Sometimes
by David Levithan

His name was Dutch. We weren't boyfriends, but we screwed all over the place. I'm serious — you name the place, odds are we screwed there. The gym. Burger King. His grandmother's house. We couldn't stop. We decided to go to the prom together to make a statement, and also to see if we could screw there, too.

There were a couple of other gay kids in our school — it was a big school — but all of the rest of them were, like, *sensitive*. With Dutch, though, everything was exactly what it was. We first hooked up at this Christmas party, senior year. You know, the kind you have with your friends a few days before everyone has to go stick it out with their parents. Anyway, the eggnog was ass-knocking. I kinda knew Dutch, but I had no idea what his story was. Me, I was a big flamer. In middle school, they wanted to cast a girl as Peter Pan but they decided to cast me instead. No real mystery there.

So it got to be about three in the morning and Dutch walked over and told me I was a little devil. I told him that he was a little devil, too. And sure enough, that's all it took for us to start making out in Kylie Peterson's little sister's bedroom. Her stuffed animals were on the bed, but we didn't care. I'd kissed guys before, but it had never been so *voracious.* I loved it. We didn't go all the way — we figured there weren't any Trojans hidden in the My Little Ponies, if you know what I mean — but it was clear we were already on the way to all the way.

It was a game. I mean, don't get me wrong — it was serious. But it was also a game. I'd say we screwed on our third date, but we didn't go on *dates. Dates* makes it sound like dinner and candlelight were the point. But the point was sex. The usual ways and places first, then getting trickier. We didn't want to get caught, but we wanted to come *this close* to getting caught. We wanted to see how far we could go before we got the shit kicked out of us. Sometimes we'd pass each other in the halls — arranging it so we'd walk by each other between every period, but not saying a word, just giving each other that *I'm going to have you soon* stare. And other times he would grab me right there by my locker and thrust his mouth onto mine, and we'd be tonguing it up for everyone to see. It was so screwed up, because the thing that made us the most powerless also gave us such power. We could make them turn away. We could bother them and challenge them and mess them up. You think people are afraid of two boys in love? To hell with that. What people are *really* afraid of is two boys screwing. And even though we weren't about to drop trou in the halls, we were going to let them know we were doing it whenever we could. We always played it safe, condom-wise. But location-wise? Safety was not the first concern.

The first floor boys' room. The showers in the locker room when everyone was in class and we were skipping. The couch in the faculty lounge. The boiler room. The

263

second floor boys' room. The lighting room in the auditorium, against the movie projector. Room 216, second
lunch block. The roof of the cafeteria when everyone
else was under us, chattering. The art room, with paints.
The third floor girls' room. The 400 aisle of the library.

We were only caught twice. Once I said I was helping
to look for his contact lens, which must have fallen on
his fly. The other time the art teacher found us. I thought
he'd been watching for a while before letting us know he
was there, but Dutch said his shock was real. He didn't say
a word to us. Just saw what was going on, turned red, and
left.

We weren't exactly the popular kids. But we were
damn popular with the unpopular kids. The girls especially, this army of goth older sisters — they didn't want
to hear about us having sex, but they admired our spirit.
We weren't the prom types, but as the time approached,
Dutch said to me, "Wouldn't it be cool to screw at the
prom?" and I said, "Yeah, I guess it would." I kinda
wanted to go anyway, but never would have told him
that. I didn't want him to think I was taking anything too
seriously. He'd already told me we were going to split up
at the end of the year, because in college there would be
new dicks to play with. He said it like he was joking, but
you can't tell a joke like that without meaning it at least
a little.

We weren't going to spend any money on the prom or
anything cheesy like that. No limo, no tuxes, no tickets.
We were just going to show up and do it our own way.
While other couples were talking about flowers and cum-
merbunds, Dutch was telling me to wear button-fly pants.
That night while biting his neck, I drew blood.

264

The prom was at some hotel, which made it very easy to crash. As everyone was pulling up to the front door in their gowns and their stretches, like it was the movie premiere of their new life, Dutch and I were smoking with some busboys by the service entrance. He was flirting, I was nervous, and when the pack was finished, the busboys pointed the way to the ballroom.

After we slipped in, I looked around the room and felt strange. It wasn't that it was beautiful — it was just a hotel ballroom, with round tableclothed tables and white balloons with our class year preprinted in orange and blue, our school colors. But seeing the room all decked out made me feel . . . sentimental, I guess. I had been to proms before, but this was the one that was supposed to be mine. This was a memory I was supposed to be having.

As I looked around at my classmates all dressed up, Dutch was scouting out a place to screw. He didn't want to start in the men's room, because that would be too obvious a choice. I insisted that going under one of the tables was a bad idea, since people would be sitting down soon, and then we'd be trapped. We walked back into the reception area. People didn't seem surprised to see us, or to see that we hadn't dressed up. They weren't disappointed in us, because their expectations had never been that high to begin with. It bothered me.

Then Dutch pulled me into the coatroom and made me feel a little better. You know what it's like to look at someone and realize they're hungry for you? The thing I loved the most about Dutch was that he never stopped grinning — even if his mouth was serious, his eyes were in on the joke. He enjoyed me, and that's what kept us going and going and going. He found the most expensive coat in that coatroom, then took it to the back, threw it on the floor, and led me on top of it. Button fly, yeah. Condom, nice to meet you. I could hear everyone outside not hearing us. I could hear the empty hangers pinging against one another as my shoulder hit into the racks again and again. Dutch would stop and smile, and I would smile back and keep quieter than usual. I'd feel his breaths catching, measure the distance between them to know he was close.

After we were done, he squeezed me tight for a moment and then said, "All right — back to the prom!" I made the foolish mistake I'd made at least a few dozen times already — I thought, for that one millisecond of hope, that this might be the moment, the occasion that he would say "I love you, Erik." Even if he didn't really mean it. We'd been screwing around for long enough that I knew it was a conscious decision on his part to never use those words with me. And because he held them back, I restrained myself, too. The two times I'd slipped and said them, he'd just smiled and said, "No, you don't."

Dutch was hungry again, this time for food. So we put our clothes all back in place and returned to the ballroom. We found our goth girls and their punk boys, and we ate off their plates, which they let us do because they thought that was punk, too. We were crashing, which was nothing new. But this time I actually felt like I was interrupting. When the DJ started spinning hip-hop and pop tunes, Dutch made fun of everyone who went to dance. I could tell that some of our friends had intended to dance, but now felt awkward about it. I kinda wanted to dance. The best I could do was lure Dutch away, so the goth girls could get down and the punk boys could shimmy to their punk hearts' content. I put my hand on Dutch's ass and whispered, "We're not done yet."

We walked into the men's room just as half the football team was peeing out the beers they'd tailgated. I thought, *We really shouldn't be doing this.* But Dutch's boldness carried me on. He held my hand and opened the stall door as if it was the door to Cinderella's carriage. When he closed it and locked it behind us, I could hear the jeers. One of the guys pounded on the door, and I jumped. Dutch looked ready to start fighting . . . but soon the jeers faded. The football players left. Other people came in, but they had no idea what we were up to — not unless they looked down and saw the two pairs of legs.

This time we just kissed and groped, and it was almost like the beginning. Only it didn't feel like the beginning, because I knew the beginning had passed a long time ago. Dutch was murmuring how hot I was, how great I was, how cool this was. Usually I could lose myself in that for hours. Usually that was how I knew I was okay. That being me, that doing this, was okay. I loved that he said these things, and I loved that when I was with him I could believe they were true. Which is different from loving him. But in some ways more powerful.

There was a spot on his back that caused him to shiver whenever I touched it a certain way. I loved that, too. I loved knowing his body that well. But it only worked when we were lying down, relaxed, quiet. When we were pressing against each other in a bathroom stall, there wasn't that kind of vulnerability, that kind of control. It was like we were now one thing, and everything outside the stall was another. As opposed to when we were truly alone together — then we were each one thing, and the wonder came from combining the two.

After a while our mouths and hands took their usual course. When we emerged from the stall, this kid I'd been friends with in seventh grade — Hector — was at the sink, washing his hands. He looked in the mirror and saw us emerge. And then he shook his head, as if to say, *What a waste*. And I thought, *You asshole*. I turned back to Dutch and gave him a long, hard kiss, right in that mirror. Us against the world.

Here's the thing — even if it was just sex, even if he didn't say "I love you," even if I knew it wouldn't last, you have to understand that I would have been alone without him. I would have been so alone.

I held his hand as we went back into the ballroom. I couldn't get him as far as the dance floor, but we found friends to talk to, joke with, tease and be teased by. I could see a few teachers and administrators wanting to say something to us about our clothing choice, but as long as we held hands, it was like we were invincible. When the prom queen and prom king were announced, I half-expected it to be us. I was a little disappointed when it wasn't, because I would've liked nothing more than to have walked on stage with Dutch, to give him that royal kiss in front of the whole school, to prove that we'd been here, unafraid.

The DJ announced that there was only one more song until the prom song, and that couples should reunite and head for the dance floor. Dutch looked over at the DJ, then grinned and sparkled even wider. He

268

held me by the hand and led me in the direction of the dance floor. Then, just as we were about to get there, he pulled me to the side, into the shadows. He pointed, and I saw what he'd found — a small crawl space under the stage, beneath the music. "Come on," he said, hunching down, heading inside. I followed.

It was a maze of dust and wires and reverb. There was barely enough room to sit upright, so Dutch stretched out on the floor, staring up as if the bottom of the stage was full of stars. I crawled next to him, and he immediately rolled on his side and kissed me. His hand ran over my back, then down below my waistband.

The first sounds of "In Your Eyes" came through — the drum and the bell, the steady heartbeat. And then Peter Gabriel's first words — *Love, I get so lost sometimes.* I heard them so deeply at that moment. Even though Dutch was pressing into me. Even though I was turned on and warm and with him . . . I thought to myself, *I'm missing something.* I stopped kissing Dutch back, and the minute I stopped kissing him back, he knew it and he stopped kissing me. But he didn't pull away. He didn't let go. Instead he pulled back enough to see me. To read me. And I stared back at him, daring him not to move. I thought it again — *I'm missing something.* A few feet away, couples were dancing to their prom song, holding each other tight. I was missing that. And at the same time, I was here, under the stage, being held in this different way. Looking into his eyes. Having him look into my eyes. Staying quiet. Just watching. Feeling our breath, his hand still on the small of my back, on the skin. I realized I would always be missing something. That no matter what I did, I would always be missing something else.

And the only way to live, the only way to be happy, was to make sure the things I didn't miss meant more to me than the things I missed. I had to think about what I wanted, outside of the heat of wanting.

I had no idea whether Dutch noticed any of this, or what he was thinking. When the song was over, we made sure we'd been hanging in the moment before a kiss, not in the moment after one. Then we crawled back out from under the stage and walked back to our friends. I forgot to hold his hand.

Later that night when we were naked in my basement, naked afterward, he said it to me. And even though it was too late, I didn't say, "No, you don't." Instead I kissed him once, quietly. Then we lay there, and I let time pass.

The Great American Morp
by John Green

Generally, I prefer floors to beds. I remember when I was about five, I'd been sleeping on the plush carpet of my old bedroom for thirty days in a row when I asked my mom, "Do you think I can set the world record for sleeping on the floor?"

And she said, "Maggie, there are a lot of people who sleep their whole lives on the floor." For about a week, I was really pissed off at all the world's homeless and/or bedless for stealing my world record.

I was not a shining example of human excellence as a five-year-old, is what I'm saying. But I've made tremendous progress.

So I'm lying on the floor reading *Moby-Dick* just for the sheer, unadulterated pleasure of reading about what has to be the longest and most metaphorical whale hunt in all of history. Or possibly because it's the topic of my AP English final — the last paper I will ever write in my high school career.

My mom comes in.

"Maggie," she says.

And I say, "Yeah?"

And she says, "What would you say if I told you that me and Dad were gonna be the photographers at your prom?"

Usually in this situation I'd correct her grammar, but — oh, sweet holy Lord. Not my parents. Not taking prom pictures. *My* parents. These are people who think the world's funniest joke is to tell photographic subjects to say *Cheez Whiz* rather than *cheese*. Don't get me wrong: They're great photographers, and I'm glad that they're good enough at it to put a roof over my head and everything. But not prom.

So I say, "No."

And she says, "Well, but, sweetie. The original photographers have another commitment, so we're gonna cover for them. It'll be fun! And also it pays well. With you about to go off to college . . ."

I don't say anything, and then after some more hemming and hawing and it-will-be-funning, she leaves. Immediately, I call Carly.

"My parents are the new prom photographers," I announce.

"Oh, God," Carly says. "I can't go. Oh, God. I'm not going." You know your parents are genuinely and truly horrible when your *friends* find them embarrassing.

"I'm not going either," I say. "I would rather die a thousand deaths."

Carly says, "I'd rather be Cleopatra and get bitten on the boob by a cobra."

"I'd rather spend months chasing after a fat white metaphor and then have that metaphor crash into my boat and kill me," I say.

"I'd rather wear a scarlet *A* to school every day," she says.

"I'd rather throw myself under a Russian train," I say.

And then she says, "I'd rather — uh, I'd rather spend a month on a raft with Huck Finn?"

And I say, "Yeah, but that doesn't make sense because you'd *love* to do that."

"True. He's such a dirty-boy-with-a-big-heart — all naughty and troubled and cute and tan."

"God, we are so cool. And by cool, I mean retarded."

"So we just won't go," Carly says after a moment. "Although that will mean turning down all of our many gentlemen callers." This is entirely a joke for me — I've had about three gentleman callers in my life, and that's only if you consider my second-grade boyfriend, Robby "The Dirt Eater" Reynolds, a gentleman. But Carly is the cutest not-horrible girl in our school — by which I mean that unlike most of the girls who guys like, Carly does not go home every night and jill off to the thought of buying a Juicy Couture bag.

The next morning before school, I'm sitting on the steps leading to the band room (I play the clarinet, and I so don't give a shit whether anyone thinks that's lame). I'm gulping Diet Mountain Dew in a vain attempt to awaken when Carly walks up and says, "We're going to have a Morp."

And I say, "A Morp?"

And she says, "It's a backwards prom."

I look at her blankly for a second and then say, "So, like, you lose your virginity and *then* go to a dance?"

Carly laughs. She always gets really into laughing — throwing back her head and pushing her shoulders back. Carly has a very loud laugh and is not entirely immune to laugh-snorts, but with her shoulders back like that, it's hard to notice anything except her unfairly good body. Like, I have always believed that God ought to give you either boobs or natural thinness. It is completely ridiculous for God to give both to, say, Carly, and then give neither to, say, me. I realize that as divine injustice goes, this is minor stuff, but still.

"No, dumb ass. It's a party *instead* of prom. We'll only have people we like, and we'll all dress up hilarious and we'll just have a party. No ridiculous theme, no hideous dresses, no DJ with a mullet, and no professional photographers. It's like prom, except without all the things that suck about prom."

The first-period bell rings, and I follow Carly through the door, asking, "Yeah, but where would we *have* a Morp? I believe the Sheraton ballroom is already booked."

We stop in the middle of a hallway, bodies all around us, pushing toward class, and Carly smiles and says, "Well, I hear your parents will be away for the evening," and before I can even say no, Carly spins around and heads off toward class. I turn in the opposite direction, off to the nonstop joy ride that is French III. My main problem with French is that it has always fallen during first period and, as it happens, I can't listen during first period.

"Maggie, *que ce porterez-vous au bal d'étudiants?*" asks Monsieur Johnson, staring at me. But if he's talking to me, I wonder, why is he speaking French? Surely by now he has noticed that I don't speak or understand the language.

"Uh," I say. "Uh. *Je ne sais pas.*" No American can say "I don't know" in French with the subtle and sophisticated accent I've managed to capture. It is the only sentence I know, but God — I know it well.

Anyway, it turns out that Monsieur Johnson is asking me what I'll be wearing to prom, which I figure out because prime prom king candidate Jesse Burns, who is, I'll admit, kind of good-looking in that I've-got-a-nice-jawline-and-not-too-much-muscle-but-enough-believe-me-although-man-am-I-ever-dumb kind of way, answers the same question by saying, "Uh, a tooxado? A tux-eedah? *Comment tu-dis*, like, tuxedo?"

I ridicule Jesse, but let's face it — he's better at French than I am. I scribble a note in my notebook:

> C,
> Hypothetical question: If Jesse Burns asked you to prom, would you still rather have a Morp or would you leave me languishing at home while you offered the esteemed Mr. Burns your cherished maiden-head?
> Luv,
> Maqs

I'm standing in line for pizza at 10:48 that morning — because for reasons that only God truly understands, school believes that it's perfectly acceptable to start lunch before 11:00 A.M. Someone bumps the back of my knee and I buckle forward for a second and then turn around scowling and it's Tyler Trumpet, whose real last name I don't know, but he plays the trumpet in our band and also plays bass in a punk band called Screw You Aunt Franny that Carly likes a lot.

"Jesus, sorry, Maggie."

"It's okay," I say, not thinking much about it either way.

And he says, "Carly said you're having a party."

"She seems to think so," I say.

"Yeah. On prom night?" Tyler is the kind of guy who says things as questions when he could just say them as statements.

"That's right."

"She said I should come?"

"Oh, yeah, you should," I say, "although I'm not totally sure we've decided to even *have* a Morp."

And Tyler says, "Well, if you do, we could play the party."

"Play the party?"

"Screw You Aunt Franny?" Tyler says/asks. I should add here that Tyler is cute, in that My-hair-is-always-in-my-face-and-I-can't-look-directly-into-your-eyes-because-it's-like-staring-at-the-sun-but-then-occasionally-you'll-see-how-blue-my-eyes-are-and-that'll-make-you-slightly-gooey-although-who-cares-because-I-can't-bring-myself-to-speak-declarative-sentences-let-alone-have-a-decent-conversation-with-you kind of way.

"I will take it under consideration," I say, and then Carly walks up and stands next to me and says, "Hey, Tyler," and he says, "Hey," and she says, "Can I cut?" and he says, "Sure."

And then she says to me, "Did Tyler tell you about Screw You Aunt Franny?"

And I say, "I don't think we can really have a *band*. I mean, my parents are only going to be gone for, like, five hours at the most."

And Tyler says, "Well, we only know twelve songs."

Carly presses a folded piece of paper against my hand. When Tyler turns around to talk to some other band kids, I unfold the paper and read it quickly.

M,
Funny you should mention that, Nostradamus: Jesse Burns cornered me by my locker after second period and asked me to prom. I told him I was sorry, but I had a Morp to attend.
C

I stare at Carly. "No shit?" I ask.

And she says, "Well, he told you, right? That's why the note."

"No. He didn't tell me. He's never even *spoken* to me. The question just popped into my head."

"Dude, you're psychic. What am I thinking right now?"

"I can't believe you rejected Jesse Burns."

We're at the front of the line finally, and I'm handed two slices of pizza with green peppers. The peppers make it good for you, see. Vegetables. Finally, Carly says, "That wasn't what I was thinking. I was thinking that, man, we had better have one hell of a good Morp now, or else I'll be, like, a forty-year-old lady working in a convenience store smoking Virginia Slims and I'll be all, like, 'Everything woulda been different if only I'd gone to prom with that Jesse Burns.'"

Honestly — and this is about the darkest secret I can imagine — I probably would have said yes to Jesse Burns. I just don't think I could have stopped myself. But that's why Carly's a superstar and I'm . . . me. And being me is neither particularly easy nor particularly hard. It just is. Put it this way: I've done lights for all the school's plays this year. I sit there, in the dark, and my job is to put the spotlight on other people.

Two weeks after her initial Morp inspiration and five days before the actual prom, Carly shows up outside the band room one morning before school. I'm sitting on the steps talking to a couple girls, and Carly hands me this note:

> M,
> Okay, here's my grocery list so far: chips, soda, air horn, plastic cups, paper plates, napkins, and raw materials for world's funniest Morp dress. Am I missing anything?
> C

"Air horn?" I ask.

And she says, "Yeah. Haven't you always wanted an air horn?"

"Not really," I say, but I'm not sure she even hears me because the air horn that is the first-period bell goes off right as I start to talk, and I'm drowned out. I head to French III, write up a note of some other things we might need, and then give it to Carly. She's doing the shopping, since I'm doing the hosting. We've already made a guest list that numbers fifteen people, counting the three members of Screw You Aunt Franny, and sent out photocopied handwritten invites:

Dear (insert your name here),
Carly and I feel that you don't suck, so you are cordially invited to attend the Great American Morp, Saturday night, at Maggie's house (2246 Leu Road), beginning at exactly 8:12 PM. There will be a prize for most hilarious costume. That prize will be seven minutes in the closet with Carly. Aww, yeah. We're going sixth grade on y'all.
Truth or Dare,
Maggie and Carly

A couple people immediately tell us that they probably won't come. So I'm vaguely worried that our Morp will consist entirely of Carly and me sitting around talking and watching TV and eating a shit ton of Doritos, but that would be okay. Better, certainly, than putting on a dress that makes me appear to have been attacked by a gigantic blue Christmas present (bow and all), and then having my dateless prom picture taken by my parents.

The Thursday before the Morp, Mom and Dad are watching this crime show on TV they like, and I sit down on the living room floor in the middle of it. Then, during the commercials, I say, "I might have a couple friends over on prom night," which is a technically true statement.

And Dad says, "Are you *sure* you don't want to go? It's a night you never forget, prom."

My mom looks askew at him and says, "Didn't you get stood up by Suzie Spears?"

Dad smirks. "And I never forgot it."

"Right, so I'm not going," I say. "But a couple other girls who aren't going might just hang out here and watch a movie or something."

"No drinking," says my dad, and I just laugh. I like the idea of drinking fine, but in practice it never works for me. Beer tastes like carbonated pee, wine tastes like spoiled grapes and gives me a headache, and anything harder than that tastes like dragon breath.

"No house messing up," my mom says.

"Don't worry," I tell them. "Nobody would ever come to my house looking for a crazy-fun party."

This prophecy seems to be coming true on Saturday afternoon. Carly drives over — keeping her supplies in her trunk so my parents won't know the scope of the get-together Carly's hoping for — and we spend the day making our Morp dresses. Mine involves black leggings and this hideous but great-fitting dress I got at a thrift store. The dress is a swirly mess of colors, but it doesn't matter because I'm slowly covering it with small squares of yellow and black duct tape. I'm going to the Morp as the world's most beautiful duct tape honeybee.

And Carly? When she gets into my room, she closes the door behind her, tosses her backpack onto the bed, and unzips it. She dumps out a plain black summer dress, glue, two dental floss containers, and somewhere in the neighborhood of five hundred condoms. "It's a condom dress," she explains. "Because the Morp is all about safe sex. So, yeah. What I'm doing is I'm using a little hole punch to put two holes in each wrapper, and then I thread the floss through it two ways, and then because that actually doesn't work that well, you glue each condom to the dress as you go. It's kinda, um, time consuming."

"Um, where did you get all those condoms?"

"They're free at the health center at Rollins," she says, which is this college close to Carly's house. "They keep them in this wicker basket in the entryway. So every day after school for the last three weeks, I walked in, grabbed, like, two handfuls of condoms, and walked out."

"They didn't look at you funny?"

"Not really. I mean, I did begin to worry that the nurses were back there talking about the girl who has sex thirty-seven times a day, but whatever."

My dress is done within an hour, but even with two full-time condom seamstresses, we don't get Carly's finished until seven, partly because we have to hide it under the bed every time we hear parental footsteps approaching my door. But once we are finished, the dress looks amazing. I carefully hold it up and she slithers into it. There are still hints of the black summer dress, particularly near the neckline and the hem at her knees, but Carly is mostly condoms.

My parents leave at seven-thirty, whereupon Carly and I immediately go out to her car and bring in two cardboard boxes full of supplies. Said supplies include snacks, fruit, soda, cups, plates, a little trophy featuring a faux-gold disco dancer that reads at the bottom MORPER OF THE YEAR, an air horn, the book *Martha Stewart's Entertaining*, a Twister mat ("in case things get desperate — or dirty!"

281

Carly explains), a Gatorade bottle filled with disturbingly brown liquid, and several sterling silver serving platters that Carly has obviously ganked without permission from her folks.

"What's the brown shit?" I ask.

"The brown shit is the normal, healthy shit," Carly answers. "Far preferable to the green or blue shit."

"You're disgusting."

"It's scotch," she says. "My dad has this gigantic scotch collection, and so what I did was I took a little bit of each bottle. It's really expensive stuff. I hope mixing it doesn't ruin it."

I unscrew the orange Gatorade cap and sniff while Carly contorts herself to get into the condom dress without dislodging any Trojans. It smells like rubbing alcohol. "Maybe later," I say, and commence to get dressed, rearrange furniture, chop up cantaloupe, and move anything that looks breakable into Mom and Dad's room, just in case.

Screw You Aunt Franny shows up at precisely 8:12. They lug in amps and a little drum set from the back of Tyler Trumpet's minivan and set up next to my kitchen. Even standing close together, the band takes up about a third of the room, which might be a problem except their entire audience consists of me and Carly. Tyler Trumpet is wearing this badass bright green tweed suit with a skinny black tie and a paisley button-down. He looks ridiculously awesome.

The singer, Dan, asks Carly, "Do you want us to, like, start now or wait till later?" And Carly says, "Let's wait a little bit."

Shortly thereafter, our friend Lesley arrives, wearing

jeans, a T-shirt, and a sandwich board that reads THIS IS A MORP GOWN. Then this goofy guy Carl, who's wearing a suit of armor constructed entirely out of aluminum foil. Fellow clarinetist Jane is next, wearing a fluffy, green A-line gown on which she's Sharpied the names of all her favorite bands and books.

And then everyone we've invited has come, and then people we didn't invite come, and then more people we didn't invite come, until I have to turn the thermostat down to 52 degrees to keep the house from boiling with body heat. There are people I've never seen here, and they keep stopping me and complimenting my dress and saying that this is a fantastic party, and I'm like, *it hasn't even started yet, just wait till Screw You Aunt Franny plays.* And it all feels so good that together we have overcome the tyranny of prom. By nine o'clock, everyone who's anyone is at prom. And everyone who *isn't* anyone — and that's an awful lot of us — is crammed into my living room.

Some kid named Frank, with whom I am passingly familiar, tells me I look cute as he hands me a cup of Coke, which I realize after approximately one tenth of one sip contains a healthy dose of Carly's dad's scotch. I put it aside, because I want to enjoy this properly. I see Carly across the room, weaving her way through the crowd, trying to keep people from brushing against her because the condom dress is more fragile than it looks. Then she comes up to me and says, "I'm going to introduce the band, so find Tyler Trumpet."

I can spot that suit across the room, so I walk up to Tyler and ask him if he can start playing now. Also I say, "Your suit is ridiculously awesome," and he smiles and

283

looks at me just enough for me to see his so-very-blue eyes, and then he's off to gather the band.

Once they're behind their instruments, the drummer bangs away for a minute until the crowd starts to quiet down and then Carly jumps behind the one microphone, and immediately everyone shuts up entirely. She says, "First, a few rules. Don't break anything. Don't spill anything. Don't do anything gross. And if at any time you hear this" — she holds up the air horn and gives it one brief but earsplitting blast — "then immediately shut up. Ladies and gentlemen. The best band at our entire school, and possibly on the entire planet. Put your hands together for Screw. You. Aunt. Franny."

Dan, the singer (and guitarist), who is cute in that I-probably-don't-shower-as-often-as-you'd-like-but-I'm-tall-and-look-sexy-when-playing-the-guitar kinda way, walks up to Carly and kisses her on the cheek. Carly goes flush for just a moment, but then laughs in that way she has, and Dan the singer takes the microphone and says, "I'm Dan, this is Tyler Trumpet, and back there is Joe Drummer. And we used to be Screw You Aunt Franny, but Tyler just renamed us Little Maggie and the Magical Morpers. Now we're going to cor the cuff out of this Morp."

And it takes me a second to realize I should reverse the *cor* and the *cuff*, and it takes me another second to register that Tyler Trumpet has possibly just renamed his band after me. They launch into something fast and loud, and I throw up my hands and dance. The bumblebee duct-tape dress wasn't made for dancing, certainly, and it isn't exactly a breathable material, so I'm starting to sweat, but I don't give a shit, because this is what prom ought to be, and I like all these people, even the ones I don't know, and everyone is just dancing, and Tyler is jumping up and down as his fingers slide around the bass. I can hardly even tell when they move from one song to another; it's just all of us dancing together, band and crowd alike, and, God, Carly is such a genius. I find myself dancing next to Carly and I say, "God, Carly, you're such a genius," and — and I hear something over the music very faintly. And then I don't hear it anymore. And then I hear it — the phone. Phone. "PHONE!" I shout to Carly.

She raises the air horn and gives it a good one-second blow. The band screeches to silence and so do the rest of us, and then I tear across the living room to the cordless, trying to beat the fifth ring. I grab it just in time.

"Hello?"

"Hey, baby. Just calling to check in."

"Hey, Mom."

"How's it goin'?"

"Pretty good."

"Did anybody end up coming over?"

"Um, it's just me, Carly, Lesley, and a couple people," I answer, and some people stifle laughter. I look up and everyone is staring silently at me. I look back to the carpet.

"Well, we miss you here. Mr. Johnson just told me that this is the fewest people they've had at prom in years."

"Yeah, that sucks, Mom. So I'll see you later tonight?"

"Yup. We'll be home around midnight."

"'Bye, Mom."

"'Bye."

In the second of silence that follows, I keep looking at the floor, but I gather the guts to say, quite loudly, what's screaming inside of me: "Monsieur Johnson just told my parents that it's the smallest prom crowd in years." The roar of approval I get in response could be measured on the goddamned Richter scale.

Little Maggie and the Magical Morpers start up again. People get to dancing, and I walk to the kitchen to get some chips. Sometimes, witnessing a party is even better than being part of one. I've always liked moments like this: quietly watching all these people having all this fun. Carly loses a couple condoms off her dress when these guys Bill and Tony raise her up so she can crowd-surf around my living room. Tyler Trumpet bounces on his toes, his sweaty hair in his face, staring down at his bass. A kid wearing a tuxedo T-shirt tries to sip from his cup without stopping his dance moves. And then the Magical Morpers transition into a new song, a soft and slow one. It's this Mr. T Experience cover — "Even Hitler Had a Girlfriend" — and the kids who smoke pull out their lighters and wave them above their heads. And I'm happy — really happy — just to watch. It's the floor instead of the bed, I know, but maybe that's just who I am: Maybe I need the littlest bit of discomfort. Maybe I need a little space between me and the life of the party.

The band takes a break then, and I watch Tyler Trumpet as he walks across the living room and right toward me, his eyes on me the whole way. And then he's close up to me and he says, "I like you."

And I say, "What?"

And he looks away then and says, "I like you? I have a crush on you?"

And I say, "Say it, don't ask it."

And he says, "I like you." And then I'm up on my tiptoes and all of a sudden I'm kissing him, just once and softly. And then he says, "Dan was going to say it into the mic if I didn't tell you," and I say, "Oh, well, I'm glad you told me," and he says, "Me, too," and then he leans down and kisses me, and his hand is against my cheek, and I sort of melt a little.

He says, "I was watching you in the kitchen and I kept wondering why you weren't dancing?"

"I think maybe I am a watcher and not a doer."

And he pauses for a second, because he's actually listening to me, and then he says, "Yeah, I understand that. I'm like that, too, sometimes. But you'd be a great doer. Wait, that came out perverted. I mean, you sorta tag along behind Carly, but you're so much funnier and prettier and more interesting than her," and I say, "Bullshit," and he says, "Seriously."

And I say, "Okay, fine, Tyler Trumpet. I'll do anything you want me to do for the next five minutes."

And he says, "Jesus, talk about perverted," and I blush and laugh.

"Well, first kiss me," he says, and I do. And I keep kissing him, even as I watch a smiling Carly rip a condom off her dress and throw it us. She tells us to get a room, but this is what I want right here — the carpet and the bed at once. And then, still kissing me, speaking directly into my lips, he says, "Get your clarinet." Which I do.

And then I'm staring out at the crowd as Little Maggie

and the Magical Morpers gather back onstage for their second set — which will include the same twelve songs as the first set. Only the songs are different this time, because it's Joe Drummer on drums, Tyler Trumpet on bass, Dan the singer on singing and guitar, and Maggie on punk rock clarinet.

Tyler Trumpet reaches an awkward hand out before they start playing and touches the small of my back, and something about him and what he said and this place and the total Morpness of the world fills me with this crazy confidence, and I realize that these people aren't going to make fun of me for this. And Tyler plays the bass line once while I watch, and then Joe Drummer says, "ONE TWO THREE FOUR" real fast, and then it's a cacophony of bass and guitar and voice and drums — and clarinet. I tear the goddamned place up with my clarinet, and Carly is right in front of me making devil horns in her condom dress and screaming, "RIP IT, MAGGIE!" and I'm only sort of following the chord changes, but I'm playing fast and loud and Tyler is smiling while he stares at his bass, and then after the second chorus, Dan the singer screams, "CLARINET SOLO!" and it's just me trying to affect punkness on the clarinet against Joe Drummer's pulsing beat, and the crowd is yelling, and I have to keep myself from smiling all goofy so I can blow into the clarinet right.

And then the band comes back, their sound washing over me, and Tyler looks up at me. He mouths *four three two one*, and then all at once our sound crescendos, and then disappears. And this is the very best part about punk music: There's a moment, right after the band stops playing all at once and right before the crowd goes

288

nuts. That's the best silence I've ever known, and I'm feeling it as a band member for the first time. Then people start yelling and clapping, and I can't stop myself from smiling. I curtsy and try to walk back into the crowd, but Tyler grabs me by my bumblebee duct-taped waist and says, "We really need you on the next one, too," and so I pick up my clarinet again.

After everything else — after Carly awards me the Morper of the Year trophy for my "heroic clarinet playing," and after everyone goes home except for me and Tyler and Carly, and after we pick everything up and put the garbage bags in Tyler's minivan, and after we put the breakables back in the living room, and after Tyler leaves me with the best kiss in my admittedly limited kissing lifetime, and after Carly and I watch TV, and after my parents come home, and after we fall asleep with Carly in the bed and me on the floor — after all that, I still feel like a punk rock Morp superstar. It's the kind of feeling that just lingers and, in lingering, makes you slightly but permanently different. Better, even.

The Prom Gallery

Jodi Lynn Anderson asked a boy named Pat to prom and never recovered from the rejection, which probably stemmed from the chunky plastic jewelry she wore and the fact that one time she accidentally drooled in front of him. She was later reprimanded by Sister Miriam for dancing too close to her date. Now she lives in Costa Rica, where she spends her time surfing and hiding from her tacky, checkered past. She is the author of the novel *Peaches*.

Holly Black is the the author of the bestselling Spiderwick Chronicles and the Modern Faerie Tale series, which include *Tithe, Valiant,* and the forthcoming *Ironside.* She is currently hard at work on a graphic novel entitled *The Good Neighbors.* Visit her on the web at www.blackholly.com.

Libba Bray did not get asked to prom. Not even after she posted her phone number in black electrical tape in a strategic location on her body. One *arranged* (*cough* pity *cough*) date later, she did manage to go to prom and has a vague memory of pogo-ing to the B-52's. Libba is the author of the novels *A Great and Terrible Beauty* and *Rebel Angels,* as well as a short story, *Bad Things,* in the upcoming anthology *Restless Dead.* She invites you to drop by her website, www.libbabray.com, where she promises you will not be forced to wear baby's breath.

Rachel Cohn did not go to prom. She did write the books *Gingerbread, Shrimp, Cupcake, Pop Princess*, and, with David Levithan, *Nick & Norah's Infinite Playlist*. Visit her on the web at www.rachelcohn.com.

Elizabeth Craft lives in Los Angeles, where she is a supervising producer on FX's *The Shield*. She and her writing partner are the authors of a young-adult novel, *Bass Ackwards and Belly Up*. Elizabeth is happy to report that despite being emotionally scarred by numerous high school dances, she has managed to meet the man of her dreams and will soon be getting married.

Melissa de la Cruz is the author of the bestselling series *The Au Pairs* and her new fabulous vampire series *Blue Bloods*. Her story is absolutely true. Just thinking of her date's beer-and-whisky-laced breath still makes her swoon. She is married to a very cute guy who never attended a prom. At their wedding they danced to Annie Lennox's "Seventeen Again" because Melissa thought of her wedding as the ultimate prom.

Daniel Ehrenhaft did not attend a prom, but he did rent an expensive tuxedo once. Now he owns a tuxedo. He is wearing it as he writes this. (Okay, he is wearing boxer shorts and a smelly T-shirt.) His wife went to an amazing prom in New York City, and her date was a really nice childhood friend who went on to become a famous screenwriter — and, yes, Mr. Ehrenhaft is jealous on a variety of levels. His novels include *Tell It to Naomi, 10 Things to Do Before I Die, Drawing a Blank*, and *The After Life*.

Aimee Friedman is the *New York Times* bestselling author of the novels *South Beach, French Kiss, Hollywood Hills, A Novel Idea,* and *Breaking Up: A Fashion High Graphic Novel.* Her work was also featured in the holiday romance collection *Mistletoe.* A native New Yorker, Aimee wore all black to her prom, and the event was held down the street from Grand Central Station. She only had one date, who was very nice, but she likes imagining what it might have been like to have three.

John Green is the author of *Looking for Alaska,* which won the Michael L. Printz Award and was a finalist for the *L.A. Times* Book Prize. His second novel, *An Abundance of Katherines,* was published in September 2006. John's high school had no prom; instead, it had this thing called "Senior Banquet." John took Amanda Key, the great love of his high school life, to Senior Banquet. Amanda, under the mistaken impression that they were going as "just friends," proceeded to break John's heart by making out with Stuart Nelson. Damn you, Stuart Nelson. Damn you to hell.

Proms, cotillions, homecoming dances: **Brent Hartinger** did them all — always with opposite-sex partners, and he was always the perfect gentleman. Which makes sense in retrospect, but which didn't make his dates feel any less fat and unattractive at the time. Brent now lives in Washington state with his appropriately gendered partner Michael. He is also the author of a bunch of books, including *Geography Club, The Last Chance Texaco, Grand & Humble, Split Screen,* and *Dreamquest.* Visit Brent online (or inquire about play production rights) at www.brenthartinger.com.

Will Leitch is the editor of <u>Deadspin.com</u>, the world's most popular sports blog, which is not a particularly impressive title. He is the author of two books, *Life as a Loser* and *Catch,* and is the founding editor of the late, great *The Black Table.* He has written for all kinds of places with italicized names, and he will keep writing for me. He wishes he could play a musical instrument.

David Levithan went to prom four times, but never really got it right. He did, however, get the idea for this anthology after writing about it. His books include *Boy Meets Boy, The Realm of Possibility, Are We There Yet?, Marly's Ghost* (a novel illustrated by Brian Selznick), *Wide Awake, The Full Spectrum* (co-edited with Billy Merrell), and, co-written with Rachel Cohn, *Nick & Norah's Infinite Playlist.* He is also the founding editor and editorial director of PUSH. Check out <u>www.davidlevithan.com</u> and <u>www.thisispush.com</u>

E. Lockhart went to prom in an embroidered 1920s flapper dress that still hangs in her office. She also wore a feather boa that turned her neck black. E. is the author of *The Boyfriend List, Fly on the Wall, The Boy Book,* and the upcoming *Dramarama.* Visit her on the web at <u>www.theboyfriendlist.com</u>

Leslie Margolis is the author of *Fix* and *Price of Admission.* Her date for her junior prom took out his retainer when dinner was served and placed it on the table between their plates. He did not put it in his retainer case first. He just left it out there. Her senior prom wasn't much better. Feel free to share your own prom disaster stories with Leslie, who can be found at <u>www.lesliemargolis.com</u>.

Billy Merrell is the author of *Talking in the Dark,* a poetry memoir, and co-editor of *The Full Spectrum.* He has been to five proms, and was even up for Prom King once, though he was defeated by an athletic jazz musician. Sigh. Visit him at www.talkinginthedark.com.

In addition to writing novels such as *Bras & Broomsticks, Frogs & French Kisses,* and *Spells & Sleeping Bags,* **Sarah Mlynowski** went to her high school's senior prom three years in a row. Was it because she was über popular? Because she had to twice repeat her final year? Because there were rumors written about her on the boy's bathroom wall? To find out the real story go to www.sarahmlynowski.com.

Lisa Ann Sandell wonders, who likes to wear a corsage? *Really?* Wilty roses, ferns, and baby's breath on an elastic band that is guaranteed to cut off any chance of blood flow to the fingers? You've got to be kidding. She did indeed go to the prom, though, and wore the corsage. As well as a navy blue, bedazzled-in-sequins-all-over sheath that probably made the whole experience that much worse. Lisa is the author of *The Weight of the Sky* and the forthcoming *Song of the Sparrow,* both novels in verse. She lives in New York City, but you can visit her online at www.lisaannsandell.com.

Ned Vizzini is the author of *It's Kind of a Funny Story, Be More Chill,* and *Teen Angst? Naaah . . .* He started writing for *New York Press* in high school, which garnered him the embarrassing status as a "writer/wunderkind" (Gawker) but has now ascended to the realm of the "former teen wunderkind" (*New York Magazine*). His work has been honored by the American Library Association, New York Is Book Country, BookSense, and the Chicago Public Library. Ned lives in Brooklyn, NY.

While in high school **Cecily von Ziegesar** never had a prom or a prom date, but if she had to pick a date for the prom she'd pick her extraordinarily handsome and devoted Cornish Rex cat, Pony Boy. Cecily prefers to dress down, but her young daughter dresses like she's headed for the prom every day, and her toddler son never leaves the house without lipstick and nail polish. Cecily and her family seem to move every few years, so it's impossible to say exactly where they're living now, but probably in or in the vicinity of New York City, where Cecily writes about people who grew up in or in the vicinity of New York City.

Due to the legendary Boy Shortage of 1992 (and so NOT due to her severe case of Shyness Cripplingica), **Adrienne Maria Vrettos** went to her senior prom in a suburban packed with the most coolest, yet most dateless, ladies you've ever met. It was wicked awesome, and they didn't need no stinking boys anyway! She is the author of *Skin* and the upcoming *Sight.* You can find her online at www.adriennemarievrettos.com.

Jacquelyn Woodson turned in her prom story just after she won the Margaret Edwards Award for achievement in teen literature. She is the author of numerous acclaimed novels, including *Behind You, Feathers, The House You Pass Along the Way, I Hadn't Meant to Tell You This, If You Come Softly, Locomotion, Miracle's Boys,* and the Newbery Honor book *Show Way.*

About Advocates for Youth

Advocates for Youth, based in Washington, DC, is the only organization that works both in the United States and in developing countries with the sole focus on helping adolescents make safe and responsible choices about sex.

Advocates promotes the core values of **Rights. Respect.Responsibility.**®

Rights: Young people have rights to accurate and complete sexual health information, confidential reproductive and sexual health services, and a secure stake in the future.

Respect: Young people deserve respect. Valuing young people means they are treated as part of the solution rather than dismissed as part of the problem. Young people should be involved in developing programs and policies that affect their well-being.

Responsibility: Society has the responsibility to provide young people with the tools they need to safeguard their sexual health, and young people have the responsibility to protect themselves from too-early childbearing and sexually transmitted infections (STIs), including HIV.

Advocates works to raise youth and adult awareness of reproductive and sexual health issues; promotes public policies that support rights, respect, and responsibility for young people; and develops youth-friendly programs for communities in the United States and developing countries.

To find out more about Advocates for Youth and its issues or to learn how you can become involved in advocating for your reproductive and sexual health, visit www.advocatesforyouth.org.

All of the authors in 21 Proms *have donated their portion of the proceeds from the sale of the book to Advocates for Youth.*